The Candy Darlings

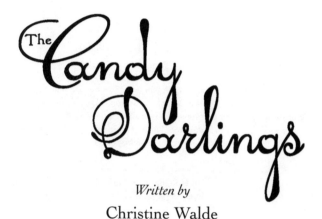

Written by
Christine Walde

G RAPHIA

AN IMPRINT OF HOUGHTON MIFFLIN COMPANY
Boston 2006

All rights reserved. Published in the United States by Graphia, an imprint
of Houghton Mifflin Company, Boston, Massachusetts
For information about permission to reproduce selections from this book,
write to Permissions, Houghton Mifflin Company, 215 Park Avenue
South, New York, New York 10003.

Graphia and the Graphia logo are registered
trademarks of Houghton Mifflin Company.
www.houghtonmifflinbooks.com

The text of this book is set in Cochin.

Library of Congress Cataloging-in-Publication Data
Walde, Christine, 1969–
   The candy darlings / written by Christine Walde.
      p. cm.
   Summary: A girl, grieving for her mother and detached from her father,
becomes fast friends with a mysterious classmate who constantly eats
sweets, as the two of them battle the vicious popular girls at school and lis-
ten to the stories of an elderly patient at the hospital where they volunteer.
   ISBN-13: 978-0-618-58969-2 (pbk. : alk. paper)
   ISBN-10: 0-618-58969-4 (pbk. : alk. paper)
   [1. Popularity—Fiction. 2. Schools—Fiction. 3. Candy—Fiction.
4. Storytelling—Fiction. 5. Death—Fiction.] I. Title.
PZ7.W1347Can 2006
[Fic]—dc22

                                                   2006004460

Manufactured in the United States of America
HAD 10 9 8 7 6 5 4 3 2 1

For Paul, my darling

Look for these other *Graphia* books

"There is no such thing as *just* a story."
—*Robert Fulford*

"Narration is as much part of human nature as breath
and the circulation of the blood."
—*A. S. Byatt*

EUGOLORP

THE REAL STORY

ONCE UPON A TIME, I saw the world the way I thought I was supposed to: as a place where the normal reigned and the weak perished under the strong. But I was wrong. And this is a story about that story. One of many tales that I must tell.

Megan would have been proud of me. For it was she who first made me see differently. She turned the world into one of stories—candy-coated, candy-colored, sweet and raw and square and round—composing words I would consume and devour, take whole inside my mouth and suck down into nothing.

What I didn't see was that there was something more behind them. More than what I had been told. More than what I had been made to understand. Because Megan made me believe that that was all they were. Stories.

In the end—whatever the truth is—this I know: whatever Megan told me, I believed it because I wanted to. Not because she made me. Megan was only doing what she had to. I was the one who didn't want to see what other truth there was. What the real story could be.

PART ONE
THE BEGINNING

HARD COMFORT

IN THE APRIL of that year, my mother died.

She had been sick for some time, in and out of the hospital, back and forth from home. My father had set up a small narrow bed for her in the spare bedroom. There, stationed in the corner next to her rocking chair and the window, was an IV pole. A puckered plastic sack of clear liquid hung from its stainless-steel hook. When she was home, I'd sit beside her on the edge of the bed and watch the drops drip slowly down the skinny tube. Once when I asked her what it was she told me glucose, a kind of sugar water.

As I thought about all that sugar running through her veins, I imagined it as a kind of liquid candy. But when I asked her if it tasted sweet, she laughed quietly and said no. It stung, she said. But she needed it. She had to have it.

Every time after that when my mother's nurse changed her medicine, I watched her with suspicion. As her nurse adjusted the tape on my mother's arm or inserted the needle into another vein I held my mother's hand. And no matter how hard I tried, every time the needle went in, I couldn't look away.

All I could imagine was that candied water burning inside

my mother. Like an invisible fire that I could not see or taste or touch or stop.

One day my father cried out for me in a voice I had never heard him use before. When I entered the spare bedroom, he was holding my mother's hand in his. He raised his head to look at me, his eyes full of anguish.

I stared at my mother lying in her bed, her eyes closed. Beside her was the IV pole: its tube dangling down beside her arm, glucose still dripping down the line. I stepped beside the bed and jerked the small needle out of her vein. Her mouth was slightly open, as if she were still breathing.

I wanted her to get up. I wanted her to come back to life. When my father looked at me again, hot jabbing waves stuck in my throat. I wanted to cry. Scream. But all I could do was watch the IV line twisting back and forth along the floor, its sugar water dripping slow as tears.

The day of the funeral it rained. My relatives came, mainly. My Uncle Sam, my father's brother. My cousins Chris and Sara. My Great-Aunt Elaine. Together we stood, heads bowed to the ground, silent with mourning as we listened to Father Joyce deliver the service.

I watched silently as my mother's coffin was lowered into the ground. All the time she was sick, I only ever thought she would get better. I couldn't believe I would never see her again.

I put my hand in the pocket of my coat and touched the plastic wrapping of the green and white striped mint that Aunt Elaine had given to me before the service. Like a pebble smoothed by waves, its tiny oval shape fit perfectly in the palm of my hand. "For later," my aunt said. "Just in case." She kissed me on top of my head and asked if I was okay. I nodded yes—not knowing what else to say—and put the mint in my pocket. Perhaps she felt she had to give me something.

Even Father Joyce had offered me something sweet. When my father and I had been in his office earlier that morning, there was a large crystal bowl of jellybeans on his desk. He joked they were the only sin he could commit. My father laughed in a sad, hopeless way. Then Father Joyce asked me if I wanted any. He stepped forward, offering the bowl with both hands, and told me I could take as many as I wanted. A broad beam of sunlight flooded his office and intersected with the bowl, casting prisms of candy-colored light against the wall.

My father leaned forward and took one. I stared at the collection of small kidney-shaped beans. Father Joyce urged me to take one. To take more than one. But when he saw my expression he put the bowl back on the corner of his desk, saying he understood if I didn't want anything just now.

Later, as Father Joyce spoke the final words of the service, I touched the piece of candy my Great-Aunt Elaine had given me and squeezed it until my hand burned with pain. And in that instant I came to believe that the glucose had been the disease, the sugar water the true cause of my mother's death. She had died full of liquid candy.

I looked down at my feet, steps away from the square edge of my mother's grave. I imagined her deep down inside that darkened box, lying on the soft bed of satin, wearing her best dress, her eyes forever closed. All that glucose still caught in her veins. Its poison seeping through her, adding to her decay.

I gripped the mint again. It was just like those bags of glucose the nurse had given my mother. But smaller. Harder. And just as deadly. And just as sweet.

It was then that I promised myself never to eat candy again. As God was my witness. So help me. Amen.

NORMAL

A FEW MONTHS LATER, my father and I moved to Woodland Hills, a quiet subdivision in a small town.

We had an average two-story house, with a paved driveway and a double-car garage. Trees stood out front: maple, birch, a couple of craggy spruce. Cedar shrubs, stiff as sentries, guarded the front door. It looked like every other two-story house on the street: neat and trim and tidy without drawing too much attention to itself. A model model home.

Great-Aunt Elaine was critical of the move. A girl my age needed stability and security, she told my father. A place to grow from. *Roots*. My father's only reply was that he couldn't live in the old house. Not anymore. Since my mother's death, the door to the spare bedroom had stayed closed. The truth was, I wanted to leave, too. I knew that nothing in that house would ever be the same.

A new reign of normalcy, I believed, would save my father and me. Events would ebb and flow in a domestic rhythm: perfect as a commercial, shiny and new. I envisioned myself gossiping on the telephone while downstairs my father drank coffee and read the weekend paper. There would be no trace of my mother's presence. Death would be reduced to nothing but a caricature: the caped crook from nightmares and comic books.

Or at least I hoped.

Shortly after we moved in, my father insisted we plant flower bulbs in memory of my mother. It was the first week of September, the last weekend before school started. Together we worked silently, side by side in the front garden, digging small dark holes in the earth.

The flowers were tulips. My mother's favorite. I watched as my father inserted the bulbs one by one into the holes, then covered them over with earth. Every now and then he stood back and wiped the sweat from his forehead with the back of his hand, his breathing strained.

His darkened shadow cast over me. I could sense the rough leanness of his face, the tense sorrow of his eyes. His whole body showed that he had been having trouble sleeping.

In the spring, he told me, things would be different. We would see the flowers bloom and we would remember her. "These sure are going to be beautiful, aren't they," he said.

I wasn't sure how to answer him. It hadn't really sounded like a question.

I looked at the black soil under my fingernails and thought about the bulbs buried in the cold ground. I couldn't bear the thought that they would be a memorial, pushing up through the earth, determined to make me remember.

The night before my first day of school, I stood naked before the mirror in my darkened room. I had grown in the past year.

"Developing," they called it, as if I were a photograph, bit by bit coming into focus.

Other landscapes of skin had appeared. Hair. Smells. Secretions. Bumps and lumps and curves. I felt weird. As if I were possessed by someone else. As if there were a whole other person growing outside of me.

Tomorrow, I told myself, I could transform into anyone I wanted to be. Nobody had to know anything about me. Nobody had to know the truth. Tomorrow I could be someone new.

My plan was simple. Be popular. Be cool. Fit in. No matter what happened: be normal.

The Woodland School was jail-like and institutional. Containment seemed to be its central architectural feature, with its cinder-block hallways painted varying shades of gray. The classrooms were militaristic. Cement-colored filing cabinets. Stainless-steel wastepaper baskets. Rows upon rows of desks, strategically arranged.

From the moment I stepped inside it, TWS seemed to me to be out of time: uncannily stuck in a previous era and, as I later came to learn, ruled by old-fashioned people and principles.

From inside the classroom, I surveyed the schoolyard. Out of the distance, a figure emerged, walking alone across the grass. A strange-looking boy. His head down.

"Hi there."

I turned around. A girl with dark skin and tight curly brown hair was smiling at me.

"Hi," I said.

"You're new, aren't you?"

I nodded.

She extended her hand. "I'm Tracey Reid. Our teacher, Mr. King, asked me to show you around." I reached out and shook her hand. Her grip was firm and dry, and she had the polite resolution of a politician.

"Nice to meet you," I said.

"That was Blake Starfield," she informed me.

"Excuse me?"

"That boy you were looking at. Walking across the yard."

I turned back around to see where he went, but he was gone.

"If I were you, I'd stay away from him," Tracey warned me. "He's *weird*."

"Well, I see someone is making somebody feel welcome."

We both turned around. In the doorway was a tall man with dark-rimmed glasses and graying hair.

"Hello, Mr. King," Tracey said, blushing.

Mr. King flashed me a quick grin, adjusting his light gray sport coat. I stared down at the floor, looking at his shoes: black loafers with little leather tassels. He was not what I expected.

"Miss Reid," he said, acknowledging Tracey. Mr. King, I later learned, always called girls by their last name if he really liked them. He put his hands in his pockets, jingling some loose change.

"If you want to know anything, just ask Miss Reid here. She knows everything." He looked down at Tracey and smiled, then winked at me. "And everybody, too."

The odor of his cologne was sharp.

"I spoke with your father last week," he said, turning to me.

"After all that's happened, I want you to know you have our support here at Woodland."

I realized this must have been the same speech my father had heard. I thought of him at the mercy of Mr. King's exacting manner, his head bowed in submission.

"If you ever need someone to talk to, I'm here," Mr. King continued.

Tracey looked at me with sympathy. "Me, too."

I looked at them both and nodded.

"Thanks. I'll remember that."

Mr. King designated our seating. Tracey sat on the other side of the room. Blake Starfield was assigned the seat behind me.

When I turned around, he stared at me and grinned. One eye looked straight at me, but his right iris was like a stray marble. I didn't know which eye to look into. Confused, I turned around, ignoring him.

Then I saw *them*.

Three girls: beautiful, beautiful, and beautiful. As they glided into the classroom, arm in arm, laughing in harmony, they seemed to me, with their pretty hair and cool clothes, the epitome of perfection. I imagined they all had complete families. Dogs and cats. Bedrooms with canopy beds edged with white lace. Jewelry boxes with ballerinas.

They were normal. And I longed to be a part of them.

After a few days, I was sitting with Tracey Reid at lunch when I was approached by two of the beautiful girls. They looked down at me and smiled.

"Hi," one said.

"Hi," I replied, noticing she didn't address Tracey.

"Meredith wants to meet you," the other one said.

"Who?" I asked.

"Meredith McKinnon." The other girl said this as if I was supposed to know who Meredith McKinnon was.

"Me?"

The girl smiled. "Right now." Tracey stood up to accompany me.

"Sit," the first girl said coldly, pushing Tracey back down. *"You* weren't invited. Newcomers only."

Tracey's eyes were bruised with hurt. I was surprised by the show of force—it seemed extreme. But I felt as if I'd been called to some secret order. As if I'd been selected.

The two girls escorted me away from Tracey. The girl who had pushed Tracey down took my arm and said, "I'm Laura Mitchell." She said this like I was supposed to know who she was, too.

"Hi—" I said.

"And this is Angela Moyer," Laura said. The other girl took my other arm.

"Hi," she said.

"Hi."

As we walked with linked arms across the school ground, everyone stared at us. Watching. Whispering. Both curious and envious. As I approached Meredith, her eyes scanned me.

"Welcome to TWS," she said. "I'm Meredith."

Meredith McKinnon had long, straight honey blond hair. Sky blue eyes. Cherry red lips. Several seconds flashed by before I realized she was waiting for me to say something.

"Thanks," I murmured. "It's great to be here."

Meredith smiled. Now flanking her, Angela and Laura also smiled. The three of them seemed inseparable, like an isosceles triangle, the two equal sides fortifying the strength of the third. Their eyes looked me over from top to bottom and back again.

"What are you doing later?" Meredith asked.

"Nothing," I said.

Meredith smiled again.

"Why don't you come hang out with us?" Laura asked.

"Yeah," Angela added. "We'll show you around."

"Sure," I said, as calmly as I could.

I had been chosen. Level One.

After school, I met Meredith and Laura and Angela outside the main entrance. With Meredith leading in the middle, they stepped through the doors, hugging their books and binders to their chests, laughing and smiling at one another. I was still surprised that I had been selected. Why me? Everything seemed to be happening so fast.

I was so nervous. I just had to play it cool. Let them take the lead. I had decided to say, in case they asked, that my father and I had moved to Woodland Hills because he had been transferred to another job. Which was partly true. But that was all I would reveal. I would pretend to be as normal as they were.

"Hi," Meredith said, smiling at me. "Glad you could join us."

"Yeah," said Laura. "Looks like you finally escaped."

I looked at them in confusion. Meredith and Angela laughed.

"From Tracey . . ." Angela explained.

"Oh." Nervous laughter. "Yeah. Thanks."

Meredith took me by the arm. "Come on. Let's go to your place."

My stomach caved. "We can't," I said, stumbling, hoping they wouldn't notice the panic in my voice.

"Why not?" Angela asked.

"Because we're not totally unpacked yet," I lied. "And the house is a mess. And since my mom's away on business she wouldn't want me to let anyone see it like that."

Meredith thought about this for a moment, then finally suggested we go to her house.

I sighed with relief. Level Two.

As we walked down the sidewalk, Meredith and Laura and Angela talked about their summer vacations. How they all went to camp together. How they learned to sail. Canoe. Throw clay. They giggled as they recalled three older boys who were junior camp counselors: Mike and Dave and Tim.

"Remember when they went skinny-dipping?" said Angela. "And then refused to come out of the water?"

Meredith and Laura squealed in delight.

"And we promised—" Laura said.

"Not to look—" Meredith continued.

"But we did!" Angela finished.

The three of them burst into laughter.

"Mike was *so* hot," Laura crooned.

"I know," echoed Angela. "Like, totally. I mean, did you *see* him?"

Meredith moaned. "Oh, yeah."

Then they turned and asked me what I had done for summer vacation. I said I'd gone to Maine. Which was in some way true—we had. But all I'd really done was spend two weeks watching TV with my cousins. Every night my father had slept on the floor beside me in a sleeping bag, snoring from drinking too much beer.

But Meredith and Laura and Angela didn't hear that. They heard the vacation I wanted to have. Boating. Sailing. Whale watching. Eating lobster, swimming in the ocean. Picture-perfect sunsets. They seemed impressed. I was glad none of them had ever been to Maine.

Meredith's house was big. Big rooms. Big bathrooms. A big indoor pool. I placed my bag at the front door and followed the three of them into the kitchen. They stood gathered around the refrigerator while Meredith gave out bottled water.

In the living room, they slumped into the matching furniture in front of the big-screen TV. I sat in a chair and listened while they talked about their hair. Their nails. Their teeth. About how fat they thought they were. Clothes. Makeup. More hair. More clothes. Then how cute Jason Cutler was. And how crazy Blake Starfield was.

"Do you remember, last year? When he climbed the roof of the school and tried to jump off?" Angela started.

"And how he said he was going to fly?" Laura answered.

Meredith laughed. "What a freak!"

I remembered the way he looked that first morning walking across the schoolyard. Then, later, in class. I thought of telling Meredith and Angela and Laura about it, but I didn't want to arouse any questions about me in their minds.

"I love those jeans," Angela said to Meredith. "They look so awesome on you."

"They don't make me look huge?" Meredith stood up and modeled them, standing on her tiptoes and turning, slowly rotating her slim hips, baring her midriff. "Now, tell me the truth—" she teased, striking a pose.

Angela and Laura fawned over her, complimenting the fit. Then Meredith looked at me. "What do you think?" she asked me.

There was not one inch of fat on her. The jeans fit perfectly.

"They look good," I stated.

Meredith glanced at me with disapproval. Obviously I had not said the right word.

"What I meant to say was, they look really good," I fumbled. "*Great*, actually."

Satisfied, Meredith tossed her hair over her shoulder. Level Three.

After more water, they talked about Tracey Reid and how they all felt sorry for me because I'd been stuck with her.

"She is such a loser."

"Did you see the way she looks at Mr. King?"

"She is so in love with him."

"It's so gross. It's like she wants to suck him off or something."

Again, they erupted in fits of laughter.

"We should do something," Angela said, brimming with mischief. "To *her*."

Meredith's eyes widened with interest. "Like what?"

Ominous silence. Then Laura looked at me.

When I didn't say anything, she looked at Angela and

Meredith with impatience. I felt my heart trip with fear. Obviously that was Level Four. But I had blown it.

"How about a letter," Laura said. "Something *really* embarrassing —"

"Yeah," Angela continued, "a dirty love letter . . ."

I knew I had to contribute something.

"How about from that guy . . . that weird guy . . ." I blurted out.

The three of them turned their heads and looked at me.

"You mean Blake Starfield?" Meredith asked.

"Yeah," Laura said. "From Blake. To Tracey."

I actually thought Tracey had been okay. But I wasn't going to tell them that.

Meredith smiled and nodded with approval. *"Perfect,"* she said.

For the rest of the afternoon, Laura dictated the letter while Angela wrote it out. Meredith made corrections and amendments, changing this word to that one, giving the letter its cruel, lurid bent.

"I want you to . . ."

"I *need* you to . . ."

"Suck . . ."

"Yeah . . ."

"My throbbing gristle . . ."

"Loving you, my Miss Meat Joy . . ."

"My Miss *Juicy Quivering* Meat Joy."

I realized they almost never finished their own sentences: they almost always did it for each other. Except, of course, for Meredith. She always had the final say.

When they had completed writing the letter, they decided I should be the one to deliver it to Tracey.

"After all, it was your idea," Angela said.

"Yeah," Laura said.

"That's OK with you, isn't it?" Meredith asked.

I swallowed nervously. "Sure," I replied. "I can do that."

That night, I lay awake in bed, staring up at the ceiling, listening to the silence. Noticing a spill of light from under my door, I got up and walked into the hallway. My father's bedroom door was open.

When I was little I used to sneak around the house at night, spying on my mother and father. I loved thinking I was invisible. I sat for hours on the stairs, watching them watch television, listening to them, waiting to see what they'd do. Sometimes I got caught and my father would chase me as I ran up the stairs, laughing as he grabbed me and threw me over his shoulder. Then he'd carry me into my bedroom and lay me down in my bed. He'd ask me about the best part and the worst part of my day. And as he listened he would stroke my hair. He'd tell me it was time for bed. Kiss me good night. And then, softly, he'd close the door.

I looked at my father now, sitting at his desk: the table lamp on, his head slumped over the open book spread out in front of him. I stared at the way the light spilled over his back. I watched the slow rise and fall of his shoulders as he breathed. I wanted him to hear me, to see me. To wake up and turn around and run after me, to lift me up into his arms and carry me back to my bed. But I knew I was too old for that now.

I walked up behind him, the floor cold under my feet.

When I was standing behind him, I gently placed my hand on his shoulder. He flinched ever so slightly, opening his eyes. He turned and looked up at me with wonder, as if I were a stranger.

"Dad," I said, "it's time to go to bed."

He nodded and stood up from the chair, holding my hand as I led him toward his bed. Without getting under the covers, he lay down on it and turned his back to me.

Down the hallway, back in my bedroom, I crawled into my own bed.

In the morning, as always, we would not speak of it.

Because, as always, he would not remember it.

The next morning I delivered the note to Tracey Reid and passed Level Five. It had been simple, really, dropping off the note on her desk. But then I watched her open it. Read it. And saw the look of hurt on her face. I felt as if I shouldn't have cared about Tracey Reid. Or Blake Starfield. That I should have been proud of what I'd done. But I wasn't. I felt awful.

Meredith and Laura and Angela had liked my idea. And me. And for that week I came and went from The Woodland School under their protective wing, privy to their conversations about hair and clothes and boys as if nothing else mattered. I was a part of them. I was almost normal. I was almost happy.

And then I met her. Megan Chalmers.

DESTINY

WHO SHE WAS or where she came from nobody knew. She just showed up the second week of school and stood cool and aloof in a corner by the outside front doors. Her mouth twisted in a sour frown, eyes pinched with suspicion.

"I'd like to introduce the newest addition to our class," Mr. King later told us, "and I expect all of you to make her feel welcome." Mr. King stood at his official post at the front of the classroom, a piece of chalk in his hand. "This is Megan Chalmers."

She was thin with white, almost bluish skin, and the bold stare of her dark blue eyes was half hidden under sharp straggles of wild spiky hair. She wore a red dress with a ruffled collar and sleeves, the elastic around the waist and wrists stretched and broken. Her eyelids were dotted with sparkling silver eye shadow, her lips glazed with a hot watermelon pink. She gave Mr. King a terse smile and put her hands in the pockets of her ripped jean jacket.

"Megan, maybe you could tell us something about yourself." I noticed that he hadn't called her "Miss Chalmers."

She studied his face with bored contempt.

"No need to be shy," Mr. King said, encouraging her. "We have other new students this year." He waved his arm in my direction. I shrank behind my desk, my shoulders leaden with embarrassment.

Megan looked me in the eye, acknowledging me, but remained silent. It was a wise, all-knowing look. And then, as I was staring at her: déjà vu. As if I had somehow dreamed her being there. As if I had known her before.

I looked over at Meredith and Angela and Laura, who were already studying Megan. Their collective gaze was charged with scorn. Mr. King waited for some response, but it was clear that Megan wasn't going to talk.

She flashed the class a fuck-you grin and took her seat.

Later that morning I looked over at Megan Chalmers sitting at her desk, her hair falling over her face, her long, thin fingers clasped around her pen. She moved her lips as she wrote, silently murmuring the words.

Then her hand went down between her legs. It was there for only a second before she lifted it up to her mouth and then hid it under her hair. As if she knew I was watching her, she turned and stared directly at me.

It was a look of pure defiance. A dare. She pursed her lips together in a kiss. Winked. Then she opened her mouth, sticking out her tongue. It was bright purple: a vivid, gaudy grape. She waggled it from side to side and then, just as quickly, slid it back in her mouth and looked away.

It wasn't until Mr. King called my name that I turned my head and faced the front.

"Since you find our new classmate so interesting," he said to me, "you can have the pleasure of showing her around the school. Today. At lunch."

Across the classroom, Meredith and Angela and Laura monitored the situation. Under my new normal status, Megan Chalmers was not the sort of person I wanted to be associated with. She was as uncool as Tracey Reid, but worse. Way worse.

But there was something about her. That feeling of déjà vu. I tried not to think of the strange specter of Megan Chalmers's purple tongue. Its dark, candied gloss.

At lunch, Megan showed up late outside the entrance to the gym, sucking a red lollipop.

"Hi there," she said and grinned, twirling the lollipop along the inside of her lips. I looked at the candy in her mouth and felt like I was going to be sick.

I led her down the halls, showing her this room and that — "This is the gym and this is the library" — while she feigned interest. Every now and then she nodded her head and said "Uh-huh" and "Hmm" or "Ah" as if she really cared where the volleyballs went or how many days she could keep a library book. For most of the tour she sauntered beside me, sucking on her lollipop.

"Want some?" she asked, pulling it out of her mouth and offering it to me.

I stared at the glistening orb, red as blood.

"No," I said. "Thank you."

She put it back in her mouth, shifting the hard round bulge from cheek to cheek. She narrowed her eyes. "C'mon. I know you want some."

"No. Thank you."

I started walking away from her. She jumped in front of me, blocking my path.

"Do you *really* like this school?" she asked. "Because I can tell you don't. C'mon! The Woodland School? Gimme a break. How retarded. It sounds like something out of a fucking Disney afterschool special." Megan took the lollipop out of her mouth and dangled it in midair. She paused for effect, waiting for my reaction. "These stuck-up bozos think it's so shit-hot. But it's just like all the other schools I've been to. The Rules are here, too."

I must have looked at her like I didn't understand.

"You know what I mean. *The Rules*. Who and what is cool and who and what is not." She paused and moved closer to me. "A small group of boys and girls who fascistically control the social dynamic of the whole, as if ruling a totalitarian state?"

I had no time to answer.

"They're everywhere," she whispered and leaned forward, then looked over her shoulder. "They have different names, but essentially they're the same. Here it's those three girls."

My heart skipped. "What three girls?"

"You know the ones I mean. The beauty queens."

"You mean Meredith, Angela, and Laura?"

Megan cracked a knowing smile. "I'm sure that's them." She paused. "Meredith, Angela, and Laura: M-A-L. *MAL.*"

Megan raised the lollipop above her head, wielding it like a sword. I hoped no one was watching us.

"What gives them their right of privilege is clear," she said, adopting a radio announcer's voice. "They're good-looking, good at sports, good in school! The kind of girls whose very nature causes their mothers' and fathers' spirits to swell with obscene, heart-puffing pride! Their parental lust almost pornographic for the power that their daughters, by right of their beauty and their privileged birth, will in the future seize! The world already belongs to them! It's only a matter of time before it's theirs to master!"

Megan clicked her heels together and raised her right arm in the air, performing a mock salute. Then she pretended to stick her finger down her throat and gag. When she had finished, she took a large bite of her lollipop, cracking it between her teeth. The sound made me wince.

"But you," Megan said, "you're different. I can tell." She looked me in the eye. "You're not like the rest of these . . ." — she paused to consider the word — "*clones*. You've been around. I knew as soon as I saw you." She thrust her lollipop into my hand. "Here, hold this. Let me look at your palm." She reached out and grabbed my other hand, holding it in both of hers. They were warm and sticky.

"Very interesting," she said, moving her finger along a groove inside my palm. "You have a deep line of the heart. And your lifeline is strong, except for here." I looked down at where she was pointing. I could see nothing.

"You've just gone through a great tragedy. A death. See how it splits in two? You're lying about who you are. You're leading a double life. At some point you'll be found out. But see here, how these two lines intersect? That means you'll have to perform an act of great courage in order to become whole again. Transformation is in your future." She turned her face to me with great seriousness and then held her own palm out for me to see. "I know because I've got the exact same lines in the exact same place. Right here. See?"

I pulled my hand away. She grabbed her lollipop back and looked me in the eye again, putting her face close to mine.

"When you first looked at me you got déjà vu, didn't you?" she whispered.

My heartbeat quickened.

"I know," Megan said, "because when I looked at you I got it, too. We're fated to be friends. It's our *destiny.*"

Anyone who could know so much about me when I knew so little about her had to be dangerous. She waved the broken lollipop back and forth in front of my eyes.

"I don't believe in fate," I told her. "Or destiny."

Megan smiled. My hand was burning.

"Sure you don't. And monkeys fly out of my ass." She laughed and stuck the lollipop back in her mouth. I didn't know what to say.

"Well, thanks for the tour," she said. "See ya around."

That day after school, Meredith and Angela and Laura wanted to know all about my tour with Megan.

"What did she say to you?" Meredith asked.

"Yeah, you were gone a long time," said Angela.

"Who is she?" Laura asked.

I thought of all the things that Megan Chalmers had said. About school. About me. About them. I remembered her acronym for them: MAL. It sounded like some multinational corporation or a radical cult. Or a new kind of cancer. But she had revealed nothing about herself.

"I don't know," I replied. "She didn't really say anything."

Meredith looked at me with immediate suspicion. "What do you mean? She must have said something."

Laura waited her turn. "She didn't tell you *anything?*" she asked.

"No, nothing," I said nervously.

"Did she say anything about us?"

"No," I lied.

Meredith's eyes narrowed. She studied me skeptically. I told myself I wouldn't panic. But I was scared.

"But you were with her all that time—" said Meredith.

"I can't believe she wouldn't say something—" Laura added.

"She's a freak," I said, defending myself. "That's all."

"She is weird, that's for sure," said Meredith.

"I know," Laura said. "I mean, did you look at what she was wearing?"

"Like, really," Angela concurred. "What was with that dress?"

"And that hair—"

"Or her makeup—"

"I know. Totally."

Laura turned to Meredith. "Perhaps we should send her a little note," Laura suggested. "Since she's new and everything. Just to make her feel, you know, *welcome.*"

Meredith smiled deviously. "What a great idea."

"Yeah, totally." Angela grinned.

Laura continued, "It could say something like, you know, about what a total skank she is . . ."

"Yeah, and how she isn't allowed to dress like that at school—" Angela said.

"Unless," Meredith interrupted, "she really, *really* wants it."

The three of them laughed. As they wrote the note, carefully crafting each sentence, I recalled what Megan had said about "The Rules." About who and what was cool and who and what was not. I listened helplessly, my silence making me complicit.

When they finished, Meredith turned and faced me. "Since you did such a good job last time . . ." she began.

"And since you say she didn't say *anything* to you . . ." Laura added.

"And because you already know her and everything . . ." Angela continued.

"*You* can deliver the note to Megan," Meredith concluded. She leaned forward and pressed the note into my hand. "Got it?"

The three of them stared at me, waiting. Obviously this was Level Six.

The following day before class started, I placed the note on Megan's desk, just as I had been instructed. Then I waited.

It was just after the morning bell when Megan came into the classroom and took her seat. While the other students streamed into the room, I watched her as she opened the folded triangle of white paper and read the words inside. When she finished reading, Megan bellowed with laughter.

Immediately, she walked over to my desk and held the note up to my face.

"What the fuck is this?" she demanded.

I stared at the hard black letters on the page. I could feel Meredith and Angela and Laura watching from across the classroom. Studying my reaction. Assessing my behavior.

"You didn't write this," Megan said as she crumpled the note into a ball. "Don't worry. I *know* you didn't write this. But *who* did? Gee, let me guess . . ." Megan turned around and scanned the classroom, tossing the ball up and down. "Our twisted little fucked-up friends MAL, maybe?"

"No, don't—" I warned.

But it was too late. I watched in horror as Megan walked over to Meredith's desk. The classroom was beginning to quiet down. Others were also watching. Listening.

"Thanks for the friendly welcome note," I heard Megan say. "That was real swell of you."

"I don't know what you're talking about," Meredith scoffed. "I didn't write you a note." Meredith looked in my direction. "*She* did—"

"Who?" Megan said, looking over her shoulder at me. "*Her?*" Megan laughed. "I don't think so. I think it was you and"—she pointed her finger first at Laura, then at Angela—"*her* and *her*." Then she pointed back at me. "It was definitely not *her*."

Sensing her audience, Megan paused slightly.

My heart was pounding.

"Let's get one thing clear right now," she explained to Meredith. "Next time you want to piss me off, don't send your little pawn to play your stupid games for you. Just be a big girl and send me the fucking note yourself."

Just then Mr. King entered the room. He stared at Megan.

"Megan Chalmers," he said sternly, "when class begins I expect you to be in your seat and ready to learn. Is that understood?"

Without reply, Megan dropped the ball of paper on Meredith's desk and casually walked back to her seat. As she did, she turned to me and winked. Meredith and Laura and Angela looked over at me and scowled. I had failed Level Seven.

At lunch, the three of them confronted me.

"What the fuck happened this morning?" Laura demanded.

"I don't know," I said. "I just did what you asked me . . ."

"No, you didn't!" Angela said. "You fucked it up."

"It was her." My stomach fluttered. "She did it. She just knew—"

"But how? How did she just know?" Meredith asked. "You must have told her something."

"I swear I didn't—"

"So what *did* you tell her?" Laura interrupted, shooting me a cold stare. "Tell us what you said."

"I didn't say anything."

"We know you're lying," Angela said. "Don't lie to us."

"Why are you lying?" Meredith demanded.

"I'm not!"

"You've been hanging out with us for almost a week. I thought you liked us. I thought you wanted to be our friend," Laura said.

"I do, I do!"

"Then why did you tell her we wrote the note?" asked Angela.

My head was dizzy with their accusations. "I didn't," I said.

Laura looked at Meredith in exasperation. "She's lying. Who knows what else she's been lying about?"

"Please," I pleaded. "You don't understand. She just knew—"

"Yeah, right," Angela said.

"Look. Whatever," Laura said to Meredith. "Let's go."

I felt desperate. Out of breath. As if I was going to cry. Laura looked at me with disgust. The tears welled in my eyes. Meredith studied me with cool detachment, silent.

"Meredith, please, wait," I pleaded.

Angela turned to Laura and smirked. *"Meredith, please, wait,"* she echoed, mimicking me.

And then, without saying anything, Meredith turned around and Laura and Angela followed behind, leaving me standing alone on the school grounds.

For days, Meredith and Laura and Angela ignored me. When I approached them at lunch, they looked at each other with disinterest and walked away. Other times, they turned their backs to me or pretended I wasn't there. I was devastated.

Then came the note, folded in a triangle, inside my desk. It was on white paper, with my name written in big black letters on the front. Inside, it said: *J BN XBUDIJOH ZPV.* There was no mode of transcription. No deciphering instructions.

I carefully looked over the letters. It was a sentence. I looked at the first letter—"J"—and thought about the letters that came before and after it and knew how to decode it. I took out a pen and wrote the correct letters underneath. When I finished, it read: *I am watching you.*

I looked up from my desk and stared at Meredith and Angela and Laura. The triangle, I knew, was no coincidence. This letter, like the one to Megan, was more than a means of intimidation. It was a measure of control, a way of putting fear in the heart of its recipient.

I am watching you. I repeated the words over and over in my mind. Like they were a knot in my brain that I couldn't untie.

DEAD GIRL

OVER THE NEXT WEEK, the notes kept coming. All written in black ink on white paper, the handwriting always the same. The only thing that varied was the message, which changed every time, using a new cryptic code that I was forced to figure out. Usually the notes were in letter code, other times in numbers. Sometimes in both.

The messages were never easy to decipher. But I managed to decode them, strangely compelled to see what they would say next. *I know what you do not know about yourself,* one said. Another: *I know what you want.*

Though they would have denied it, I knew the notes had to be from Meredith and Angela and Laura. But they continued to ignore me when I tried to talk to them, pretending I didn't exist at all.

I wished being ignored was something I was used to. But I had a thin skin, and every time they did it, it hurt. And they knew it. And even though I knew they hated me, I still wanted to be their friend. They had made me feel a part of something. A part of them. Normal. But now that was all over.

Every day after school, I went home to my room and stared

up at the ceiling. I hated my life. And I hated Megan Chalmers. She had ruined everything.

The next week, I was in the washroom, alone, when I heard the door open. When I looked up in the mirror, my heart froze.

"Well, look who's here," said Meredith, walking up behind me, finally talking to me.

"Hi," I replied nervously. I felt her eyes burn straight through me. Angela and Laura moved beside her.

"I really like your outfit," Meredith began.

"Yeah," Laura echoed.

I said nothing.

"I mean, it fits you so well. That top—and the pants are so fashionable, too. Where'd you get it? The Salvation Army?"

Angela laughed.

"Oh, no. I know what it is," Angela continued. "It belonged to someone else—someone who died. I mean, it probably belonged to a dead girl, right? A girl who was killed in a terrible accident—"

"Or who had cancer . . ." said Laura.

"Or who had been *murdered*," said Angela.

"*Yeah.*" Meredith's eyes sparkled. "A girl who'd been *murdered.*" Meredith savored the word and then reached out and touched the sleeve of my shirt. "It was really too bad. She was walking home from school one day—"

"Through the woods," Angela interrupted, improvising.

"And suddenly, out from behind this tree, there was this man—" Laura added.

"Yeah, a bearded man, with bushy black eyebrows and glowing black eyes and sharp yellow teeth," Meredith said.

"And he crept behind the girl, following her as she walked through the woods."

"And she wasn't looking to see who might have been behind her—"

"And," Meredith interrupted, "just when she was at the edge of the woods he grabbed her by the hair and forced her to her knees and told her to suck him off."

"Yeah," Laura said, filling the left side of her cheek with her tongue and curling her hand into a tight ball, moving it back and forth from her mouth in a lewd gesture. "And he said '*Suck it, girl, suck it real good.*'"

Meredith looked at Laura and erupted into high-pitched laughter. Angela joined them.

Paralyzed with humiliation, I stood there before them, tears welling in my eyes.

And then a toilet flushed.

I looked at Meredith. She looked at me. Then all four of us turned in the direction of the stall. As the door opened, out walked Megan Chalmers, zipping up her fly. She beamed at Meredith. "So then what happens?" she asked.

"Wh-what?" Meredith stammered.

"What happens to the dead girl? How does she die?"

There was an awkward silence. I'd had no idea Megan was in the washroom. Her presence was entirely coincidental. But I knew Meredith and Angela and Laura wouldn't see it that way.

Laura moved and stood in front of Megan, staring her in the face. "She dies because after the man shoots off his load he takes out an ax and chops her into little bits and buries her in a box in the woods."

Megan stepped away from Laura and washed her hands in the sink beside me.

"Charming. And then?"

"And then one day when some kids are playing in the woods they find the box."

"And?"

"And," Meredith said, stepping away from me and directing her stare toward Megan, "they open it. And inside are all the bloody bits of the dead girl." Meredith looked back at me and narrowed her eyes, a twisted grin on her lips. "Later, when the police tell the dead girl's mother what happened, the mother cries and gives away all the girl's clothing, all her books and toys. Everything.

"And then *she*," Meredith continued, pointing her finger at me, "goes shopping at the Sally Ann, and guess what? *She's* wearing the clothes of a dead girl."

Megan ripped off a sheet of paper towel and dried her hands. "Leave her alone," she said.

"What?"

"You heard me, bitch. Leave her alone."

"Look," I said to Megan, "I can fight my own battles—"

"Shut up, dead girl," Angela fired at me.

"Yeah, shut the fuck up," Meredith said, looking at me and then at Megan. "Just who do you think you are?"

Megan turned to her and smiled. "The biggest pickle you're ever going to have rammed up your ass, princess."

There was silence. Then Laura stepped in front of Megan.

"No one," she started, "and I mean *no one*, talks to my best friend that way."

"Yeah?" Megan replied. "And who says? *You?*" She laughed at them. "I can say whatever the fuck I want. Especially to you."

"Now, listen, you," Laura said, pausing for the right word, "you *pussy*—"

Megan burst into laughter. "Now don't go using big words you don't understand," she shot back.

"You . . ." Meredith said, standing there, enraged, speechless. The bell rang.

"Saved by the bell," I murmured.

"Shut up, dead girl," Angela told me again.

"Yeah, shut up," Laura said. "C'mon, Meredith." She tugged on Meredith's arm, pulling her away.

"I'm not through with you," Meredith threatened Megan. "Or you," she said to me.

"Just watch your backs," Angela added.

"Yeah," Laura agreed. "Or else."

Megan narrowed her eyes and gave them a surly like-you're-really-scaring-me kind of look. Then the three of them turned and walked out.

"Thanks a lot," I said, "but I don't need your help—"

"Looks like you needed all the goddamn help you could get." She reached into her pocket and pulled out a clear plastic roll of Rain-Blo chewing gum. "Bubblegum?"

I looked down at the long and slender package in her hands, flinching at the sight of it.

"No," I said, turning away.

She shrugged. "Suit yourself."

I watched as Megan split open the side seam of the plastic wrapper and tilted her head back. One by one the gumballs barreled into her mouth.

"You know, to anyone else," Megan said, chewing, "they look like nothing more than three pretty, perfect girls. But MAL have been given what only girls like them get: unquestionable authority; the gross pink talons of supremacy."

Megan chewed the gum, grinding her jaw in a rough circular motion.

"Like a beast at the gates of hell, their three-headed, hydra-like oneness will rise up from the miry wastelands before lost souls . . ." She gave me a wicked smile. "Like I said. E-V-I-L."

Megan chewed again, forcing the gum out with her tongue, forming a large dark purple bubble. As it popped and deflated, shriveling against her lips, I was struck again by the same feeling of déjà vu that I had when I had first seen her. She reached into her pocket and offered me another package of gum. I shook my head no. She looked at me with total confusion.

"I don't like candy," I lied, not wanting to explain why.

Her face dropped. *"What?"*

"I just don't like it," I repeated.

"Impossible," Megan said. "Everyone likes candy. Whether they want to or not. Everyone *wants* candy."

"I don't."

"I don't believe you," she said. "Here, try one of these." She put the gum back and reached into her pocket again, this time pulling out a package of M&M's.

"No," I said, "I don't want any. Thank you. I should be getting back to class."

I started to walk away, but Megan stepped in front of me.

"One tiny little piece isn't going to kill you. C'mon, try it. I promise, you'll like it."

"I can't," I said, making up something to tell her. "I'm allergic to it. To dextrose. The corn-based additive—"

"I know what it is," she said. "What's it do to you?"

"What do you mean?" I asked uncomfortably, looking at the door. I wanted to leave, but Megan was blocking my way.

"Do you freak out?"

"Sort of," I lied. "A doctor once told my father that it makes me hyperactive . . ."

Megan laughed and put the M&M's back in her pocket. "Candy makes all kids like that. Don't you know there's a conspiracy of adults against kids having candy? It's because they want to control us. Control our minds and bodies, shape our lives and destinies." She blew another bubble. After it popped, she sucked the gum back into her mouth and said, "It wouldn't surprise me if your doctor just said that so your parents would have an excuse not to give you any."

"No," I said. "You really don't understand. It really does . . . I don't know . . . make me kind of crazy."

Megan looked at me and grinned. "So?"

"I should really be getting back to class," I said, moving toward the door.

"Yeah, I guess so," Megan said. "But who the fuck wants to? That Mr. King is a real asshole."

"I don't know," I said. "He seems OK."

"Yeah, right," replied Megan. "He's just as backward as everything else in this bum-fuck school." She paused, adopting the tone of Mr. King's voice. *"Megan Chalmers,"* she imitated, *"when class begins I expect you to be in your seat and ready to learn. Is that understood?"* She snorted. "I've seen his type before. Just wait. He'll be licking MAL's boots before you know it."

There was a break in our conversation, but I seemed unable to move.

"Sure you don't want any?" she offered again, rustling the M&M's in her pocket. "Just one. Take it home. Try it. See if you like it. And if you want more, I can get it for you. I can get you whatever you want. *Anytime.*"

"No," I said, moving toward the door. "Please. Just leave me alone."

"OK, but just think about what I said," she told me. "You're probably not allergic to candy at all. And just remember this word: C-O-N-S-P-I-R-A-C-Y."

As if things couldn't get any worse, that afternoon I noticed Blake Starfield staring at me.

At first I thought it was accidental. But over the next few days I realized that every time I turned in his direction he was looking at me. I began to wonder if he was the one sending the notes.

I soon learned that Blake was a special student. Which meant that he was not developmentally challenged, exactly, but just — or so everyone thought — slow. Blake had problems. Problems with paying attention. Problems with his behavior. Problems with authority.

His lazy eye did not help. And it was this outward evidence of defect that earned him the most scorn. Most of it came from Jason Cutler and Adam Diamond and David Pierce, the most popular boys in the class. They had christened Blake "Slug Bait," "'Tard," and their all-time favorite, "Quasi." Every day they taunted Blake, their laughter cruel and mocking. In the throes of my own torture from Meredith and Angela and

Laura, I felt sorry for him. But I knew that to express sympathy for him would be a social death sentence.

Blake was the kind of student teachers whispered about in staff rooms. It was rumored that he had been expelled from three other schools before coming to TWS. Exactly where he had been and what he had done remained a mystery—only the teachers were privy to such information—but it was clear that Blake's "special" problems had been the cause.

He always looked as if he had just rolled out of bed right before coming to school. His clothes were constantly rumpled. His hair regularly stood up on end. And in his eyes was a perpetual look of bewilderment, as if he were both simultaneously confused and amused by everything around him.

The truth was, I didn't think Blake was "slow" at all. Rather, I thought, as his last name implied, he was actually moving at light speed. He was like a meteor hurtling through space, with the universe around him so large that it only made him seem slow, drifting along as lazy as a tumbleweed in the cosmos.

One afternoon a black jawbreaker was left in the pencil tray of my desk. There was no packaging. No evidence of who might have touched it, in whose hands it may have traveled. It was simply a naked, innocuous black jawbreaker. A tiny bomb.

To my shame, I wanted to take it in my mouth. To feel my cheek bulge and my teeth ache. To taste the sugar melt as I moved it from side to side, rolling it over my tongue, imagining each layer a different sensation, altering from one flavor to another before it exploded in a big sour bang of gum.

I walked home with it, clutching it tightly. When I was far

enough away from school and I was sure no one was watching me, I held it between my thumb and index finger and studied its strange beauty.

I could have had it. But when I saw myself reflected in it, like a crystal ball, I saw how I was tempted by it. By its potency. By its sweetness. Horrified and ashamed, I threw it away, tossing it into someone's bushes.

When I got home, I went straight into the bathroom and washed my hands. I watched the gray candied water swirl down the drain as I rubbed the stain of the jawbreaker away, erasing its black mark of death.

The next morning there was another note. The first part read: *J IPQF ZPV MJLFE JU*, which I translated as *I hope you liked it.* The second part, which I realized was each word written backwards, said: *TEEM EM TA EHT ECNEF YB EHT SEERT NI EHT DRAYLOOHCS TA HCNUL.* And then, below: *RUOY TERCES DNEIRF.*

At lunch I stood in the schoolyard, at the fence, by the trees, waiting; the note was folded in my hand. What had started out as a sunny day had turned to a cloudy one, and now there was a sudden rain. Kids ran toward the shelter of the school doors, but I remained in the cold drizzle, waiting.

It was her. Carrying a yellow umbrella, walking across the field. Streaks of purple accented her eyes; her lips were a bright fuchsia. That morning I'd noticed her hair was dyed electric pink and the roots were a deep red. She was wearing a pink patent leather miniskirt. A black T-shirt with the words LICK ME glittered in silver on the front.

I should have known.

Megan Chalmers.

Her face came into focus: the two dark blue eyes as alert as a starling's. When she was close enough to face me, she stopped and stood in front of me. At that moment I knew I had no choice but to relinquish myself to her, to accept my fate. Our destiny.

"So," she said, smiling. She stuck her tongue out at me, revealing a tiny "O" of transparent orange candy looped around the tip. "Did you know they were from me?"

I nodded.

"Ha! Like shit you did," Megan said. "You thought they were from Meredith and Angela and Laura, didn't you?"

"MAL?" I said.

Megan grinned.

"Maybe," I admitted.

I looked down at the ground, watching the rain dive-bomb the grass. She smelled like a combination of cotton candy and candied popcorn, an intoxicating mixture.

"Did you get the jawbreaker?"

I nodded again.

"I got more candy, you know," Megan said, stepping forward so that her face was almost touching mine. "At home. *Lots*. Want some?"

I looked into her eyes. "I told you. I don't eat candy. I'm allergic."

Megan smiled. I could smell the sweetness of her breath, her lips shimmering with sugary gloss, as bright as berry punch. The rain beat down around us.

"Yeah, right," she said. "Sure you are."

CANDY JUNKIE

THAT AFTERNOON AFTER SCHOOL, we went to Megan's house. She lived in another part of Woodland Hills, in a brown brick bungalow that she said was the color of fecal matter. As we walked, Megan told me her mother traveled. On business. A lot.

"She works as some high-powered executive for some huge-ass corporation," Megan said. "It's called K-C-U-F Inc." She spelled out the letters slowly and deliberately, waiting for my reaction, as if I was supposed to know who they were. I shrugged and said I had never heard of them.

"C'mon," Megan groaned. "Think about it. K-C-U-F. Get it?" she said. "It's a joke!"

I stared at Megan. "Ha ha. Very funny."

Her mother, Megan told me, bought the house because she liked the neighborhood. It was a good move. A good investment. Or something like that. Of course, it meant another new school and another new neighborhood, but Megan didn't care. She said she had gotten accustomed to moving around for her mother's work.

"What's your dad do?" I asked.

Megan rummaged in her pockets. "He's dead," she said. "He died three years ago. In a plane crash."

"Oh," I said, surprised. "I'm sorry."

"Yeah," Megan said sadly as she pulled out a piece of Bazooka. "Me, too."

I knew it would have been a good time to tell Megan about my mother, but I couldn't. We walked on.

Once inside her front door, the first thing I noticed was the stale lemony smell, like that of a hotel room. There was hardly any furniture in the living room except for a couple of chairs and a coffee table. Stacked in the corner was an assortment of boxes. There were no pictures on the walls, no drapes on the windows. The whole house seemed unlived in.

"My mom's out of town," she explained. "And she still hasn't unpacked everything yet." She grabbed my hand. "C'mon," she said. "Let's go to my room."

Megan was the standard latchkey kid, as well as a self-confessed candy junkie. As an only child, she said she'd grown up with the minimum amount of adult supervision and parent-child "quality time." And whatever time she got was only to maintain her mother's illusion that they were a "normal" family unit.

"Who wants to be *normal?*" Megan asked. "Fuck, I hate that. It's *so* bourgeois."

Every surface of Megan's bedroom was personalized by the hurricane of her private activity. Clothes, stuffed animals, and candy wrappers were scattered everywhere on the pink carpet. Then there were the books. Volumes of them. Everywhere. Words, words, words.

On the wall above her bed was a giant collage of images: a

poster of Iggy Pop, his hand down his pants, salivating into a microphone; a sad-looking man with white hair standing next to a picture of a Campbell's tomato soup can; a black-and-white photograph of the Buddha. A mask. A movie poster from *Willy Wonka and the Chocolate Factory*. The album cover from *Magical Mystery Tour*. Tickets. Postcards from around the world: LA. Bangkok. Cairo. Kathmandu.

"Want a Sour Cherry Blaster?" Megan asked, wading through the detritus toward me.

"No," I replied, bending down to pick up a book. I turned it over in my hands: *Jane Eyre*. I stared at the glossy red cover, the busty raven-headed heroine, her upturned face in firelight, looking at her lover.

"Ever read that?" Megan said. "Very cool."

I thought of my books at home, carefully arranged and left unread in my small bookcase by the window. I saw their titles appear in my mind: *Little Women*. *Little House on the Prairie*. *The Littles*. My own room at home was nothing special, just an arrangement of a desk and a bookcase, a dresser and a bed. The sheets and pillowcases didn't even match. There wasn't even a rug on the floor. In contrast to Megan's room, everything about it seemed small and uninspired.

Megan walked across the room to her closet and opened the door. Inside, amid a maze of clothes, were more books. She reached up into a stuffed oversize pillowcase and pulled out a bag of Sour Cherry Blasters.

"Here," she said, throwing them across the room. "Help yourself."

The bag landed with a thud next to a copy of *Frankenstein*. The book shifted to reveal other titles: *Grimm's Fairy Tales*. *Alice in Wonderland. Wuthering Heights. Dr. Jekyll and Mr. Hyde.* I cringed as I thought about the sudden sour hit of sugar.

"You didn't eat the jawbreaker, did you?" she asked.

The jawbreaker. I remembered its dark temptation.

"No," I replied, lowering my head.

"But you wanted to. Didn't you?"

I stepped over a volume of *Leaves of Grass* and stood beside Megan in front of her closet. Above our heads on the upper shelf was another large stuffed pillowcase.

"What's in *there?*" I asked, changing the subject.

"Last year's Halloween candy." She grinned proudly. "At first I had four pillowcases. But now I'm down to my last two."

Megan stepped across the room to her stereo and put on some music. I looked at the title on the cover: *Raw Power.*

"Iggy," she said, breathlessly, "makes me cream my jeans. His voice is *so* sexy."

I stared back at the pillowcase and took a deep breath. Everywhere I looked, I was surrounded by candy.

"Don't you think you're a little too old to go trick-or-treating?"

"What! Are you crazy?" Megan balked, offended by my question. "Of course I'm not too old! I'll never be too old! I plan to go out trick-or-treating every Halloween night until the day I die!"

"So how do you do it?" I asked.

"Do what?" Megan said coolly.

"Get so much?"

"Easy," Megan said, walking across the room and sitting on her bed. "First of all, I get four different costumes and four different pillowcases. Then I start real early, before all the little kiddies come out." Megan pulled out an orange lollipop and threw away the plastic wrapper. "I hide the costumes and the pillowcases in a secret place earlier in the day, and then I do my four rounds, each in a different costume, with a different pillowcase." Megan stopped and drew the lollipop out of her mouth and flashed me a sly grin. "No one ever knows it's me again and again and again, because every round I look totally different. And by the time I get to the end of the night I've got all the candy I could ever want. For the year. *Free.*"

I stared at her, pretending that I didn't think it was weird that someone our age still went out trick-or-treating. I imagined her changing costumes in the dark, alternating different masks with different props, grabbing the next pillowcase before heading off again. She was four different people in one night: a shape shifter.

Megan sucked on her orange lollipop, taking it whole inside her mouth.

"You really like candy, don't you?" I said.

"Doesn't everybody?" she replied.

I remembered my mother lying prone on her bed.

"No," I said quietly. "No, not everybody."

Later that same afternoon as we sat cross-legged on the floor of her room, Megan told me all about herself.

Her full name was Megan Somerset Chalmers: Somerset being her mother's maiden name, Megan meaning "strong." Born six weeks premature, she weighed just four pounds, five ounces, and had almost died during delivery. After three weeks in an incubator, she screamed and howled, her little cry so piercing that the nurses in the maternity ward had to wear earplugs. Finally, out of desperation, one of the nurses stuck a lollipop in her mouth. It was then, Megan told me, that she finally stopped crying.

Her favorite color was pink. Cotton candy pink, to be precise. Her sign was Leo. She didn't like TV. She liked music. Old-school punk, mainly. She hated competitive sports. But she liked swimming in the ocean. She liked to read. Her favorite book was still *Charlie and the Chocolate Factory.*

Astonishingly, she said she had already done "it." That summer, with a boy named Lars Eriikson, a foreign exchange student from Finland. He walked her home from school one afternoon and, thinking she was sixteen, took her back to his host-parents' house, where they did "it" on his bed, a black satin Led Zeppelin flag draped over their heads. It hadn't hurt at all, Megan boasted. And she didn't bleed. Not even a little.

Then she told me about her father.

The day he died, Megan was in class at her old school, listening to her teacher talk about the mating habits of birds, when she was told to go to the principal's office. When she got there, she was surprised to see her mother sitting in one of a pair of matching black vinyl chairs, talking low and seriously with the principal.

Seeing Megan at the door, the principal waved her in. Dim fluorescent lights flickered in his office. A black leather ink blotter rested under his hands. The principal carefully clasped his hands together, as if he was going to say a prayer. Megan wondered what she had done wrong. But he only quietly excused himself from the room. It was then that her mother told her that her father had died that morning in a plane crash.

The news walloped her in the stomach like a wrecking ball. It was all she could do just to breathe. She sat perfectly still, watching her mother's lips move.

The morning he left, Megan's father had come to say goodbye to her when she was still asleep. As he did before every trip, he put some candy under her pillow, and Megan, as always, pretended to stay asleep. She loved to listen to her father's footsteps as he entered her room and said goodbye, his hand slipping under her head. When the door closed and she knew he had gone, she reached under the pillow to see what he had chosen to leave. Each time it was something different. On that day, it was a roll of Life Savers.

As she sat there in the principal's office, the only thing Megan could think about was the Life Savers she had devoured on her way to school. She had emptied the entire roll into her mouth until her tongue was blanketed with their sweet fruity tang. Within moments, they were gone. Just like her father.

All she could imagine was her father falling from the sky, encased within the aircraft, while gravity, like the sharp-toothed mouth of a monster, pulled him down into fire and flames, toward the impact of explosion.

And yet she envisioned her father inside sipping his drink, his seat belt still fastened as the plane tilted down on its nose, every object held in place above in the overhead compartments, miraculously defying gravity. As the flight attendants walked upright in the aisles, they pushed their stainless-steel carts and politely offered passengers peanuts and soda pop as the earth came perilously closer and closer. When the plane crashed, exploding into a fiery mess in a farmer's field, she decided her father had not felt a thing.

Megan said that for years she thought that maybe if she hadn't eaten them all—if only she had eaten them one at a time and kept just one Life Saver, just for him—maybe her father would still be alive.

When I went home that night, I thought about how Megan didn't have a father and I didn't have a mother. Somehow, despite our differences, we mirrored each other, our missing pieces fitting into one another, like two halves making a whole.

I found my father asleep on the sofa in front of the television. He had been up again the night before. And since he was sleeping now, he probably would be up again tonight. I walked over to him and gently nudged him on the shoulder. At least I still had him.

"Dad, wake up."

His eyes fluttered open.

"Where have you been?" he asked.

"A friend's."

"What time is it?"

"I don't know."

"What do you want for dinner?"

"I already ate," I lied.

"Good," he said, not moving, his eyes closing again. "That's good."

He crossed his arms over his chest and fell back asleep. I tried to wake him again, but he turned away from me. What he always did when he wanted me to let him sleep.

∽◌∾

I went up to my room and closed the door. Then I pulled out a small white box I had hidden under my bed. In it were some photographs of me and my mother. I pulled out one of us on a vacation to Disneyland.

We are standing together, smiling. My father must have taken it, because he's not in the picture. Beside us, but not really with us, is Mickey Mouse. The color is dizzying: vivid pinks and reds and yellows, clashing against one another. In my hands I am holding a bright red balloon. The white of Cinderella's castle is directly behind us, blocking a section of sky. I study my mother's face, then mine.

We look ridiculous. And happy. I search my mother's eyes for some evidence of weakness, some sign of illness, something that could have foreshadowed what was to come. But her expression was nothing but normal, infuriating happiness. Part of me could still remember how light the balloon had felt in my hand in the chaos of that warm afternoon.

I put the photograph away, sealing it in the white box. Then I crawled into bed and shut my eyes tight, trying hard to sleep, trying hard not to cry.

GIVE ME CANDY OR GIVE ME DEATH

THE NEXT DAY AFTER SCHOOL, Megan showed me the vacant basement apartment in her house. Fully furnished, with its own separate entrance, it had been a big selling feature for Megan's mother—a way to help pay the mortgage. But Megan, of course, had other ideas.

"Check it out," she said, leading me downstairs. "It's the ultimate swinging crash pad."

Locked in time, the apartment had not been redecorated since the early seventies. Brown polyester lace curtains. Thick orange shag carpet. Dark wood paneling. Avocado-colored appliances. Abstract, psychedelic wallpaper.

In the living room there were white swivel chairs. Bulbous silver lamps. A built-in mirrored bar. And on the wall, a photographic mural of a forest scene with towering redwood trees and shiny red toadstools on the dark, mossy ground.

"So? What do you think?" Megan asked. "Isn't it the fucking coolest?"

It was damp and moldy-smelling. The windows were hung with spider webs. It felt as if we were trapped in time, buried underground. But it was there, in the forest of the living room, that Megan told me the first candy story.

"This," Megan said, "is called 'Genesis.'"

In the faint blue half-light from the basement windows I saw the outline of Megan's body as she skulked around the room. She turned on a table lamp and placed it on the floor, casting backlight against the forest wall behind her. Clearing her throat with an exaggerated flourish, she sat down in one of the white swivel chairs.

"Once upon a time there was a man called Adamo and a woman named Evelyn. They lived in a magical wonderland called the Garden of Eating. The man and the woman spent all their days and nights eating all the food that was in the garden. There were clouds made of marshmallows and trees made of chocolate, and the sand was made of cinnamon sugar and the rocks were hard candy, and the man and the woman could eat whatever they wanted, whenever they wanted, and Adamo and Evelyn were very happy.

"Then one day Evelyn went out by herself and came upon a tree she had never seen before. It was decorated with candy hearts that hung like little leaves from its branches. They were oh so pretty and looked oh so good to eat, so Evelyn reached out to put one in her mouth, and all of a sudden the little heart cried, 'Oh, no! No! No! No! Beware! You can't eat me!' And Evelyn asked, 'Why not?' and the heart said, 'Because I am a sacred heart of the Sacred Heart tree.' The little heart explained that the tree was owned by Goddo, an almighty lord and powerful wizard, and that if she should try to eat a sacred heart it would be like stealing from him, and it would be impossible for her to eat just one and that she would only want more and more and more and would not be able to stop. Evelyn looked at the little talking heart and began to laugh. 'Ha! Ha! Ha! Little heart,' she said, 'you're very silly!' But then another little heart hanging on the tree said to Evelyn, 'Oh, but you mustn't laugh! It's true! If you eat just one, it will never be enough!'

"But Evelyn just laughed and laughed, because it was very funny that the hearts on the tree could talk, and as she listened to them chatter and natter and say this and that, she thought how rude the little hearts were, telling her what she could and couldn't do, and, besides, she was hungry and they were just a bunch of stupid candy hearts. And so, with that, Evelyn reached out and plucked one of the hearts off a branch as easily as if it were an apple, and she popped it into her mouth, pressing her tongue down upon it, sucking hard."

Megan stopped and pulled a lollipop out of her pocket and unwrapped it. She looked at me and grinned.

"All of a sudden Evelyn's eyes went all wonky and her head went all woozy and she felt all tingly inside, because the candy heart was the most delicious thing she had ever tasted. And so she ate another one, and it was even more delicious than the last one, and so she just kept eating and stealing, stealing and eating—one after another after another until every little candied heart on the tree was gone but one. And the last little candied heart cried out to Evelyn, begging, 'Oh, please don't eat me! Please, please! I am the last candy heart, and Goddo will punish thee!'

"But Evelyn ignored the little heart and was just about to pick it for herself when Adamo, who had been wandering around the garden, came up to the tree and asked Evelyn what she had been eating. So Evelyn told Adamo, and then she picked the last candy heart left on the tree and gave it to him, and Adamo ate it and indeed, it was just as Evelyn had said. It was the most delicious thing he had ever tasted.

"Suddenly, in a great blast of lightning, the tree split apart and a mystical being appeared before them in a blinding ray of light. Evelyn and Adamo shielded their eyes. 'Who are you?' they asked in terror. 'I am Goddo the all-knowing and powerful,' he boomed, his voice as loud as thunder. 'And you have eaten all the sacred hearts of my Sacred Heart tree, and for that you will be eternally punished!'

"Then Goddo pointed his finger at Adamo and struck him down with a single blast of fire. Evelyn screamed and flung herself upon the dead body of her lover. 'Why, why, why?' she cried. 'Why have you done this?' Goddo turned on Evelyn in fury. 'Because you stole from me and did not heed the words of the Sacred Heart tree, and thought only of yourselves and your greed and hunger! No one steals from Goddo and gets away with it!' Evelyn fell to her knees and wept at Goddo's feet. 'Please, please,' she pleaded. 'Give him life, and take mine! Please, please, I beg of you!'

"'Never!' Goddo thundered. 'You had your chance! You were warned! Besides, your life isn't worth anything! From this day forward you are forever banished from this garden, doomed to a life of struggle and hardship!' Yet Goddo was not without mercy, and he took pity on Evelyn. 'But you shall not be alone,' he commanded, and he pointed his finger at Evelyn's belly and she instantly gave birth to a baby girl. 'Let this child be a lesson to you,' he ordered, 'as a constant reminder of your crime and as a symbol of your gluttony and selfishness! May it always be hungry for candy!'

"Evelyn looked down and cradled the child in her arms. Immediately it began to cry, ravenous with hunger. Goddo quickly disappeared, vanishing into the air. 'No, no!' cried Evelyn, weeping. 'Please, please! Don't go!' But it was too late: Goddo had spoken and the rocks became rocks and the trees became trees and the sand was sand once more."

For a moment Megan paused.

Then she said quietly: "The End."

I learned more about Megan with each passing day. Walking to school together. Walking home together. At lunchtime. Anytime. All the time.

"After my dad died, my mother stopped giving me candy," Megan said as we walked home from school one day. "She said it would make me fat. Make my skin bad. Rot my teeth. And no man would ever want to marry me and I'd end up a lonely old maid who would have to look after my dying mother." Megan laughed. *"And is that what you really want?"* she said, imitating what must have been her mother's voice.

So Megan told me she was forced to stop eating candy. And she said it was like something was cut out of her, like a heart or a lung or another vital organ. Eating it gave her more than just comfort. It numbed her. Protected her. Made her feel safe.

"After that, I started sneaking candy behind my mother's back," Megan confessed. "You know, just when I needed it. After my mother would go to sleep, I'd eat candy and hide the wrappers under my bed." Megan said how she loved going to sleep with candy in her mouth, the sweetness numbing her tongue. Then one day her mother found the candy wrappers, pressed flat under the mattress. "You should have seen her." Megan laughed. "She *freaked*."

So she learned to be more cautious. She carried mouthwash to disguise the smell, and ate as much as possible when she was away from home.

She also began hoarding it. What she was doing she said was not just out of necessity, but was insurance—a way of protecting herself against the unknown, guaranteeing that there would be candy there when she needed it.

"So what happens when you don't have it?" I asked.

A look of horror passed over Megan's face. "When I don't have candy?" she replied. "Impossible. I always have it. I have to."

"But let's just say you don't."

She paused, thinking about it. Then she turned and faced me. "I die."

I stared into her face. "You die?" I asked in disbelief.

"Yes," she said, looking at me with total seriousness. "Give me candy or give me death."

The next week, every day after school, we went to Megan's house. Since I wouldn't eat candy, Megan shared her stories with me instead, telling them as quickly as I could consume them, as if the words were edible.

She was fearless in a way I had never known anyone to be, and I became fascinated by her, seduced by her confessions and her secrets. But most of all by her stories.

"This," said Megan, "is called 'Satin Chocolate-Covered Chicken Bones.'"

We were in the downstairs apartment again, with me seated on the floor and Megan on a swivel chair.

"Once," Megan began, "there was a girl who went to live with her grandmother in a house in the city. One afternoon the grandmother invited some of her friends over for lunch. After everything had been prepared, the girl and her grandmother sat in the front room and waited for their guests to arrive. It got later. And later. Impatiently, the grandmother scrutinized the girl.

"'Stop that fidgeting!'" Megan said in a thin, high screech, imitating the voice of the old woman. "'Very soon our guests will be arriving, and I want everything to be just right.'

"The girl sat up straight on the hard vinyl ottoman at her grandmother's feet and stared across the room. On the table before the window, the girl could see the plate of warm tuna sandwiches. There were potato chips in a plastic green bowl, and vanilla ice cream cake. Celery sticks stuffed with cheese.

"The clock struck three. Weak from hunger, the girl felt the chimes thudding in her brain. The grandmother sat unmoving in her armchair as she watched the girl.

"'I said *stop* that fidgeting!'" Megan said, again assuming the grandmother's voice. "'Can't you sit still for just one minute?'

"Springing from the seat of her chair, the grandmother leaned forward and slapped the girl's face, hard, with her hand. The girl's cheek stung with pain. Satisfied, the grandmother settled back into her chair and reached into the glass dish beside her for a satin candy that was shaped like a chicken bone.

"Tears burned in the back of the girl's throat as she watched her grandmother suck a chicken bone, moving it back and forth from cheek to cheek, savoring its fake chocolate flavor.

"After a moment, the girl heard a thin, raspy sound coming from the grandmother's throat. The old woman's eyes bulged with panic; blood rushed from her face. Her hands grabbed her neck and she dropped to the floor and slumped forward on the carpet. Eyes wide with panic, the grandmother looked up at the girl, a long string of pink saliva mixed with blood dripping slowly from the corner of her mouth. On her knees, clutching her throat, she strained for breath, imploring her granddaughter with her eyes.

"The girl sat absolutely, perfectly still. Not even daring to breathe. Behind her, on the table, in the late-afternoon sun, the vanilla ice cream cake melted into a white puddle. The End."

Megan spun around in the white swivel chair, then looked at me and grinned.

"Does everyone die in your stories?" I asked.

"Almost always," she replied, and spun around in the chair again.

"Why?" I asked.

"Because," she answered as she took one last final spin, "death makes all the best stories."

As I walked home from Megan's house that day, I remembered this girl I knew in kindergarten. Her name was Wendy.

Wendy and I had played house together. It was a world in miniature, sensible and orderly, and we would pretend to cook and clean, acting the way we thought we were supposed to while the boys played with their trucks and tools, guns and shovels, to kill and to scale mountains, to stage wars and to conquer cities.

I did not know Wendy outside the little world we created at school. I knew nothing about where she lived or what her family was like. I didn't even know her last name. All I knew about Wendy was what I knew from our games of make-believe at school. Somehow that always seemed enough.

One day Wendy stood in front of me and said: "I know how to spell 'yes.' Y-E-S. Yes. I know how to spell 'no.' N-O. No." I remembered how it seemed almost superhuman.

Then I asked Wendy if she knew how to spell any other words. But those were the only two. I looked at her and felt cheated. Why couldn't she spell anything else other than "yes" and "no"? I was profoundly disappointed.

What I realized about Wendy — and myself, too — was that those two words were all we had been given to understand. Within our sheltered world, language functioned only as a way of defining what was right and what was wrong, how we were supposed to play and behave, yes and no.

In many ways, I still felt confined by those two words. In how I was supposed to act. In who I was expected to be. But Megan changed all that. Through her stories, I could dispel the notion of right and wrong. She made me feel free.

Whether it was in defense against MAL or in retaliation to Mr. King, Megan knew how to use more than just those two words. How she told her candy stories was her way of breaking through "yes" and "no." Of exploring language, of exploiting it. Of using it as a weapon. As a means of escape. As a chance to dream. To get what she wanted. To define her world.

For Megan Chalmers, language was power.

STORIES FOR GIRLS

INITIALLY, I REALIZED, I had been fearful of Megan. She was not normal. Far from it. But as we spent more time together, I admired her more and more. Our friendship was by no choice of mine. It was, as Megan said, our destiny.

MAL was still around. But with Megan, I felt that I didn't have anything to worry about. Friendship with her had its privileges.

She was everything I wasn't and nothing I wanted to be. And what began as an aversion to her became a total and complete immersion in her world. I succumbed absolutely, like a parachutist forced out of a plane into the open sky.

After school, we always went to her house. As she had told me from the beginning, her mother was never home. I began to wonder when I would meet Mrs. Chalmers, although I secretly hoped Megan would never have to meet my father. I still hadn't told Megan the truth. About me. About my mother. Once when Megan suggested we go to my house, I even told her that my mother was at home working and that she was expecting company. She seemed to think nothing of it and never asked again.

Most of the time we went downstairs to the basement

apartment. Megan would sit on the shag carpet with her back against the forest mural, and I'd sit cross-legged in front of her, listening. Her words swam in the heavy syrup of the candy she ate as she told her stories; the spaces between her teeth and gums were cemented with gooey watermelon or lime, cherry or orange.

At first I was a reluctant disciple. But my mood soon changed. Because with each passing day—with the telling of each story—we each got what we wanted. Megan found that telling the stories was like prolonging the candy's effect, and I got to savor each letter, each word, each sentence. And, to my shame, I became addicted to the feeling I got every time. Remarkably, I was shedding my fear. And Megan knew it.

"Listen to this one," Megan said with a wicked smile, one afternoon after school.

"One day Madeline went and bought a Ring Pop. When Lawrence, the boy who lived next door, saw what Madeline had bought, he got all hot and turned on and said to Madeline, 'Stick it up my bum.'

"And then Madeline said, 'Oh, no, Lawrence, I couldn't do that!' But Lawrence said, 'Oh, please, Madeline, please stick it up my bum,' and still Madeline said no, but Lawrence begged and begged and begged, crawling around on the ground on his hands and knees and poking his bum in her face. So Madeline said OK and then she told him to pull down his pants, and as he did this, Madeline put the shiny red Ring Pop on her finger.

"Madeline had been hoping that maybe they could have had a pretend wedding and that Lawrence would put the Ring Pop on her finger and they would kiss and pretend like they were going to live happily ever after, but all Lawrence could say was 'Stick it up my bum,' so Madeline did just that.

"Lawrence oohed and aahed and said it felt real good, but could Madeline move it around a bit? So she did, and then she started to wonder what would happen if she put her hand in deep, as far as it could go, and so she did that, too. Lawrence groaned and Madeline thought, 'Why not?' and put her whole arm inside. Lawrence just grunted faster, saying, 'More more more.' So Madeline gathered herself up and slid right through, into his insides, and moved all around inside him. On her finger she could still see the juicy red Ring Pop, sparkling like a dazzling ruby.

"And it looked beautiful to her, being inside Lawrence, his veins crisscrossing this way and that, in and out of roped muscles and nerves. Madeline leaned against Lawrence's heart and listened to it beat, pumping the bright fiery soup of his blood and glowing with scarlet light. And it occurred to Madeline that she really did love Lawrence and that no other boy in the world could be more beautiful than him. So Madeline took off the Ring Pop and looked at how soft and smooth and worn it was, just like a piece of glass polished by the sea, and she placed it right inside Lawrence's heart. There it shattered and divided into prisms of light, arching in a rainbow under the surface of his skin."

Megan stopped and pulled out a Ring Pop from her breast pocket. She took a long deep breath and stared at it, removing its plastic wrapping with her thumb and index finger. I watched as she placed the ring thoughtfully on her baby finger. The room was silent.

"Did you like it?" she asked.

I was bewildered, but enchanted. "Yeah," I said, quietly. "Yeah, I did. But it was, you know—"

"What? Kinky?" Megan smiled knowingly and licked the Ring Pop. "Yeah, I know."

They were not nice stories. They did not have happy endings. They were not what people might think girls would write stories about, or what stories about candy would be like. They were dark and rude and outrageous, as bizarre as they could be. And each time she told them Megan always tried to upstage herself, injecting into the vein of every story some gross, horrific detail.

It was the only way she knew to tell a tale.

That following Saturday, while we were sitting around her bedroom listening to music, Megan said, "C'mon, let's go to the store. I want to show you something."

The store was T'n'T Variety, the only corner convenience store in our subdivision. It had a bright neon sign out front, sizzling red sticks of dynamite at both ends, the slogan "More Bang for Your Buck" written above in big yellow letters.

On our way there, Megan said, "Now listen. This is what we're going to do. You just go to the back of the store, where the porn is. And when the chick at the front has to step out from behind the cash register and tell you to stop looking at the skin mags, leave. Just walk out. But don't look at me. Pretend you don't even know me. Then wait for me outside, up the street. Got it?"

"But why?" I asked. "I don't want to look at pornographic

magazines." I wondered if this was what she wanted to show me. Megan rolled her eyes.

"You're not going to actually look at them. You're just going to pretend to look at them."

"But why?" I couldn't figure out what it was we were supposed to be doing.

"To create a diversion, dummy," Megan said, annoyed.

"But why?" I asked again. "What are you going to do?"

Megan cracked a wicked smile. "Don't worry. You'll see."

When we got there, I went in first. As I walked in, the cashier turned and looked at me from behind the counter.

"Hi there," she said. She was a round, heavy woman with brassy orange hair that matched her red and yellow smock.

"Hi," I replied nervously.

I went straight to the back of the store, just as Megan had told me to. The magazine stand was right where she said it would be, except that the porn magazines were on the highest shelf, up top, out of reach.

I stood on the bottom shelf of the stand, stretched my arm up, and grabbed whatever I could. Just then Megan came in through the front door and hung around up front.

In my hands was a magazine called *Fantasia*. On the cover was a woman naked except for a red cape and red stilettos, carrying a basket full of shiny red apples, her bright red mouth open, just about to take a bite.

I had never looked at pornography before. Inside were vaginas of every imaginable shape and size and color, hairy and nonhairy, shaved and nonshaved, pierced and nonpierced, peeping out from every glossy page. I felt queasy.

Then something caught my attention. A story called "Enchanted Evening."

It was about a woman named Cindy who lived with her stepmother and two stepsisters. On the first page Cindy was chained to a fireplace, her hands and feet and mouth bound with black tape. She was wearing a chain and a dog collar while two other women, dressed in black leather, brandished whips. Behind them a large black dog lurked ominously in the shadows.

I quickly flipped to the next page. It was a ballroom scene, with Cindy on her knees sitting on top of a handsome prince. Facing that page: she is punished, locked in a darkened dungeon, alone with the big black dog. On the next and final page was a picture of her, naked but for a diamond-studded tiara, lying in a mountain of satin white pillows, the prince sitting on top of her. Below, in fancy italicized script, were these six words: *"And they lived happily ever after . . ."*

"Hey!" I heard. "You there, put that back!" It was the woman from behind the counter. She stepped away from the cash register, away from the front of the store, just as Megan said she would. She walked toward me until she was standing only a few feet from me, her back turned to Megan. She looked down at me with shock and disgust.

"Didn't you hear me?" she said as she snatched the magazine out of my hands and put it back on the shelf. "That's for *adults only.*" She shook her head angrily. "Now get out of here, before I call the cops."

I nodded silently and walked out. On my way out the door, I watched Megan from the corner of my eye, hanging around the counter. I pretended not to know her.

Just as she had instructed, I waited for her. A moment later, she walked up the street to meet me.

"That was perfect!" she said as she beamed proudly.

"What did you do?" I asked.

"Look," she said, opening her coat pocket. There were handfuls of Slime Balls.

"You *stole* those—"

"Yeah," she said.

"But . . ."

"But what? Do you really think that I would *pay* for candy?" She laughed, as if stealing were so easy, permissible, even. "Look, it was there for the taking, and so I took it. Just like that."

When we got back to her place, Megan laid all the candy out on the floor and counted the pieces, splitting it all down the middle. Then she gave me half.

"I've told you," I said. "I don't eat candy."

"Doesn't matter. Fair's fair."

I looked at the row of green gumballs in their plastic wrappers, dotting the carpet.

"Just have one," Megan said. "It won't kill you."

I surveyed one of the Slime Balls as if it were a small planet.

"I can't—" I said.

"C'mon," she pleaded, "I'm here. If anything happens—"

"No, I can't."

"Why not?" she asked.

I turned and looked at her. "Because . . ."

"Yes?"

I wanted to have it. I wanted to tell her. About everything.

Instead I told her about Cindy in *Fantasia.* As she listened,

Megan lay down on the floor and ate one Slime Ball after another, sucking each one hard and slow. I watched with a curious envy, longing to savor the same punch of lime green slime exploding and oozing inside my mouth.

The day after the convenience store raid, Megan told me another story.

"Once, in a subdivision far, far away," she said, "there was a girl named Moira. One day, Moira went to the store to buy some Garbage Can-dy. Garbage Can-dy was Moira's favorite. She loved the little plastic garbage can full of fish heads and old sneakers and tiny little bones.

"When she went up to the front to pay for her Garbage Can-dy, the guy behind the counter looked at her and smiled. He had bloodshot eyes and greasy thinning gray hair and a soft pouch of a belly that made his shirt buttons poke out. Moira could see the dimpled, hairy fat flesh sticking out through his buttonholes.

"'So you like candy?'" Megan said, imitating a man's voice.

"Moira could smell the vinegary dampness of the man's aftershave. As he punched in the price on the cash register, his fat-knuckled fingers picked up Moira's Garbage Can-dy.

"'I know many girls who like candy,' he said to her, 'girls who would do anything for candy.'

"Behind him, next to the cash register, Moira could see the pages of a skin mag cracked open at the centerfold.

"'I have lots of candy in the backroom of my store for girls like you,' the man said, smiling. 'For girls who like candy. *Free.*'

"Moira couldn't believe what she was hearing. An entire backroom full of *free candy.* It sounded like paradise.

"The man stepped out from behind the counter and surveyed the front of the store, eyeballing the parking lot. Then he asked Moira if she wanted to see how much candy he had. So Moira said 'sure,' and she followed him into the backroom.

"He was right: there were walls and walls of it, boxes from floor to ceiling, wrapped in plastic and stacked like bricks. Row upon row, untouched and unopened. There was more candy than Moira could ever have imagined.

"The man stood close behind her, watching. Moira could smell his sweat. His breathing turned hard and rapid.

"She told the man she wanted to leave. There was a small dirty line of sweat on his forehead. He brought a cigarette up to his lips and lit it, inhaling deeply, staring at her, his eyes gleaming. At the top of his shirt Moira could see coarse spirals of gray hair snaking over his chest.

"'So you don't want any?' he asked.

"Moira said she didn't know what he meant.

"He laughed gently, inhaling his cigarette nervously, smoothing his hand back and forth over the bald crown of his head. *'Candy.'*

"Next thing Moira knew, he had grabbed her hand and was rubbing it against the front of his pants. Then he unzipped his fly and pushed her hand through it.

"He moaned, saying how didn't all girls like candy and didn't that feel good and wouldn't Moira like to suck on some candy. Moira struggled to pull away, but her whole body felt frozen. He moved her hand faster. He moaned louder. Then he pushed her down on her knees."

Megan paused to clear her throat.

"Then he forced open Moira's jaw and put his thing in her

mouth. Moira bit down. Hot liquid filled her mouth. Blood. The man screamed. He dropped to the floor, and Moira kicked him once, twice, three times in the crotch and ran from the backroom. On her way out the front door of the store, she grabbed all the candy she could.

"When she got home, Moira shoved each piece of stolen candy into her mouth. Then she went straight into the bathroom and puked. All she could see in the toilet bowl was the man's face. His twisted mouth. She remembered his smell. The taste of his blood at the back of her throat."

Megan popped a Slime Ball into her mouth.

"Sick fuck. The End."

I was shocked.

"Did that really happen?" I asked.

Megan looked at me in dead seriousness, her eyes narrowing with suspicion. "Of course it did. Do you think I would lie to you about something like that?" she said.

"N-no," I stammered. "I just thought—"

"You just thought what?"

Megan was silent. Then she collapsed on the floor, bursting with laughter.

"Of course it didn't happen, you freak. It's a *story.*"

The whole thing had seemed somewhat improbable. But things like that happened. I couldn't get the picture of Moira's mouth full of blood out of my mind.

Megan was still laughing. "Oh, Mr. Creepy Variety Store Guy," she moaned. "Oh, please, please—*I want your candy.*"

"It's not funny," I said.

Megan stopped laughing and looked at me with the same seriousness that she had before.

"OK, OK. Look. You're right. It's not funny." She paused a moment. "It's fucking *hilarious.*"

She exploded into vicious laughter again.

"You know, you shouldn't believe everything you hear," she goaded me. "Especially from me."

When I was little, my mother read stories to me at bedtime. Almost every night, she sat down beside me in my bed and we held the storybook together. When she was sure I had fallen asleep, she lifted the book out of my hands and tucked me under the covers.

I loved listening to her, sharing the story together. Many times I wanted her to read the same one over and over again. Somehow the way she told a story was always enchanting, and I never tired of hearing her voice. I trusted her. And I trusted the story she was telling me.

The books she read to me seemed like magical doors that could open endlessly into other worlds that I believed were, in all truth, *real.* I never questioned the possibility that girls like me couldn't fall down a rabbit hole into the underworld, mad tea parties awaiting. I never suspected what was real and what wasn't. I believed everything, unquestionably.

For the first time in my life, Megan Chalmers made me suspect stories. Like my mother, she made me listen. But in a radically different way. She made me think about what was *not* being said. With Megan, I would eventually come to learn that there was always another story behind the story, another version of the truth in the shadow of the words.

THE FORCES OF DARKNESS

MEGAN AND I WERE THERE the day Rose moved into the basement apartment.

She was an older, heavyset woman with short graying hair and what appeared to be a mustache above her upper lip. There was a mysterious limp in her walk. I wasn't sure whether it was because of the weight of the boxes she was carrying out of the tiny trunk of her tan Chevette, or if she had it from some previous injury. All I knew for sure was that Megan and I were getting kicked out. We would have to find another place to go.

Megan and I looked out the window and watched Rose unload her car.

"What do you think she does?" I asked.

"I dunno," Megan said, uninterested. "I think my mother said she teaches or something."

"Is she married?"

Megan snorted. "Yeah, right. *Not.*"

We watched Rose walk down the driveway and stand at the foot of her trunk, bend over, lift out a box. When she turned around, there was a look of strain on her face.

"That must be a heavy one," Megan said.

"What's her last name?"

"Why do you care?"

"I don't. I just want to know, that's all."

"I don't know, exactly. Red-something-or-other."

"Do you think we should go out there and help her?" I suggested.

"What are you, crazy? No way!"

We continued our watch from Megan's bedroom window. Rose appeared at her car again. I tried to imagine her in our darkened basement, sitting in one of the white swivel chairs in front of the forest mural.

"What does she teach?" I asked.

"I don't know," Megan said. "How should I know?"

I wondered why Megan was so hostile toward Rose. She didn't even know her. I watched Rose lift out the last few boxes and slam the trunk shut with her elbow before disappearing from view.

Megan and I slumped back down on her bed. Then Megan asked me to hand her a Tootsie Pop from the bunch of lollipops on her bedside table.

"Go on," Megan urged. "It's not going to bite you."

My hand wavered as I reached above the table.

"Cherry, please," she said.

I picked one up and tossed it toward her. It catapulted through the air before hitting the wall above her head and falling to the floor.

"Watch it," she warned, smiling. "Maybe next time you could just hand it to me." She bent down to rescue the Tootsie Pop among the piles of books and then removed the wrapper.

"We could go introduce ourselves to her," I suggested.

"Who?"

"Rose."

Megan put the Tootsie Pop in her mouth.

"Let's not and say we did, OK?" she said.

She moved the Tootsie Pop to the side of her mouth and chewed on it before she cracked it between her teeth. I squirmed as she bit down on the chewy candy center and gooey dribbles of chocolate leaked from the corner of her mouth. Then she chewed some more and swallowed, and it was gone.

Megan stared sadly at the waxy white candy stick.

"You always eat your candy so fast," I observed.

Megan stuck out her tongue.

"Ewwww, gross! It looks like—"

"Like *poo?*" Megan teased, laughing. "Yummy yummy!"

Megan sprang across the room and opened her closet, ripping into her Halloween stash. She grabbed a handful of mini–chocolate bars and peeled them open, stuffing them into her mouth, shrieking with delight. Then she leapt back to the bed and stuck her face in front of mine, opening her mouth as wide as she could. I stared at the brown cud of half-chewed chocolate in her mouth.

Laughing, I turned my face from her, kicking my feet in protest, slapping her away.

"Gross!" I said.

"Mmmmmmmmmm . . . ooooooooo . . . poooooooooo," she cooed.

She threw herself onto the bed and pulled me down with her. Tears were running from my eyes, I was laughing so hard.

And then, before I knew what was happening, I was crying. Really crying.

Megan stopped laughing. After a moment she asked, "Why don't you really eat candy?"

I had known that eventually I would have to tell her the truth about my mother, but I had thought it would happen in another way. When I would have the right words to say. Whenever that would be. When I stopped crying, I rolled over onto my back.

Then I told her: "Because when my mom died, I thought it was candy that killed her."

My words hung in the air.

"Oh," Megan said finally as she rolled over on her side. "Is that all?"

I hadn't told anybody about my mother. Not one person. Not until now. The words had just spilled out of me.

"Can I tell you something?" I asked.

"Sure," Megan said. "Anything. Or don't you remember what I said when we first met?" Megan lifted up my hand and pressed her palm to my palm. "Fate. Destiny. Like two streams of the same river. Each half making a whole."

I looked into Megan's eyes and told her everything: about how my mother got sick and died and why I promised myself that I would never eat candy again. Megan didn't question why I had lied. Why I had so desperately wanted to be normal. She didn't judge me. And for the first time in a long time, I almost felt like myself again.

Almost.

෴

The next morning at school I found a note in my desk that said: *135520 135 1620518 1938151512 191135 209135 191135 1612135 119 25519205184125.* Numeric code for *Meet me after school same time same place as yesterday.*

Using the same piece of paper, I wrote my reply underneath: *166918131209225. Affirmative.* Then I folded it up and wrote Megan's name on the front. I passed it forward and watched as it made its way across the classroom. Then, while it was with Tracey Reid, Angela Moyer leaned over and snatched it from her hands. She then passed it to Laura Mitchell, who handed it over to Meredith McKinnon. Victorious, Meredith looked over at me and smiled, toying with the note in her hand.

Later, at lunch, MAL cornered Megan and me.

"So," Meredith said, holding up the note. "Got yourselves a little secret club, do you?"

"Yeah," Laura said, fulfilling her duty as second-in-command. "A secret club. For *lezzies.*"

Angela threw in her insult: "Yeah, *lezzies.*"

Megan was cool. "For your information, asswipes, you interpreted the message incorrectly. What it actually says is what a bunch of stupid twats you are."

Laura snorted at Megan. Then Meredith turned around and looked at me.

"You know, I've been thinking," she said. "Why don't you come hang out with us after school?"

"What?" I said.

Meredith and Angela and Laura looped their arms around me, pulling me a short distance away from Megan. I turned and looked back. Megan followed nonchalantly behind us.

"We didn't really mean what we said," Meredith said. "About not wanting you to be our friend."

"But I—"

"We were only testing you." Meredith smiled. "After all, you don't really think that we'd allow just anyone to join us, do you?"

I thought of how they had used me. Ignored me.

"Thanks," I said nervously. "But I don't think so."

Meredith's smile dropped.

"Did you hear that?" she said to Laura and Angela. "She doesn't think so! She thinks she's too good for us!" Meredith grabbed my arm and held it tight. "Who do you think you are, anyway?" she said, seething. "How *dare* you."

"Let go of me."

Megan stepped behind Meredith, grabbing a handful of her hair.

"You heard her. *Let. Go.*"

Meredith released me and swung around to confront Megan. "You know, we could end this all right here, right now. Then you'll never have to worry about what might happen."

"Oh, yeah? And what might happen?" Megan asked.

Meredith leaned toward Megan. "You know the story."

"I do?" Megan sarcastically replied. "And what story is that?"

"You know. The one about the dead girl." Meredith looked at me. "*Girls.*"

"Oh. *That* story," Megan said. "I thought you were talking about the *other* story. You know, of the three girls who were actually Nazi test-tube babies?"

Meredith fumed. "You think you're so clever, don't you?" she said.

"Yep," Megan replied.

Angela and Laura and Meredith locked arms and moved toward Megan and me.

"Like, omigod!" Megan exclaimed sarcastically, pretending to cower from them. "You're, like, trying to *corner* us!"

"Get out of our way," Meredith snarled. *"Now."*

"Oh, yeah?" Megan laughed. "Make me."

"Let's see how clever you really are," Meredith said to Megan, her eyes narrowing, "when we find out about your secret club." Meredith smirked. "And you can try to keep your mouths shut and you can try to keep it secret. But eventually we'll find where you are and we'll destroy you."

"Oooh," Megan said, screwing up her face in a mask of fear. "I'm soooooo, like, scared."

"Think about it," Meredith said. "Before it's too late. Or else you'll be—"

"What?" Megan taunted.

"Very . . ." Laura said, joining Meredith.

"Very . . ." Angela added.

"Sorry," the three of them chanted together.

"Sorry *you* were ever fucking born, is what you mean," Megan said.

Meredith gave Laura and Angela a signal to back away from us. Then she stepped in front of Megan.

"We're warning you," she hissed. "When we're through with you, you'll wish you were already dead."

And that was that. Before Megan had a chance to respond, they turned their backs and walked away.

"And don't forget," Megan shouted after them, "to give my regards to SATAN!"

She turned and looked at me with anger. "Can you fucking believe that?" she said. "Now they're finishing each other's sentences, speaking as one tongue. It's a definite sign of evil. Possession, for sure. Any minute now, they're going to projectile vomit and turn their heads three hundred and sixty degrees."

As I watched MAL walk toward the school doors, I saw Blake Starfield wandering alone along the fence. He was pacing up and down the edge, stopping every now and then to gaze up into the sky. It was strange, because even though he sat directly behind me, our daily interaction was limited. Yet he fascinated me nevertheless.

"You like him, don't you?" Megan said.

I turned around. "What?"

"Captain Bizarro. King Freak. Quasi. You like him. I can tell."

I felt myself blushing and turned away. "I do not!"

"Do, too!" she taunted.

I turned and faced Megan. "I do *not* like him," I insisted.

"OK, OK, whatever, " Megan said. "Jheesh." She rummaged in her pockets and found a pouch of Big League Chew and wedged a small wad of gum into her cheek.

"Where'd you get that?" I asked, changing the subject.

"Where do you think?"

She offered me some. I shook my head. That was fine by Megan. It just meant more for her.

"Do you think MAL really meant it?" I asked.

"Meant what?"

"What they said?"

Megan chewed her gum in serious contemplation, then held her hand against her heart. "No doubt about it," she answered with mock patriotic fervor. "From now on, we must be very careful. We must protect ourselves from the forces of darkness."

Later, when we arrived at Megan's house, we saw Rose in the driveway.

"Hello, girls," she said. It was the first time she had talked to us.

"Hey, Rose," Megan replied. "Going to work?" Obviously they had met.

"Yes, as a matter of fact, I am," she answered, opening her car door and sliding into the driver's seat. She looked at me with interest, sizing me up.

"This is my friend," Megan said, introducing me through the open door.

"Hi, friend," Rose said, extending her hand. It was soft and cold, with a fresh soapy odor. She smiled at me and her mustache came into focus.

"Well, I must be going," she said, inserting her keys into the ignition and turning on the car. "See you girls later."

She closed her door and waved at us as she pulled out of the driveway.

"When did you meet her?" I asked.

"Last night."

"Last night?"

"Yeah, so?"

"You never told me."

"You think I have to tell you everything?"

"No. It's just that—"

"What? She's just some old dyke that lives downstairs. What do you care whether or not I told you if I've met her before?"

"I don't know," I said. I didn't know why Megan was acting this way. "I just thought you might tell me, that's all."

"Whatever."

Megan watched the car drive down the street and disappear into the distance. There was a moment of silence.

"So what do you want to do now?" I asked.

"I've got an idea," Megan said, turning and looking at me with a devious grin. "Follow me."

It was Megan's idea to snoop in Rose's stuff. As she searched for the key to Rose's apartment in the kitchen, I noticed a number of broken-down boxes piled up in a corner.

"I see your mom got some time to unpack," I said.

"Huh?" Megan eyed the pile of cardboard. "Oh, yeah, that." She continued searching. "That's my mom. A real homebody."

Opening a cupboard drawer, Megan dug under boxed rolls of aluminum foil and plastic wrap. "Aha," she exclaimed, lifting a small silver key. "Our access is authorized."

Downstairs, the apartment looked almost exactly as it did before. But now there was someone filling out its space with odd, particular smells. Megan and I moved in stealth from room to room, carefully inspecting the evidence.

"C'mere," Megan whispered to me. "Let's look in here."

I followed Megan into the bedroom. She stood beside the bed with her hand frozen on the handle of Rose's bedside table.

"What is it?" I came up behind Megan and peered down, looking into the open drawer.

There, underneath an assortment of cards and paper and jewelry, was a long white cylindrical object. Beside it, in the left-hand corner of the drawer, was a small black Bible. We gaped at the white thing. We stared at the black Bible.

"What is that?" I whispered.

"A dildo," Megan replied nonchalantly.

"What does she do with it?"

"What do you think?" Megan replied. "She, you know, does *stuff* with it."

"Like what kind of stuff?"

Megan looked at me, lowering her eyebrows.

"*Duh*. You know. *Stuff*."

"You mean—"

"That's right! Masturbation for the nation! Batteries included!"

I looked down at the cylinder again, and I had the weird feeling that I was going to be sick.

Megan laughed.

"C'mon, you freak," she said, tugging my arm. "Let's go scope out the kitchen."

We checked out the fridge and the freezer but were disappointed when we found nothing more than a plate of cold ham and some Diet Coke. Megan fished in the garbage, looking at some old receipts and other pieces of paper.

"What are you looking for?" I asked.

"Oh, you know, skeletons, dark secrets, body parts."

The apartment seemed smaller with all of Rose's things crammed inside it. I recognized some of the items she had carried in from her car the day she moved in: a lamp, an ottoman, a magazine rack. Things had the look of being untidy but organized. On top of a bookshelf was a thin, craggy plant in dire need of water.

On the small coffee table in front of the television, Megan found several multicolored candy wrappers, scrunched up tightly into hard little balls. Beside them was a large bag of toffees. Megan switched on the television. A documentary about bulimia and anorexia nervosa was being shown. The girl on the screen was pale and emaciated. Her skin was stretched like a drum, translucent and white, over her bones. Her name was Mary.

Megan sat down on the floor in front of the television and watched, taking a handful of toffees out of the bag. Without looking down, she untwisted the ends of one and put it in her mouth.

Mary had been starving herself for the past month. I watched Megan as she stuck her finger absentmindedly into her mouth, loosening the toffee from her teeth. It made me shudder.

"I think we should go now," I said nervously, standing behind her.

"Aw, come on. Sit down. I was just getting into this." She untwisted another toffee, pointing at the television. "See? Mary's at death's door! Look at her!"

"What if Rose comes back?"

"She won't come back. She's gone to work."

"But what if she's forgotten something?"

"Like what? Her dildo?"

Mary was lying down on a small cot. Her spine was permanently deformed from malnutrition.

"I don't know! Anything. Megan, please," I said. "Let's get out of here!"

Megan turned around and stared at me, grinning. "What's eating you?" She reached across the table and grabbed the remote, pressing the mute button.

"Megan," I warned. But it was no use. She kneeled beside the television screen. Mary was standing in a room, her gaunt, thin face looking out a window.

"In the beginning Mary's mother had thought it was wild and kinky," Megan began. "But now it was turning her tongue blue."

"Megan," I said. "No stories. Not now —"

"Her mother had promised Mary that the next time Joey asked for it she'd try to say no, suggesting they maybe try something else to get him excited, like watching a porno or something. But it was no good. Joey insisted; he absolutely had to have the Fun Dip. It was the only thing that worked."

The camera moved away from Mary, showing her surroundings. There was the cot. The white sheet. A chair.

"Sometimes," continued Megan, "her mother made Mary buy four or five, just in case she and Joey might need them later, when they'd be feeling unexpectedly horny and too stoned to move. Besides, it was better buying them in bulk that way — then Mary didn't have to deal with the clerk's weird vibe every time she was at the store."

"Megan," I pleaded. "Please . . ."

She glared at me and continued.

"Mary looked at the innocuous package, feeling the rib of the candy stick inside. She thought of the extras in her mother's bedside drawer, rattling like broken bones, chalky with the powder of their sweet dust. At the store, Mary bought her mother and Joey lemon-lime, a change. The cashier gave her a wary look.

"What Mary thought her mother really should be doing," Megan rambled on, "is trying powdered Jell-O. Or maybe she and Joey should just switch to chocolate pudding. Or whipped cream."

On the television, the camera moved outside, panning the hospital grounds before zooming in on Mary's window, catching her sad, lifeless expression.

"Mary stepped out onto the sidewalk, into the sunny afternoon. It was really too bad she hadn't seen more of the neighborhood during the day, she thought. It really was pretty."

Megan grabbed another toffee and shut off the TV, adopting the voice of Porky Pig. *"Th-th-that's all, folks!"*

"You're sick," I said.

"I'm sick?" Megan came back. *"I'm* sick? Did you check *Mary* out?"

Then, suddenly: a noise.

"Shit! Did you hear that?" she whispered. "C'mon!"

We ran down the hallway and up the stairs to Megan's bedroom, quickly closing the door behind us. As we jumped on her bed to look out the window, sure enough, there was Rose's car in the driveway.

"I told you!" I said, pushing Megan over on her bed. "I knew she was coming back!"

"Don't push me!" Megan said, standing up, smiling and pushing me back.

I fell into the mess of sheets and pillows while Megan straddled me from above. Picking up a stuffed white rabbit by the ears, she whapped me in the head with it.

"It's not funny!" I said between wallops.

"Oh, yes it is!" Megan said, raising the bunny into the air. I reached for some defense, grabbing hold of a pink teddy bear. As it collided in the air with the bunny, the bear let out an odd wheeze, kind of like a squeak but damaged somehow, broken.

"Oh, no!" Megan cried in mock horror, raising a hand over her mouth. "No! No! No! Not *Bubbles!*"

As Megan wielded the bunny by the ears and I clutched Bubbles by the legs, we thrashed the stuffed animals in midair—each of us taking turns at whopping each other's head. We laughed, thrilled, screaming and cowering from each other's blows.

Finally, Megan grabbed Bubbles away from me and threw the bear behind her. I snatched the bunny out of her hands and held it up in front of my face.

"Bunny didn't think that was very funny," I said.

Megan fell over on top of me, laughing. "I give up. Stop, stop," she said breathlessly.

I could feel the strength of her heartbeat against the wall of my chest, smell the candied strawberry scent of her skin and hair. After a moment she rolled over onto her back and lay beside me on the bed. Silent, we stared up at the ceiling.

"Do you ever wonder what heaven is like?" Megan said.

"Sometimes," I answered quietly.

"I know it sounds crazy," Megan continued, "but I had this dream last night. I must have been in heaven. There were these glass dump trucks full of candy. And like in a parade, they drove up and down the highways, through towns and cities, through financial districts and meatpacking districts. Through suburbs. Parks. Past movie theaters and shopping malls: glass dump trucks, clear as Cinderella's slipper, carrying truckloads of candy.

"And everyone leaned out of windows as they watched the glass dump trucks roll past, their dump bodies brimming with billions of candies as colorful as confetti.

"Finally they pulled up into a field. A green field so flat and wide, the sky could be seen from end to end. And then, all together, the glass buckets rose in the air and all the candy fell to earth, turning into a giant candy mountain. Then all the people ran toward it, diving right into the center. The rich. The poor. The old and the young—everyone—plunged in their hands and arms and toes. Everywhere there was candy."

Megan let her words linger on her tongue.

"After they all had eaten their fill, they climbed hand in hand in peace together to the summit of the candy mountain, forming a human chain to the top. And there they could see for miles and miles, over the hills and the fields into the forests and the trees . . ." Megan's voice faded, then suddenly she sat up, breaking out of her reverie. "That's it! I know where we can go!"

"Where?" I asked.

Megan rolled over and looked at me, her eyes twinkling. *"The forest."*

ONE OF THE ONLY REASONS FOR LIVING

THE FOREST WAS NOT FAR from where we lived. It bordered the edge of our subdivision. From a distance, it looked like any other forest: a clump of trees, squarish and green. But beyond the first line of sight, it was deep and dark and endless, full of shadows and long light.

What was not visible from the road was the old path Megan and I found, the solitary trail in the grass that weaved through the field into the trees. At the end of it, we discovered an abandoned fort camouflaged among the trees. It was built from found wood that had long succumbed to a slow crawl of moss and graffiti. The floor was a sea of broken glass; garbage was strewn everywhere.

In front of the fort was an abandoned fire pit. I picked up an old beer bottle. It was full of black water and cigarette butts, mashed and swollen. Megan grabbed it out of my hands and smashed it against a tree. Then she picked up another bottle and did the same thing. Again and again.

When she couldn't find any more bottles to smash, Megan sat down on a rock and reached into her pocket. "Here. Why don't you have one of these," she said slyly, "if you want."

They were Necco Wafers. Megan opened the package and offered me some as she put one into her mouth. She sucked for a moment and smiled.

"Good?" I said as I sat down on another rock beside her.

She nodded, opening her mouth and showing me the thin disk of candy on the end of her tongue.

"You know what I wish I had right now?" she said to me, eyes gleaming. "Popeye Cigarettes. Man, I love those! Although they're not called Popeye Cigarettes anymore. They're called Popeye Candy Sticks."

"Yeah, I remember those," I said.

"You've had them?" Megan asked.

"I didn't not eat candy all my life, you know," I said.

"I know, I know," Megan said. "I was just teasing."

Megan stood up and struck a pose.

"Undt vat are dese?" she said in a high-pitched voice, pretending to hold up a package in the air. She then turned her head as if she were simultaneously two people having a conversation. "Vat do you zink zey are?" she replied to herself. "Popeye Zigarettes?" She did her best to sound outraged, hysterical. Like a zany Nazi's, her voice rose to a controlled frenzy.

"Zey're not zigarettes anymore," she said indignantly, then turned to look the other way. "Zey're Kandy Stix."

She turned her head again: "Kant you eet karot stiks?"

"Nein," she continued to herself. "I detest za peeling."

"Selery stiks?"

"Ugh."

"Strawze?"

Megan raised her eyebrows in mock horror. "Yoo must be jhoking."

She turned once more. "Zey youse to bee Popeye Zigarettes—"

"But zey're not anymore, are zey?" Megan shrieked to her other self. "Zey're Popeye Kandy Stix now!"

Megan took a breath. Then she said, "Vell, zey look za zame to me. Zo. Vat I vant to know ees, how ees dat helping you queet?"

Megan spun around and faced her imaginary foe with exaggerated fury, eyeballs bulging. As she lunged for the package of candy cigarettes from her own hands, she fumbled and tore it open, placing one between her lips, sucking impetuously.

"Eet iz helping me," Megan pleaded, pretending to exhale a long stream of smoke. "EET IZ!"

I clapped. The sound of my applause made a distant echo in the trees.

"So," Megan said after a minute, sitting back down on the rock, "what are you going to be for Halloween?"

If you really thought about it, Megan said, the entire year revolved around candy. From one holiday to another, the calendar was a succession of sugary orgies, each providing the opportunity to eat as much candy as possible. If one planned it right, one could be supplied with free candy throughout the whole year.

In Megan's mind, Christmas, with its candy canes and gingerbread houses and chocolate Advent calendars, was the inaugural event. Then there was Valentine's Day, with its cinnamon hearts and heart-shaped boxes of chocolates. Following that, there was Easter, with its chocolate bunnies and eggs, which Megan thought looked like turds when hidden in wads of plastic pink grass.

And then there was Halloween.

Halloween was not an ordinary holiday. It was not a celebration of a religious ritual disguised as something else. Halloween was for the demonic. And for kids. It was, she confessed, perhaps one of the only reasons for living.

"Let's get one thing straight," Megan said. "When I go out trick-or-treating, it's not in the traditional way. I'm not in it to waddle up and down the streets with my stupid pumpkin pail, wearing a goofy costume. I'm in it to accumulate mass, to get as much fucking candy as I can."

The real, hard-core Halloween junkie, Megan insisted, did not care what kind of candy she got, just as long as she got it and got lots of it. Which is what Megan planned to do.

"The first time I went out trick-or-treating," Megan said, "I was three. I can still remember the way it felt, holding my father's hand, walking up and down the street, going up to one house after another. All these strangers giving me candy. Free. I couldn't believe it." Megan popped some more Necco Wafers into her mouth. "After a couple of years, my father stopped taking me out. Then I started going out with other kids. But I found out that I could get more if I went alone. I was eight when I went out all by myself."

Megan grinned, waiting for my reaction. She enjoyed boasting of her past accomplishments, as if there were a Candy Hall of Fame where only she was featured.

"Since then I've always gone out alone," Megan said. "That way I always get the most candy."

Megan took Halloween seriously. *Very* seriously. From the time she was eight she'd gone trick-or-treating the same way, changing from one costume to another, exchanging one set of pillowcases for another, doing the same loop of neighborhood over and over to get as much candy as she could. As focused and efficient as a long-distance runner, she chose only costumes that were quick and easy to change in and out of. No nylons, no makeup. Nothing fancy.

From her experience, she knew that most people didn't remember who came and went. They just saw a bunch of kids standing at the door. People gave out candy mostly because of fear, she believed. Because if they didn't, shit would happen. Those were the rules. Trick or treat.

"This year I want to try something new," Megan told me. "All I have to do is take around two pillowcases: one for me and one for my kid sister who is sick in the hospital with tonsillitis. People are such suckers for a sappy story. They'll ooh and aah and say *Well, gee, isn't that nice?* and then give you more, not even thinking that maybe a kid who just got their tonsils ripped out shouldn't be eating candy anyway."

Megan never considered that she might be too old to go out trick-or-treating. Age was immaterial. Halloween was the crescendo, the climax, the mother lode of the candy year.

"So are you in, or what?" she asked.

I wasn't sure if Megan was daring or testing me. But I was afraid that if I said no to her—even though I knew I was too old to go out trick-or-treating—it might threaten our friendship. And I was still confused. I didn't know if I was ready to eat candy. Not yet.

"I don't know," I replied. "I'll have to think about it."

Megan said nothing. Then she stood up and led the way back. There was just enough light to see where we were going. As we walked through the forest there was only the sound of our footsteps as they fell upon the flat muddied path. It was dark by the time we got back to the edge of the field.

Just before we went our separate ways, Megan turned and faced me.

"You know, you don't have to blame yourself for your mother's death," she said. "It's not your fault."

Megan looked back toward the forest. I didn't know what to say.

"I know you're afraid," she continued, "that if you forgive yourself you'll stop remembering her. But you won't. Trust me. You don't have to keep punishing yourself."

Tears stuck in my throat. "But how do you know?" I asked.

"Because," she answered with a sad, strange smile, "when my father died, I felt the same way."

Later that night I heard my father through the wall, quietly crying. It was not the first time. He often woke up in the middle of the night now. I listened helplessly, thinking about what Megan had said.

My father blamed himself, too. But for what I didn't know. I pulled the covers over my head and curled up on my side, shutting my eyes and closing my ears to the sound. I wished he would stop. But he didn't. I knew I should have gone to him, but what would we say to each other? My mother's death grew like a chasm between us. Eventually I drifted back to sleep.

And then I had a dream.

It was a winter day. Bright and white, a piercing blue sky. All around the schoolyard at TWS, kids were building snow forts and having snowball fights, running and jumping, frenzied by the cold. I was eating snow, my hands cupped together like a bowl, crystals melting in my mouth.

Then, they came. MAL.

They walked across the field toward me, all rosy cheeks and rosy lips and waves of golden hair. But as they drew nearer their eyes deadened to blackened hollow pits; their teeth turned into fangs; their tongues twisted into snakes. Beetles and snakes and rats festered in their hair.

Weave cum tew kil yew, they said, hissing and cackling.

But I was not scared. I felt powerful and free. Then I did an extraordinary thing: I laughed. At them and at everything. And with one great breath I froze MAL, turning them into silent sculptures, their features as fine as marble, frozen in time.

I bent down and scooped up more snow in my hands. It was crunchy and hard and cold, but sweet, unlike anything I had ever tasted. Then I looked down at my hands.

It was not snow I had been eating, but sugar.

Pure white sugar.

The next morning I told Megan that I wanted to taste candy again.

Her eyes glassed over. Then she screamed and hugged me.

"Now?" she said ecstatically.

"No," I said. "On Halloween night."

Megan screamed again.

"The first thing we have to do is plan our costume changes."

Her voice fluttered with nervous excitement. "We've only got four good hours. So that means four costumes, one for each hour." Megan put a piece of gum in her mouth, chewing and then forming a giant bubble. It popped and collapsed against her face like a mask. She peeled the gum off her nose and re-inserted it into her mouth.

"Have you thought about what you want to be?" she asked.

"Sort of," I answered. "First a housewife, then a witch."

Megan pondered this for a moment. "OK. What next?"

"Then a princess."

Megan blew another bubble. It swelled, bulbous and glassy, and then popped loudly, deflating. "Nope. No princesses. Too frou-frou. Try something else."

"How about a ghost?"

"OK. Great. Then?"

I shrugged.

"C'mon! Think about it—something else white."

I tried to think of what I had been in years past, but I could not remember. I hadn't gone out trick-or-treating in a long time.

"An angel?" I guessed.

Megan grinned. "Perfect. We'll use the forest as a change area and drop-off zone. But we don't have much time."

"What are you going to be?" I asked Megan.

"Easy. Exactly what I was last year. First a hobo, then Frankenstein, then an alien, then Death."

For the next week, Megan and I busied ourselves with getting our costumes ready, timing our changes, going over routes, charting the course of our evening.

We would waste no time stopping between houses,

lollygagging over what candy we got, Megan commanded. We would move quickly from house to house. We would cut through yards, jump over fences. And we would not walk; we would run. We would alternate being the designated doorbell-ringer. That way there would be no hesitation and we would not waste time.

No matter how much we wanted to, we would resist the temptation to snack. It was this precise tactic of abstinence that Megan believed was essential to our success. We would not become idle and placated. We would be driven by hunger and desire, by the manic, all-consuming lust for candy.

The night before Halloween, I was sitting at the kitchen table eating a bowl of Alpha-Getti when my father entered the kitchen. I was surprised to see him. I thought he would be at work.

"I need you to stay in tomorrow night and give out Halloween candy," he said. "I have to work late."

I couldn't understand why he was telling me this now.

"I can't," I said, not looking at him. "I'm going out. Trick-or-treating."

"With who?"

"Megan Chalmers."

"And who is Megan Chalmers?"

"A friend."

My father sighed quietly with disappointment. "Don't you think you're a little old for that?"

"What?" I said, pretending that I didn't know what he was talking about. I stared at the letters swimming in the tomato sauce. Bored, I chased an F with my spoon.

"You're a teenager now," he said, his tone incredulous. He bent over and looked inside the fridge.

"Why aren't you at work?" I said, changing the subject. I spooned together a C and a K and placed them at the edge of my bowl.

Beer in hand, my father straightened up and closed the door. "I thought you'd be happy to see me," he replied.

I wanted to tell him I was, but I had become comfortable with his not being around. I had developed my own routines and schedules, my own way of working around his absences. His patterns of sleep. His grief.

There was an uncomfortable silence. I collected a stranded U in the center of my bowl.

"Well, I don't think you should go," he said finally.

"Why?"

"Because you're too old, that's why. You can tell your friend Megan you can go out another time."

He was right, of course. I was too old. But I didn't care what he thought. Not now. Megan and I had worked too hard to prepare for this night.

I looked down at the letters and grouped them together on my spoon, staring at the word with a perverse pleasure. My father raised his beer up to his lips. I wanted to stand up and throw my bowl across the room at him, but I kept my head down, not looking at him.

"Is that clear?" he demanded.

I slowly spooned the word into my mouth, each letter fat and cold and spongy on my tongue.

"*I said*, is that clear?" he repeated.

"Yes," I replied, swallowing the word whole.

The next morning at school, a few kids paraded up and down the halls in costumes, faces painted in fierce palettes. Even some of the teachers got dressed up. Mr. King came in an Elvis costume and insisted we call him "The King."

Megan and I had agreed in advance not to dress up, so we could save our energy during the day.

MAL, however, had dressed up as fairies and flitted around in sheer white skirts over solid white body suits, glittering gold crowns secured in their hair, wands poised in their hands. All day long they went around granting wishes, touching the tops of people's heads with the tips of their "magic" wands.

While we were standing on the school grounds, Megan observed MAL's behavior with a bored look of disgust. "Can you believe that?" she said to me. "Granting wishes? How fucking pathetic."

Tracey Reid walked up to us, dressed as Little Bo-Peep. "Isn't that nice?" she said, looking at MAL with glowing admiration. Meredith had just touched the top of someone's head with her wand as if she were Tinkerbell.

Megan shot her a look of disbelief. "You have got to be kidding."

"I think it's very sweet," she said to Megan.

"Puh-leeze. They're hell spawn. Can't you see their wands are instruments of the devil?"

Megan opened a handful of individual bite-size chocolate bars and ate one after the other.

"I like candy, too, you know," Tracey said.

"Oh, yeah?" Megan said sarcastically, raising her eyebrow at her. As if she cared. "How interesting."

"My favorite is Fun Dip. You know, with the little candy stick?"

Megan looked at her and smirked.

"And what do you like to do with your Fun Dip, Tracey?" Megan asked.

Tracey scrunched up her face in confusion. "I dip it—" she began.

"In and out, in and out?" Megan said, trying to control herself.

"Yes," Tracey said. "What else am I supposed to do with it?"

Megan collapsed with laughter.

"I don't see what's so funny," Tracey said. "Besides, I know how you get your candy."

Megan stopped laughing.

"I saw you," Tracey went on, "the other day. At T'n'T. I watched you do it."

"Do what?"

"*Steal* it."

"You wish," Megan scoffed. "You don't know what you're talking about."

"You didn't see me. But I was there. I saw everything. And that's not all I know—"

"Hey, Bo-Peep," Megan interrupted, "don't you have to find some lost sheep?"

MAL drifted up behind Megan and me, circling around us and standing beside Tracey.

"Everything OK, Tracey?" Meredith asked in her good-fairy voice, looking at Megan.

"Would you like to make a wish?" Angela asked Tracey.

"Gee, I wouldn't know what to wish for," Tracey gushed.

Beside me, Megan rolled her eyes.

"Why don't you let us make it for you," suggested Laura.

"OK," Tracey agreed.

Laura started walking around Megan and me, waving her wand over our heads.

"Don't you dare use that on me," Megan threatened, "you minion of Lucifer."

Laura's eyes widened with anger. "Oh, yeah? And what are you going to do about it?"

Megan grabbed Laura's wand. "Look, I said *don't.* So *don't.* Why don't you just get lost?"

"Please, just leave us alone — " I said.

Laura swung around and leered at me. "Why don't you just stay out of this," she said, pushing me. *"Dead girl."*

"Mr. King's coming. Mr. King's coming," Angela warned.

All of us turned around. Mr. King was walking across the field toward us, dressed in his white jumpsuit. With his dark sunglasses on, he looked almost like the real Elvis.

"Everything all right here?" he said to MAL with a soft southern twang.

"Oh, we're fine, Mr. King," Meredith politely replied. "Angela and Laura and I were just trying to grant Tracey her Halloween wish."

Mr. King tipped his sunglasses down on his nose and looked around the circle, staring at Megan and me.

"Nothing else going on here, Miss McKinnon?"

"No, Mr. King," Meredith said sweetly. "Nothing at all."

Mr. King rocked back and forth on his heels, then put his sunglasses back over his eyes.

"Well, all right then," he crooned in a low voice, flipping up his collar and striking a pose. "Let's break it up." The bell rang. "Thank ya, thank ya very much."

As he turned his back, MAL smirked at us and followed after him. We trailed behind them, Megan goose-stepping toward the doors.

That afternoon, as I passed a handout to Blake Starfield, I found myself staring down at his hands. They were large for a boy's, broad and wide, with long, strong fingers. Blake lifted his head and met my gaze with a soft, innocent smile. For an instant I thought I could see a kind of light around him. He took the sheet of paper from me, accidentally brushing my hand.

Then Mr. King asked me if there was something that Blake and I wanted to share with the rest of the class. I quickly turned around and faced the blackboard. I muttered "No," the back of my neck burning.

CANDY, GLORIOUS CANDY

THE TRUTH WAS, I DIDN'T CARE what my father said. I was going out for Halloween. I wanted to taste candy again.

That afternoon after school, I packed everything I needed, including my masks and costumes and pillowcases, in a large black garbage bag and headed out to meet Megan.

As I walked toward the forest, I saw her standing under the trees. She was dressed in her hobo outfit, an old felt brown hat on her head, and she was clutching a brown paper bag.

"What's in there?" I asked.

"Jolt. Want a slug?"

"No, thanks," I said.

"Suit yourself."

I watched Megan take a long drink. Dark drops fell from the can onto her coat as she lifted the rim away from her lips. I could sense the sugar, inch by inch, roaring through her blood.

"You ready?" she said.

I was nervous. But excited, too. I nodded. "Ready."

As we walked along our planned route, the toddlers and their parents were just beginning to come out trick-or-treating. They all looked so harmless, all the little ghosts and devils walking beside their mothers and fathers in the late-afternoon light. I watched as the kids stood in the doorways, holding out their pails and pillowcases. When they turned around, their expressions were of absolute joy. And greed.

As we hurried from house to house, Megan told me a story about this girl, Melinda Foster, who wanted Halloween to come so badly one year that she broke out in hives. She'd anticipated the event for weeks and weeks, talking about what costume she was going to wear and how much candy she was going to eat and how she was going to get so much more than anyone else. And the day before Halloween these big red lumps broke out all over her face. They were too big to be chickenpox, too small to be measles. And when Melinda Foster's mother took her to the doctor and she was diagnosed with hives, she was not allowed to go out for Halloween. Melinda Foster cried and cried, but her mother's mind was made up. Melinda would have to spend the night in bed.

Halloween night, Melinda Foster sat up in bed and watched outside her bedroom window all the kids trick-or-treating, gorging on Halloween treats. And as she thought about all the candy she was missing, Melinda Foster's hives flared even more. All she could do was apply and reapply calamine lotion to stop them from itching.

She had not contracted the hives, catching them like the flu or conjunctivitis or any other contagious disease. In her excitement and anticipation, she had given them to herself. Melinda Foster had made herself sick.

When Megan finished telling me the story, I stopped and looked at her.

"Did she get better?" I asked.

"Who?"

"Melinda Foster."

A look of vague confusion passed over Megan's face. "Oh, her. Oh, yeah. Yeah. Of course she did. Why do you ask?"

"I just wanted to know how the story ended," I said. "Who did you think I was talking about?"

"C'mon," Megan said. "Let's keep moving."

In order to maximize our opportunity, Megan chose a densely populated neighborhood next to the forest. At first I was flattered that Megan had invited me along, since she had spoken so proudly of going out alone. Because we had agreed to split everything fifty-fifty, she still needed me to help get as much candy as possible.

For each round, we each carried one pillowcase. An additional pillowcase alternated between us. This was known as the best-friend-with-chickenpox/brother-with-the-broken-leg/cousin-in-the-wheelchair/kid-sister-with-tonsillitis pillowcase. At the end of the evening, Megan concluded, we would have a total of twelve pillowcases of candy. Pure bliss.

Changing our costumes proved easy. All we had to do was run and drop off our pillowcases at the edge of the forest and quickly pull on the next costume. Megan and I ran back and forth from the woods into the neighborhood. As we went from house to house, monsters drifted across people's lawns under the dull burn of streetlights and moon glow.

Everything went off just as we planned. No one said we were too old. No one commented on our costumes. Every time we went to a house, the people did just what they were supposed to do, open their door and put candy in our pillowcases. Every time.

Only once did a woman on Woodland Avenue suspect our

plan. When she saw the third pillowcase, she raised her eyebrow at us.

"For my brother," Megan explained. "He broke his leg three weeks ago."

The woman dropped a piece of gum in the pillowcase. "He wouldn't be related to your other sister, the one with tonsillitis, now, would he?"

Megan didn't miss a beat.

"Yes, ma'am!" Megan replied in a ridiculous southern accent, grinning ear to ear. "My ma says it's a good thing I got two legs for both of them or else they wouldn't get a thing."

The woman looked down at Megan and smiled ruefully. "Well then," she said, "your brother and sister had better share with you, shouldn't they?"

Shameless, Megan continued grinning. "Yes, ma'am!"

When we completed the last round, we returned to the forest to collect our loot. We each carried six pillowcases over our shoulders, our backs stooped as low as old ladies'. I imagined how we must have looked emerging from the forest, me outfitted as an angel and Megan dressed as Death, walking side by side, hunched over with the weight of our enormous sacks.

As we walked, I watched my costume sparkle in the light. Ahead of me, Megan's black hood flapped behind her, the inky outline of her body disappearing within the dark tangle of shadows.

I was exhausted. All night Megan had kept a grueling pace, not stopping once. It was the longest amount of time I'd seen her go without candy. And now that we'd done all the work, we were going back to her place to take inventory of our stash, and when we'd done that, it was finally going to happen.

I was going to eat candy.

My stomach buckled, filled with dread and anticipation. It had been six months since I'd tasted anything sweet. What would I have? My mind swam with the possibilities. As Megan and I reached the edge of the field, we stepped onto the sidewalk and stood under the streetlight, adjusting the weight of our pillowcases.

"You OK?" Megan asked me.

I nodded.

"Tired?"

I nodded again.

"Yeah, me, too."

"Can we take a break?" I asked.

Megan looked at me through the peepholes of her skeleton mask. "No," she said. "We can't afford to stop. Not now."

I heaved my pillowcases up higher on my shoulders, the weight cutting into my back.

No doubt my father would be waiting up for me. I'd have to explain why I'd gone against his wishes, why I'd deliberately defied him. There would be his stern silence, the cool, authoritative way that he would express his disappointment. It all seemed so predictable: the way he would act, the way I would react. As I balled the ends of the pillowcases in my hands and switched shoulders, I realized I didn't care what would happen when I got home. I would just go straight up to my room and close my door, avoiding all the drama.

"Eyes up," Megan said. "Behind us."

I turned and looked. Behind us were three costumed figures moving toward us. As they got closer I could see they were wearing all black, with long black trench coats and black turtlenecks and black gloves. As they passed under the streetlight, I saw their identical pig masks become illuminated, then vanish into the darkness before reappearing under the next steetlight.

"Who are they?" I asked Megan. My heart was racing.

"I don't know," Megan said, pushing against me, grabbing my elbow. "But I've got a pretty good idea."

"What are you doing?"

"Getting us the fuck out of here," she said, guiding me into the middle of the street.

"Are they following us?"

"Don't turn around. Just play it cool. Keep walking," she urged.

I looked behind us. The pigs were marching shoulder to shoulder, quickly and evenly.

Megan yanked my arm. "I said, *don't* turn around."

"They're gaining on us."

"Walk faster."

I walked beside Megan, trying to keep up.

"C'mon," she said. "Can't you walk any faster than that?"

"I'm trying—"

"Try harder."

I could feel the weight of the candy like a blade digging into my shoulder. In the grip of my sweating hands, the ends of the pillowcases twisted in my palms, burning like fire. I turned around again.

"I told you, *don't fucking turn around*," Megan said angrily. "Just keep cool."

The three pigs were now running toward us, elbows joined like riot guards, three snouted pink heads bobbing in a sea of black.

"But they're coming for us," I said anxiously.

This time, Megan turned around.

"Oh, shit," I heard her say. "RUN!" she yelled.

At first it looked like Megan might get away. But just as all things terrible seem to stand still in time, it was as if she were moving in slow motion, charging ahead of me in the street. But then she tripped on her costume and two of the pigs caught up to her. Hard and sudden, they knocked her down. Then me. As my knee hit the pavement, my pillowcases went flying. Candy sprayed everywhere.

I tried to stand, but I got caught up in my angel costume. Before I knew what was happening, I was pinned face-down to the ground. I struggled to free myself, but it was no use. I couldn't lift my head. The pig that had knocked me down was sitting on my back, straddling me, locking my arms at my sides, holding my head down from behind. I kicked my legs and tried to roll over, but each time I moved the pig pushed my face down harder into the pavement. I could hear Megan screaming maniacally, ordering them to let us go.

Finally the pig released me. As I looked up I saw all three pigs scrambling to collect our pillowcases of candy. Then they took off with them, laughing, spilling some of our hard-earned treasure. Howling like a wounded animal, Megan pulled herself up and ran after them.

I tried to keep up with Megan. But my knee was shot through with pain. I looked down. A pinkish blur of blood was seeping through the silver and white sparkled cloth of my gown.

After that, my feet went out from under me. There was a bright flash of light. Then darkness.

❦

When I opened my eyes, I was lying in the middle of the street, staring up into the face of Death.

As she removed her mask, Megan's own face came into focus above me.

"You OK?" she asked.

"My leg," I replied. "It hurts."

"You scraped your knee," Megan said, lying down on the road beside me. "That's all."

I felt her body next to mine, our shoulders touching.

"Did they take everything?"

Megan's voice was choked with anger. "Almost. Yes."

She held up her hands and showed me: only two handfuls of candy were left behind.

I couldn't believe it. "That's it?"

"Yes. Bitches."

"Do you think it was —"

"Yes."

I couldn't even say their names.

In the distance, we heard the far-off sounds of the last remaining kids still out wandering the neighborhood. They sounded like a bizarre herd of animals, whooping and hollering in their high voices, barking out strange signals into the darkness.

The street under my back was hard and cold; my knee throbbed with pain.

"Do we have enough time?" I said. "To do another round?"

She considered this for a moment. "No," she said. "It's too late."

I sensed the weight of her disappointment, our colossal failure.

After a moment she said, "You know, I've actually never done four rounds before. This was the first year that I was going to try."

"But you've done three, right?"

"Honest?" Megan said. She shook her head, then held up two fingers. "Nope. Just two."

I was thinking about all the candy I had wanted to have. M&M's, Mike and Ikes, Hershey's Kisses, Tootsie Pops.

"Do you really think that woman knew it was us again?" I said.

"Of course," Megan answered.

"Why do you think she gave us more?"

"Because it's trick or treat. She chose the treat."

"What would we have done?" I asked. I was curious to know what we were capable of doing.

"I dunno. Maybe we could have soaped her windows, egged her car or something," Megan joked.

I imagined us running through the streets, vandalizing cars with rotten eggs or soaping someone's windows. Throwing toilet paper into people's pools. Leaving flaming bags of poo on their front steps. Maybe we, too, would steal other kids' candy. But it seemed improbable. We weren't that diabolical.

"What's going on out there?" said a voice in the darkness.

Megan and I sat up.

At one of the houses an older man stood in his doorway, holding open the screen door, staring out into the street. Megan and I watched as he sauntered down his driveway toward us, his hands in his pockets.

We stood up. I was groggy on my feet and leaned into Megan for support.

"Everything all right?" he asked from the end of the driveway. Suspicion hung in his voice as he raised his hand to his forehead and peered out at us.

"Our candy was stolen," Megan explained.

"Oh," the man said. "Well then —"

"By three pigs," she added.

The man chuckled lightly, rocking back and forth on his heels. "Three pigs, eh?"

"Yes," Megan said. "Did you see them?"

"Well, no, now, no, I didn't," he said with obvious amusement. "But don't sweat it, girls. It's just candy. And besides, there's always next year."

Megan glared at the man.

"'Just candy'?" she said. "There is no such thing as 'just candy.' Only boring old fuckers like you think that."

The man stopped rocking on his heels. I could tell that he was preparing to say something, but Megan was already walking away from him, her back turned. When she was far enough away, she turned around and gave him the finger.

As I hobbled after her, I heard the man yelling something about insolence and respect as he headed back up his driveway, the fury constricting his throat.

When I got home, my father was waiting for me.

"Where have you been?" he demanded. "Do you know what time it is?"

I started up the stairs to my bedroom.

"Where do you think you're going?" he asked.

"To my room," I answered.

"Get back here right now," he ordered.

I went and stood at the bottom of the stairs, hoping he'd finish whatever it was he had to say and say it fast. "You were supposed to give out candy tonight," he said firmly. I stared at the empty bowl on the table by the front door. Beside it were several unopened bags of miniature packets of Bottle Caps — my favorite candy as a child. I felt a pang of guilt.

"I forgot." I shrugged.

Then my father droned on about how I had disobeyed him, how I had disrespected his decision, how I disappointed him. I stared at the carpet on the bottom stair, my arms folded over my chest.

"Look at me when I'm talking to you!" he said. I turned my face to him and looked him in the eye. For a second his expression was so fragile, as if he was going to cry, but then it became a mask of anger once more.

"You're grounded until further notice. Do you understand?"

I nodded. It was exactly as I predicted.

Megan mourned the loss of our Halloween stash as if it were pirates' treasure. Obsessed, she spun intricate tales of vengeance about putting our assailants to justice, their faces unmasked before death squadrons, their identities finally revealed.

Much to Megan's disappointment, however, I'd taken it as some kind of sign that I hadn't really been ready to eat candy yet. Obviously there were greater forces at work. It just wasn't meant to be.

But Megan still believed that candy could make the difference between an ordinary and an extraordinary day. Between being happy and sad. It alone had the power to transform a moment in time into something memorable and sweet.

Candy was not like ordinary food, she assured me. And even though we had almost none after all our efforts, Megan insisted that there would be other opportunities. For her. For me.

After all, it was everywhere: in penny machines at the grocery stores, at eye level in the variety stores, at the cash register in restaurants, at parades, in doctors' offices. Candy as a treat, candy as a reward. Candy, glorious candy.

Our time would come.

TRAP OWT

EHT ELDDIM

ECSTASY

Enough was enough, my father decided. I needed something to do after school, something that would teach me old-fashioned values and respect. Ground me. Just hanging out after school was not getting me anywhere. Volunteering was the answer.

After some phone calls, my father arranged for me to work as a volunteer at St. Teresa's Hospital. After my behavior on Halloween, it was not coincidental that he decided I should be a candy striper, pushing a cart of sweets and magazines up and down the hospital floors to sell to the patients. Furthermore, it was determined and agreed among all parties—except myself, of course—that the convalescent environment at St. Teresa's would be of the greatest benefit to me spiritually. My participation, although voluntary, was non-negotiable. I would learn my lesson. Sister Catherine assured my father of that.

The only compensation was that, if she desired, Megan would be allowed to volunteer with me.

At first, Megan was skeptical.

"Nuns?" she cried. *"No fucking way."*

"It's the only way," I pleaded.

"Only way to what, exactly?" Megan charged. "Salvation?" Closing her eyes, Megan dropped to her knees, rolling her eyes back in her head. "Hail Mary, full of grace, may the Lord be forever with thee," she incanted.

"It's the only way of appeasing my father," I explained. "The only way we would be *allowed* to see each other."

Megan kept chanting.

"There's candy, too," I said.

Megan stopped praying and opened her eyes. "Really. How much?"

"As much as you want."

"Really?"

"Of course. We are going to be candy stripers, after all."

Megan's face warped into a grin.

"OK," she said, rising to her feet. "I'll do it. But just so you know, I don't need to be saved. By anybody. Not even God. *Especially* God."

St. Teresa's Hospital was an ancient building of square stone blocks and straight columns that sat on a grassy green hill. Founded and operated exclusively by nuns, it was named in honor of their spiritual patron, Saint Teresa of Avila, a visionary and mystic nun of the Carmelite order.

It was an antiquated structure, with small, stale-smelling rooms and dark winding hallways, ancient offices and uncomfortable sitting rooms. It was cold, too, due to the marble floors and high ceilings and tall windows. Most of the patients who came to St. Teresa's were elderly. Everything that could be done for them had been done for them. They came to die.

On our first day, Sister Catherine welcomed Megan and me in the foyer.

Megan had outdone herself in dressing for the occasion,

sporting a tight black leather miniskirt, red fishnet stockings, and her usual pink high-top sneakers. She had styled her normally unkempt hair into a startling coiffure of bright pink spikes. To complete the ensemble she wore a ripped Sex Pistols T-shirt that proclaimed I AM AN ANTICHRIST.

Sister Catherine was as old as I had expected her to be, with a moon-shaped face and steady blue-green eyes. Dressed in her long dark habit, she was a tall, sturdy woman with a calm, easygoing manner. Startled and bemused, she looked down on us.

"Good afternoon, girls," she said calmly. "Welcome to St. Teresa's."

As she gave us a tour of the hospital, she informed us that our duty would be the same each week: to push a cart up and down the hallways, wheeling our way through the wards, knocking on every door, asking if anyone wanted to buy any candy or magazines.

We got the cart and cash float from Sister Maria, the nun who operated the gift shop. She was a nervous and absent-minded woman, with thin blue veins that snaked under the liver-spotted skin of her hands. It never seemed as if she really checked the candy or the float before or after our shift, so Megan could always get away with stealing something. Megan loved Sister Maria.

Our uniforms were pale pink and white striped smocks with ties on the sides. Velcroed around the inside of the elastic waist were stubbly little bits of balled lint. Megan said they creeped her out, that it was as if she were trying on a pair of department store underwear. She hated wearing them.

Then there was the hospital smell. That was what bothered

me the most: a warm, urine-saturated sort of vinegar that went straight up my nose and lingered in the center of my head. Everywhere Megan and I went, we smelled that smell. That slow erosion of life, the premature scent of death.

Some patients treated us with a vague, drug-addled suspicion, not exactly sure who we were or what we were selling. Others just refused us entry, shaking their bleary-eyed heads.

Some, though, were happy to see us. Eyes gleaming, they would usher us into their rooms, their bodies bristling with excitement as they sat perched like birds on the edge of their beds. With trembling hands they would select tins of hard candy—in elegant flavors like lemon and black currant—and ask us to open them. Then they'd sit and wait, licking their lips with expectation. After we opened the tins, they would dig in and select a piece as if it were a rare jewel, and pop it into their mouths. Then they'd lie back on their beds and smile, staring out the window while the candy burst with flavor.

And then came Edie.

We met her during our first shift at St. Teresa's. It was getting late in the afternoon and we were almost at the end of our rounds. Sitting upright in her bed, Edie was dressed in a blue satin dressing gown, pillows fluffed up around her, doing a crossword puzzle. When she heard us at the door, she motioned us in.

"Darlings," she said. "Six-letter word for 'an act of passage.'" She looked at us and then looked down at her newspaper. Megan and I looked at each other.

"Well?" she demanded, scrutinizing us.

We shrugged.

"Hmpf," she said, writing down the word. "It's *ritual*, darlings. R-I-T-U-A-L." When she finished, she tapped her pen on the newspaper page with satisfaction and lifted her head to look at us again.

"Well," she demanded, "what are you afraid of? I'm not going to bite."

Edie had snow white hair and mischievous blue eyes that sparkled from within the deep lines in her face. She had a petite, fairylike body with tiny feet and hands.

"Come closer, come closer," she said.

We wheeled the cart to the edge of her bed so she could have a better look.

Her room was an oasis: she was surrounded by a lush jungle of greenery, tropical potted plants, orchids, and hanging baskets. Above the foot of her bed, fastened to the ceiling, was a small TV, its wall-mounted retractable arm covered with creeping vines. Plants crowded the window, taking every available inch of sunlight.

"That's better," Edie said, leaning forward, carefully inspecting us and the cart.

Among the potted plants on her bedside table were tins of hard candy—scotch mints and butterscotch melt-aways—as well as boxes of Russell Stover chocolates, jars of Jelly Belly jellybeans, and boxes of raisin Glossettes. There was also a large bag of peanut M&M's, some Reese's Peanut Butter Cups, and a roll of BreathSavers. In the middle of everything was an assortment of different-colored pills in various shapes and sizes in small clear plastic containers with white screw-top lids.

Edie eyed us with a calculating, stern expression. "Well, what's the matter with you two? Cat got your tongues?"

"No," Megan said defensively.

"Oh, they speak!" Edie exclaimed, lifting up her arms in exaltation. "Hallelujah!"

Megan turned and looked at me. I could tell I was going to hear about this later.

"Now, darlings," Edie said, pointing to the candy, "I want a box of these. And a tin of that. And these and these." She stopped for a moment and then said, "Oh, and this, and this, too." She pointed again. "And these and these and these."

Most people got only a packet of gum, some breath mints. But not Edie. She handed us a crisp fifty-dollar bill.

Megan and I were astonished. We returned her change.

Edie leaned back into her pillow and opened a new tin of butterscotch melt-aways. She closed her eyes and took a long sniff.

"Delicious," she announced. "I love that smell. So sweet and fresh—like a dream." She carefully watched our reaction. "Would you like one?" she asked.

Without hesitation, Megan reached out and plucked one from the tin.

Edie looked at me. "How about you?"

I stared into the caramel-colored abyss.

"No, thank you," I said quietly.

Edie laughed. "Don't be so shy! Go on, darling. Have one—"

"She doesn't eat candy," Megan interrupted.

Edie raised her eyebrows at me. "What? Darling! Why? Are you crazy?"

Megan sighed. "I know. Tragic, isn't it? I've been trying to tell her. But she just won't listen."

Edie looked me up and down and grabbed my hand, giving it a little squeeze.

"Don't worry," she said kindly. "All in good time."

Edie leaned over her bedside table and selected some of the clear plastic containers and emptied out a handful of pills. Green, blue, yellow, and red ones jumbled in the palm of her hand. We watched as she carefully placed the tin of candy on the left-hand side of her bed and then slowly and methodically laid out each pill on the right-hand side. Then she closed her eyes, took a deep breath, and stared up at the TV. "I'm ready," she said.

Looking at Megan, she said, "Be a dear and bring me a glass of water, will you?"

As Megan went to the bathroom, Edie reached for the remote control and turned on the TV. It was *The Price Is Right*. A giant smile floated over her face.

"I do love *The Price is Right*," she said, not looking away from the television screen. "Don't you?" She sighed. "It's the only place on TV where you can see the true face of human happiness."

In the small bathroom that adjoined Edie's room, Megan dispensed some water into a small paper cone and then handed it to Edie.

"Thank you, darling," Edie said, taking the cone from Megan as if she were holding fine china. Using the remote with her other hand, Edie turned up the volume. The theme song for *The Price Is Right* got louder.

Edie raised her paper cup to the screen. Then, one by one, she took each pill with a small sip of water, followed by a piece of candy. And so it went. Pill. Drink. Candy. Pill. Drink.

Candy. As she did this, she stared at the screen. A woman who had just been called down to play was running toward Bob Barker, arms outstretched, ecstatic.

Mesmerized, Megan and I watched Edie in silence.

"Well," she said, turning and looking at us, "what are you staring at? It says right here on the bottle — *Take with food*."

Megan gave me a look that said we should go. Now.

Just before we turned around to leave, Edie said, "Before you go, one more thing." Her eyes twinkled. "Do you like stories, darlings?"

Megan looked at me, eyes big.

"Yeah," she answered slowly. "Yeah, we do."

"I knew it!" exclaimed Edie. She turned back to the television screen. Another woman had come running down from the studio audience, her face radiant. "As soon as you walked in the room, darlings, I could just tell!"

That Friday my first period came in the middle of the night. When I woke up, I had the peculiar feeling that something inside me had been cut or come untied, like a dark red ribbon was loosened. I stared with a sense of dread and embarrassment at the stain of reddish-brown gunk in the white square crotch of my underwear.

I had known it was coming, of course. Last year at my other school, all the girls had to sit together in the dark with the curtains drawn on a sunny afternoon, staring up at a giant overhead projection, learning all about the bloody business of our bodies, the ins and outs, the raw symmetry.

At the time, the female pelvis seemed to me to be made of words that sounded like the parts of a prayer. *Coccyx, sacrum, il-*

ium, ischium, intoned like a mantra inside my mind. I stared at the diagram of the fallopian tubes as if they were reckless snakes twisted into Medusa braids.

I had seen books that would help me with my burgeoning womanhood. Books with titles like *Your Changing Body* and *Becoming a Woman.* Most of them were basic textbook material with outdated illustrations that made the female body look like a scientific specimen. I might as well have been looking at the cross-section of a frog.

Once I found a book called *The Miracle of Life.* In it were pictures of animals mating: elephants atop elephants, dogs behind dogs. There were pages about different gestation periods and complex diagrams about mating rituals, including those of salmon, with little arrows pointing everywhere showing their life cycle. At the end of the book was a picture of a human fetus. There were no photos of humans mating, no complex drawings with arrows. Somehow, mysteriously, humans just did something and the result was a tiny little person curled up in a sac of fluid, sucking its own thumb.

Maybe through a microscope my blood would have looked interesting. But I could only study it with a vague sense of confusion and alienation.

I knew that in some parts of the world when a girl gets her period she is considered too powerful and has to leave the village until she has completed her first cycle. On her journey she is accompanied by other women who adorn her with flowers and perfume, initiating her into womanhood. It is a grand event, an important rite of passage in the girl's life.

So when I told Megan on Sunday about getting my period, it was she who suggested the ceremony.

It began with a blindfold at the edge of the forest, me holding on to Megan's shoulder. It was a dark November day, cold and wet and gray. Megan had kept the details of the ceremony a secret, requesting only that I bring the stained underwear.

When we stopped, she told me to remove my blindfold. We were in the forest, although I did not know where. In a somber voice she told me to kneel on the forest floor, and then she ordered me to give her my underwear. I reached into my pocket and passed them up to her.

"Now," she said, "do as I say. Open your mouth and stick out your tongue."

I did. She reached into her pocket and pulled something out, concealed within her closed fist.

"First," she said, "you must listen." Megan raised my underwear above my head, then uttered in a low moaning: "Forever and now, remember this blood."

She looked down at me and winked.

"OK," Megan said as she placed something on my tongue. *"Now."*

"Wha?"

"Now you may taste your true essence."

So I did.

It was hard at first, hard and square in my mouth, dense with flavor and very, very sweet. I hadn't sucked on it for more than a moment before it began to leak a foamy syrup, bubbling like lava on my tongue. An instant after that, it cracked and the pieces melted in my mouth.

It was a cherry-flavored Lotsa Fizz.

I looked up at Megan, at the dark blur of her holding my underwear up in the air. I had forsaken my mother. Broken my promise. Been tempted and surrendered. Shame flooded through me. And then, as the candy melted in my mouth, I felt relief. Refreshing, blissful relief. Like a big wave had come up and crashed down over me, taking me away in its lovely swell.

For the first time, I didn't care what anyone thought. My mother. MAL. God. My father. And I didn't care what anyone would ever think of me again.

Satisfied, I sank to the forest floor and lay there in ecstasy.

Above me against the canopy of trees, Megan howled with laughter.

I walked home that afternoon feeling as if I were flying far above the earth, bouncing on clouds. I was invincible.

I reached inside my pocket, touching the small brown paper bag that Megan had given me. Inside was an assortment of jellybeans and Jujubes, sours, licorice, bubblegum, and lollipops. This, according to Megan, was in case I ran out and needed an emergency fix in the middle of the night. I said that that would be unlikely, but she gave it to me anyway, admitting that she always woke up in the night to eat candy.

I imagined her reaching out for a peppermint in the darkness and putting it in her mouth before drifting off to sleep again. From the bag I pulled out a Sour Cherry Blaster. The sour crystals stung my tongue, sending jolts of pleasure rippling through my mouth. I couldn't believe I'd waited so long—all those months afraid of eating candy, forbidden from tasting such sweetness.

I swallowed the Sour Cherry Blaster and bit down hard on another, then another, and another. With each bite I felt my fear fade away, the guilt of my mother's death diminishing.

A few days later, on Veterans Day, our class went to the gymnasium for the annual assembly. As we entered the gym in single file, we took our chairs quietly and carefully. If we had to speak we would speak in hushed voices, Mr. King instructed us, or we would not speak at all.

Megan sat two rows behind me, dressed all in white, with a small lapel pin that declared THE WAR IS OVER! When I turned around to look at her, she rolled her eyes. She was sitting next to Tracey Reid.

I sat next to Blake Starfield. We did not speak.

Mr. Carter, the principal, climbed the narrow wooden steps toward the stage. He was an elderly man with narrow shoulders. When he reached the podium he faced everyone with a terse, authoritative expression.

"Would you please rise for the national anthem," he said, and everyone got up from the chairs. As the music began, Mr. Carter took a step aside on the platform and looked ahead into the distance as if he were seeing something very great, like a passing ship or a rare bird flying into the sun. The rest of us reluctantly joined in, our voices deadened by habit.

When we were finished, we all sat down again.

"Ladies and gentlemen, boys and girls, we are here today to remember and mourn those who so valiantly lost their lives in war so that we might stand here in freedom today." As he spoke, Mr. Carter's face twisted with a kind of sour expression. I imagined the words coming out of the small dark hole of his mouth as colors: one gray, one black, then a stream of red—bang bang bang—like bullets punctuating the space of air.

After he said a few more words about freedom and democracy, Mr. Carter told us we would be watching a film about war. The gym went dark. The reels of a projector turned and a voice, slow and plodding, spoke over heavily orchestrated music. Black-and-white footage showed men marching through fields. I tried to think of their sacrifice. But all I could think of was my mother.

I started to cry, silent tears rolling down my cheeks.

Then, suddenly, I felt a hand slip into mine. Blake Starfield's hand. I stared ahead at the film, feeling the gentle pressure of his fingers rest against the inside of my palm.

To my surprise, my heart was racing.

I did not let go.

The next day, Megan and I were invited to a surprise birthday party at Meredith McKinnon's.

"Un-fucking-believable," Megan said, digging her hand into a box of Nerds. She passed me the box. I took a handful, too. We stared down in disbelief at our identical invitations and read:

YOU'RE INVITED
TO A SURPRISE BIRTHDAY PARTY
FOR MEREDITH MCKINNON
FRIDAY AT 5:30 P.M.
DON'T FORGET TO BRING YOUR SWIMSUIT

(AND REMEMBER, IT'S A SURPRISE!!!)

Megan and I couldn't understand why we'd been invited. We weren't friends with Meredith. It was a trick, we concluded. A sick joke. A hoax.

But, as we later learned from Tracey Reid, we were not

alone. Every girl in our class had been invited. Apparently Meredith McKinnon's mother hadn't wanted to leave anyone out.

"We're not actually going to go, are we?" I asked.

Megan's eyes narrowed with mischief. I'd seen that look before.

"Why not?" said Megan. "I think we should."

I reached for more Nerds. "But—"

"But what?" Megan countered with a smile, hoarding the box. "We were invited, just like everyone else."

"What about Angela and Laura?" I asked.

"What about them?" replied Megan.

"Don't you think they'll tell Meredith?"

"*Of course* they'll tell Meredith," Megan said. "There's not going to be any surprise for anyone, that's for sure. Except maybe for Meredith's mom."

Megan laughed and emptied the remaining Nerds into her palm, burying her face in her hand.

"Besides," Megan said in a mock English accent as she raised her head between bites. "It would be such a dreadful shame for us to miss her birthday. We can't be party poopers, now can we?"

FRANCESCA AND THE CAVE OF SECRETS

THE NEXT TIME Megan and I went to St. Teresa's, Edie was waiting for us.

"Where have you been?" she asked. "I've been watching for you all week." As we wheeled the cart beside the bed, she picked out the same selection of sweets she had the previous week. When she was finished, she put everything on her bedside table.

"Now," Edie said to Megan, "close the door."

As she turned around, Megan gave me an I-can't-believe-I'm-fucking-doing-this kind of look. When she closed the door, Edie smiled and patted the side of the bed. "Now sit down. Right here."

Megan looked at me, raising her eyebrows. Slowly we edged toward the bed. We sat down—me on one side and Megan on the other.

"Comfy, darlings?" Edie asked.

We watched as she leaned over and opened the drawer of her bedside table, removing a small black book. Then she looked at us with complete seriousness and said: "I am going to tell you a story. A very special kind of story. A story that was told to me when I was your age. Very long ago. During a very dark time. It is the kind of story one remembers for a lifetime. A *magic* story."

Edie adjusted the pillows behind her back, opened the book, and turned the first few pages.

"Here it is," she said, her fingers resting on a page. "'Francesca and the Cave of Secrets.'"

Edie was silent for a moment and then cleared her throat. Finally she spoke, her voice reverently filling the room.

"Once upon a time, in a land not so far away, there was a girl named Francesca. Some years ago, Francesca's mother had passed away, and the girl lived with her father in a tiny cottage in the woods. They were very poor, and Francesca and her father lived a life of struggle and hardship.

"Every morning, Francesca's father labored in the fields while Francesca toiled at home and prepared the meals and looked after the tiny cottage. It was difficult work, but sometimes when Francesca had finished her many chores for the day she wandered through the forest before her father came home for dinner."

Edie stopped and looked up at us. "Everything all right, darlings?" she asked.

Megan smiled while I nodded politely. Edie returned to the story.

"The forest was Francesca's favorite place to walk. And she had spent many a happy moment there, strolling under the giant pine trees that towered into the sky.

"She had heard tales from long ago, of kings and princes who had traveled through the forest but were robbed by thieves. There was one such legend about a mysterious cache of gold that had been stolen. Some said it had been taken by an evil witch.

"According to the legend, the gold was buried in the forest, and although Francesca didn't imagine she would ever find it, she dreamed about the life of luxury it could bring her and her father. Her father would never have to work again. All their struggles would be over.

"One day as Francesca walked through the forest, she saw hundreds of butterflies of every size and shape and color flying above her. Entranced, she followed them, wondering where they were going.

"Deep into the woods she went, through swampy bogs and dark stretches of forest. Finally, after a great distance, Francesca saw the butterflies squeeze through a tiny opening in a wall of rock.

"Now, Francesca was a very curious girl. She just had to see where those butterflies were going. She made herself as small as possible and crawled through the opening and into the damp darkness of a cave. When she finally came to its center, she couldn't believe her eyes. There, seated on the ground, was an old woman. She was surrounded by the butterflies, who were slowly opening and closing their wings.

"'Where am I?' Francesca asked the old woman. 'Are these your butterflies?'

"'No. I am only their guardian,' the old woman replied. 'This is the Cave of Secrets, where every butterfly has a tale to tell and holds a mysterious secret.'

"'What kind of secrets?' Francesca asked with wonder.

"'Some good. Some bad.' The old woman smiled. 'If you

wish to hear one, you may pick one yourself. But only one,' she warned.

"Francesca turned around, looking at the inner wall of the cave. Thousands of butterflies clung to the dark wet wall, fastened to rocks and boulders, their wings slowly fluttering.

"Then one butterfly caught her eye. It was red, with golden tips on its wings that sparkled as it fanned them. Francesca approached it, studying its small, fragile body. She was spellbound: she had never seen anything so beautiful before. She wondered what its secret could be.

"'Is that the one you choose?' asked the old woman.

"'Yes,' Francesca replied.

"'Then do as I say. Stand before the butterfly. Close your eyes and open your mouth. When the butterfly senses you are ready, it will fly into your mouth and up into your mind. There, it will open its wings and release its secret to you. When it is finished, open your mouth again and let it fly away.'

"Francesca looked at the old woman with confusion.

"'Do not be afraid, my child,' the woman said, laughing. 'It will not hurt you.'

"Francesca was afraid that once the butterfly had flown up into her mind that it would stay there forever. But she wanted to know the secret. So she did as the old woman said and stood with her mouth open and her eyes closed.

"Flitting its wings, the butterfly lifted off from the wall and hovered in midair. Then it circled around Francesca's head and flew straight into her open mouth and up into her head, just as the old woman had said. Francesca was surprised at how little she felt; it was just like a small tickle inside her throat. When

Francesca opened her mouth again, the butterfly came out, flying away as quickly as it had gone in.

"'Now,' said the old woman, 'if you open your eyes, the butterfly's secret will be revealed to you.'

"Again, Francesca did as the old woman told her. And there, floating in the center of her mind, was this thought: *In the forest under the tallest tree, here you will find the most precious treasure of me.*

"'Remember,' the old woman warned gravely, 'that this is the Cave of Secrets. Whatever the butterfly told you must remain a secret. Tell no one. Or suffer the consequences. For if you speak of it, you will lose your voice. Forever.'"

Edie stopped reading and closed the small black book.

"Is that it?" Megan asked.

"Oh, no, darling," Edie said, gently easing the book into the drawer of her bedside table. "No, no. It's only just beginning. When you come back next week, I'll tell you more. But not right now."

Picking up the remote, Edie looked up at the screen and turned on the television.

"*The Price is Right* is on," she informed us.

As we walked home from St. Teresa's, I asked Megan what she thought of Edie.

"I like her. But she's whacked," Megan replied with her usual candor. She twirled her finger in the air beside her head. "Abso-fucking-lutely loo-loo. I mean, did you listen to that? Butterflies flying in and out of that chick's brain? Wee-ird."

I remembered the beautiful red and gold butterfly. Its majestic splendor.

"Your stories are just as weird," I said.

Megan popped a succession of Whoppers into her mouth, her cheeks bulging.

"Old ladies who call everyone 'Darling' and pop lots of little pills and tell stories about butterflies are whacked." She chewed, swallowed. "And you're right. My stories are weird. But I make them that way on purpose."

"So then you're whacked, too," I replied.

"Yes, I am." She smiled proudly, emptying more Whoppers into her mouth.

"Gimme those," I said, grabbing the bag from her hand.

"Cursed thief!" Megan said with a grin, in her best Shakespearean accent. "How darest thou steal my Whoppers! Thou dost offend me greatly!" She stomped her foot and raised her fist in outrage. "I challenge thee to a duel! Do you accept?"

I grinned back. "I do."

"Art thou ready to meet thy maker?" Megan challenged.

"I am," I replied. "But art thou?"

Without another word, we stood back to back, squaring our shoulders together. Then we walked five paces away from each other and turned around and stuck out our tongues at each other. *"Aaaaaaarrrrrrrrrrrrggggghhhhhhhhhhhh!"*

Later that evening, I stared out my bedroom window into the night sky and thought about Blake Starfield.

I had told no one of what had happened in the gym. Not even Megan. I was too afraid of what she might have thought. To pay him special attention was dangerous. No one who knew better would dare to be seen or associated with Blake Starfield.

To most other kids, there was something about him that just

seemed wrong, as if he'd been born without the right number of fingers and toes. A biological error. That was how they saw him: *Quasi.*

I remembered the touch of his hand in the darkness. His gentle calm.

Not that I liked him, I told myself. At least not in that way. Boys were like aliens, with strange smells and secretions. I wasn't interested in boys.

That's all some girls ever talked about: boys, boys, boys. What boys were cute and what boys weren't. I once knew this girl who drew a graph in her notebook with all the boys in the class listed alphabetically on one side of the page. Above, in neat columns, were the categories that they fell into: Nice, OK, Not Nice, and Gross. All the way down were neat little check marks beside each boy's name. I couldn't figure out what the big deal was.

I had been kissed by a boy, once. At a dance at summer camp. He had been a Boy Scout and talked a lot about knots and wood, and when no one was looking he pushed me up against a tree and kissed me. He tasted like BBQ chips. I don't even remember his name.

But Blake Starfield was different. He was no ordinary boy. Even his name sounded magical, as if he had come from another world.

I looked up into the starry night and wondered where he was, what he was doing. And if he was thinking of me the way I was thinking of him.

GIRLS, GIRLS, GIRLS

MEGAN AND I WALKED to Meredith McKinnon's house late after school on Friday. When we rang the bell, a woman who
must have been Meredith's mother answered the door. She
looked at me and Megan with a forced, cheery grin.

Mrs. McKinnon was thin and tanned, with shoulder-length
bleached-blond hair. As she stood at the door and ushered us
in, pieces of chunky silver jewelry jangled when she moved her
arms.

"All the presents over there on the table, girls!" she directed.

After everyone arrived, Meredith's mom distributed party
hats and noisemakers and announced that Meredith was being
dropped off by her father in less than ten minutes. Most of the
girls in our class, including Tracey Reid, were there. Some had
come because they wanted MAL to like them. Others just
wanted MAL not to hate them. Megan and I didn't fit into either group. We just wanted free cake.

I watched Tracey bristle with excitement as Mrs. McKinnon
informed us that Laura and Angela were also with Meredith.
Our instructions were to hide in the darkened living room, to
huddle behind the couches and chairs. When Meredith and

Angela and Laura came in, Mrs. McKinnon would give us the signal and we were all going to jump up and yell *"SURPRISE!"*

"Oh, it's going to be a big surprise, all right," Megan said, muffling a laugh.

Mrs. McKinnon checked her watch and went to the window.

"They're here, they're here!" she cried, turning around. "Hurry, hurry!"

We all scurried to our hiding places. Beside Megan and me, Mrs. McKinnon ducked behind the couch. We heard Meredith and Angela and Laura come through the door.

"Bye, Dad!" Meredith yelled.

"Bye, Mr. McKinnon," Laura and Angela echoed.

The front door closed.

"Your dad is so nice," Angela said.

"Yeah," Laura said. "He's so sweet."

Mrs. McKinnon grew rigid beside me, the smile gone from her face. We heard Meredith and Laura and Angela whispering.

"So," Laura said. "where's your mom?"

"Yeah," Angela said. "Isn't she supposed to be here?"

"Oh, I don't know," Meredith said. "She's around here somewhere—"

Meredith's mom gave the signal.

"SURPRISE!"

Noisemakers erupted. Everyone shouted. Meredith looked into the living room with a practiced expression of bored surprise. It was obvious Laura and Angela had told her about the party from the beginning.

Mrs. McKinnon jumped out from behind the couch.

"Happy birthday, sweetie!" she shouted. "Surprise!"

Meredith looked at all of us again—including Megan and me—and frowned, her mouth a small line. Ignoring her daughter's expression, Mrs. McKinnon beamed emphatically as she did a little dance around her daughter, clapping her hands with delight.

After Meredith's "shock" had worn off, Mrs. McKinnon announced that we would eat, play a few games, and then, "surprise, surprise," head off to the bowling lanes. I watched as she bustled between the living room and the kitchen, ferrying us trays of lukewarm hot dogs and bowls of potato chips.

As Megan and I took our seats in the dining room, Meredith sat at the head of the table, flanked by Laura and Angela. I watched as Tracey Reid offered Meredith her congratulations, her eyes lowered as if she were approaching a monarch.

"Look at this," Megan said to me, taking the hot dog out of the bun and standing it upright between her legs. I watched it wobble between her hands, a pale pink plastic dancer.

Tracey Reid looked down with shock and disgust. "Omigod, that is so gross," she said.

"Oh, yeah?" Megan said, jiggling it between her fingers. *"Bite me."*

After the cake had been brought out and all the candles blown out, Meredith opened her presents. In between bites of cake, she tore open each gift and passed the wrapping paper on to Laura or Angela, who stuffed it into two large garbage bags. MAL glossed over each present with vague interest.

Mrs. McKinnon came back into the dining room and surveyed her daughter's gifts. "Oh, isn't that pretty?" she said, picking out a pink scarf and holding it up against Meredith's face. "That's so nice. Did you thank all the girls, sweetie?"

Meredith looked up at her mother, her eyes impatient.

"Yes, Mother," she said.

I noted the quick hurt in Mrs. McKinnon's eyes. But she said, "OK, girls! Let's play Twister!"

Meredith groaned audibly. "But Mother, that's so *dumb!* No one plays Twister anymore!"

"It is not dumb, sweetie," Meredith's mom replied. "It's fun! Who wants to play?"

Instantly, Megan shot up her hand. "I do, I do!"

"See, sweetie? She wants to play!"

Meredith shot Megan a death stare down the length of the table. "But she's the only one!" Meredith said. "No one else wants to play! And I don't want to go out bowling, either. Only *losers* go bowling, Mother."

There was a hint of desperation in Meredith's voice, as if she were a small wounded animal. Her face was becoming red and blotchy; tears in the wings of her eyes, ready to make their dramatic, watery entrance.

Meredith's mom crouched down and kissed Meredith's cheek, putting her arm around her daughter's shoulders, hugging her tightly.

"OK, sweetie. You're right," Mrs. McKinnon said. "It's your birthday and you can do whatever you want."

Victorious, Meredith leaned into her mother, smiling falsely.

As Meredith led everyone down the short flight of stairs to the indoor pool, the smell of chlorine was sharp. Tracey Reid turned to me on the pool deck and said breathily, "Isn't it beautiful?"

Megan, finishing the last of a can of Coke, belched loudly. "Yeah, whatever."

Tracey looked at her, affronted. "You are so gross," she said. "Why can't you be normal?"

"Oh, but I am normal," replied Megan, batting her eyelashes at Tracey. "Just. Like. You." Megan belched in Tracey's face again, then followed a small group of girls into the changing room.

"And there's the sauna," said Meredith, pointing to a door at the end of the room.

"Can we go in?" chirped Tracey.

"If you really want to," Laura said, answering for Meredith, "but *we're* just going swimming."

Then, side by side, in the changing room, in front of the wooden benches, facing each other, MAL began removing their clothes. I froze. Some of the other girls started undressing. Fear hammered inside my chest. I had assumed that we would be allowed to change privately, in a washroom or a bedroom with the door closed, where no one else, particularly MAL, would be watching. I noticed the gazes of some of the girls, looking at one another, seeing what one had and another did not.

I turned my back to the others and took everything off except my T-shirt and rolled my underwear down my legs, trying to appear as if this were the most natural way of undressing. I quickly pulled on my swimsuit under my T-shirt and adjusted the shoulder straps. Megan didn't care who saw what as she took everything off and changed into a black bikini. As I looked over my shoulder, I noticed Laura watching us.

"I can't believe your mother invited *everyone*," Laura said to Meredith in a voice that was loud enough for us to hear.

"I know," Meredith replied. "It's so *embarrassing*."

"Nice ass, dead girl," Angela said to me.

"Yeah, it's sooooo tight," Laura said.

I turned away, silent with embarrassment.

"Look," Megan said, "just leave her alone."

Out of the corner of my eye, I noticed all the other girls in the dressing room had quickly changed and walked out, leaving MAL and Megan and me alone. Fearlessly, Megan puffed out her chest and stood with her hands on her hips, deflecting their comments: the new Wonder Girl. But MAL was on the offensive.

"Good thing you've got your girlfriend with you," Laura said to me.

"Yeah," Angela added. "You couldn't defend yourself to save your life, could you, dead girl?"

Before I could answer, Meredith's mom came into the changing room. She was wearing a black one-piece bathing suit and had silver tasseled flip-flops on her feet. In her hand she clasped a large glass tumbler full of ice and what looked like water, a drowned olive at the bottom. A white towel was slung over her right shoulder.

"Meredith," Mrs. McKinnon said to her daughter politely, "what's going on here? You're ignoring your other guests."

Meredith gave her mother an anxious, worried look. "But, Mother —"

"No buts. Now *go*."

Meredith pouted and made her way toward the door, Laura

and Angela following behind. On their way out, they gave us their usual I-hate-your-fucking-guts-and-want-to-kill-you look. Megan and I stood there with Meredith's mom and watched their exit.

Mrs. McKinnon tilted her glass to her lips.

"Having a good time, girls?" she asked, opening an antique case and lighting a cigarette. She took another sip of her drink and inhaled the cigarette deeply. A thin blue stream of smoke hung suspended in the air of the small room. As we stared with fascination, Mrs. McKinnon offered us the case. "Cigarette?" she said.

It was elaborately embossed with birds.

"Oh, go on. I won't tell anyone."

Megan and I reached for the small sticks. Neither one of us had ever smoked cigarettes with any adult, let alone somebody like Meredith McKinnon's mom. As we held the cigarettes to our mouths, she lit them with her lighter. First Megan's, then mine.

"*Gall-waz,*" Mrs. McKinnon said, waving the cigarette in the air. "They're *French.*"

I inhaled deeply, sucking in the thick, ratty stench of the cigarette, pretending I knew what she was talking about. All I really knew was that France was somewhere other than where I was—smoking cigarettes in a changing room with Megan and Meredith's mom. And I felt as though, for that moment, we were not her daughter's friends—which she could obviously tell by now—but *her* friends.

When we had finished she looked at us and smiled, saying, "Don't worry. It'll be our little secret. I'll promise not to tell if you will. Meredith would *kill* me."

"Thanks, Mrs. McKinnon," Megan said.

"Please, call me *Margaret*."

"Thanks, Margaret," I said.

Mrs. McKinnon drank from the tumbler again. When it was empty, she lowered the rim from her lips and winced slightly, her eyelashes fluttering. With a glazed look, she stared down into the empty glass.

When we emerged, the other girls were standing around the pool, wrapped in their towels, shivering. Tracey Reid stood at the edge of the deep end, her teeth chattering.

Meredith glared at us. "What have you two been doing?"

Because she knew Meredith would never believe her, Megan told her the truth. "Smoking French cigarettes with your mother," she answered.

Meredith's eyes narrowed with suspicion. "Yeah, right."

"It's true," I said.

"Oh, why don't you just fucking shut your mouth, dead girl," Laura said, standing at Meredith's side. "You weren't asked."

"Yeah," said Angela, stepping up behind Laura and Meredith.

"Let's just get one thing straight," Meredith said to Megan. "You were *never* invited to my party. I'd *never* invite a loser like you." Behind her, the swimming pool rippled; ribbons of reflected light danced on the walls. "Or *you*," she said, turning to me. I noticed the pool water was the same color as Meredith's eyes, a sort of fake toilet-water blue.

"*You* didn't invite us," Megan said. "Your mother did." Megan stepped forward. "Happy birthday, party girl," she said. Then she pushed Meredith into the water.

For a moment there was a horrified silence as everyone watched Meredith fall backwards into the pool, a look of panic frozen on her face. Meredith squawked in protest as she helplessly tried to prevent herself from falling, her arms flapping at her sides. As she landed spread-eagle on her back, Megan stood at the edge of the pool and laughed.

Before Meredith's head emerged, Laura and Angela grabbed Megan by the arms and pushed her into the pool. There was a brief struggle before all three of them collapsed and fell in the water. As Megan gasped for breath, the three of them surrounded her and held her head down.

"Put her under!" Meredith yelled.

I dove in after Megan and clawed at Laura and Angela. As I tore at their bathing suits, I heard Megan coughing and gagging, spitting up water. I turned to the side of the pool and pleaded desperately to Tracey Reid.

"Please!" I screamed. "Help us!" But Tracey Reid only stood there dumbfounded, her towel drawn over her skinny shoulders.

I felt someone tug at my hair and try to push me under. I turned back. It was Angela. As she gripped my head with both hands, my face hit the water. I twisted under her grip while Megan's and Meredith's and Laura's arms and legs sparred under the water, performing a slow, violent dance. All of a sudden Angela's grip released and the tangle of Megan and Meredith and Laura stopped. I raised my head up out of the water and gulped some air.

Mrs. McKinnon was standing over the edge of the pool with a shocked expression on her face. "Girls, girls, girls!" she yelled. "What is going on here?"

In her hand she cradled another full tumbler. This time there were two olives.

Meredith looked at her mother and smiled innocently. "Nothing, Mother," she said breathlessly.

"We were just playing around, Mrs. McKinnon," Laura said, panting. "Really—"

"Yeah," said Angela. "We were just testing to see who could hold their breath the longest—"

"And it was me!" bragged Megan defiantly.

Silently, Mrs. McKinnon fixed her eye on Megan. Then she took a long drink and eyed her daughter critically. Megan flashed MAL a dazzling, arrogant smirk.

Turning around, Mrs. McKinnon looked at Tracey Reid and all the other girls standing beside her poolside. They averted their eyes and Tracey hung her head in shame. Mrs. McKinnon swung slowly around again and looked at Megan, then me.

I stood in the pool, hugging my sides, shivering with cold.

"Are you all right?" Meredith's mom asked me.

I looked at MAL, then Megan. Her eyes told me to say nothing.

"Yes," I said quietly.

"Well, girls," Mrs. McKinnon said, tilting the glass up to her lips, "I guess that settles that."

CONNECTING THE DOTS

THE NEXT TIME WE VISITED EDIE at St. Teresa's, she was dressed in a green Chinese dressing gown, standing at the window, watering her plants.

"You're late," she said, slowly turning around as we came through the door.

Megan pushed the cart into the room. "You're not the only candy freak in this joint, you know," she retorted.

Edie's shoulders shook with laughter. As she raised her watering can over a miniature jade plant, sunlight filtered through the window. The room was silent but for the sound of sprinkling water.

"You know, plants are just like people," Edie said, putting down the watering can and picking up a spray bottle. "They need water. Food. Sun." She misted an orchid, caressing its flower. "And love, too."

Megan and I were silent.

"Do you remember where we were last week?" Edie asked. "With our story?"

I remembered bits: Francesca, the cottage, the forest. The old woman in the cave. And the butterfly.

"We finished with the secret," Edie said.

"Huh?" Megan answered.

"Don't you remember?" Edie asked, turning around, a smile on her lips. *"In the forest under the tallest tree, here you will find the most precious treasure of me."*

Maybe Megan was right, I thought. Maybe Edie was whacked.

Edie walked across the room to the cart and picked out her candy for the week. Then she went back to her bedside table and opened the drawer, paying us with another fifty-dollar bill. When we gave her her change, she deposited the money and candy inside the drawer and took out her small black book. She sat on her bed and leaned back against the pillows. When Megan and I didn't move, she looked at us with consternation.

"Well, what are you waiting for?" she said. "If we're going to continue with our story, we have to start right now!"

Megan looked at me as if to say, *What the hell — we've got nothing better to do.* So, just as we had done the week before, Megan and I sat down on either side of Edie's bed and listened. Edie's story might have been weird, but if we were lucky, she would give us some free candy.

"Ready, darlings?" she cooed.

We nodded our heads.

Edie opened the book and began:

"Francesca was not an idle creature. Neither was she foolish. But when she heard that there was precious treasure under the tallest tree, she instantly thought of the legendary gold and hidden riches. Leaving the old woman in the cave, Francesca went off into the woods, in search of the tallest tree.

"As she trekked through the forest, she discovered a clearing in the woods. It was a field, flat and green and full of wildflowers. She walked into the middle of it and stopped to look around. She could see the whole forest before her. Then Francesca gasped, for she could see the tallest tree, many miles away on the outer edge of the woods, towering above all the other trees.

"Suddenly Francesca felt very weak. She looked down at the ground. The soft green leaves of grass looked so inviting. Overcome with fatigue, Francesca sank into the field and a deep, deep sleep."

Edie stopped and cleared her throat and glanced up.

"Everything all right, darlings?" she asked.

"Yessiree," Megan replied.

Edie looked at me. "And you?"

"Yes," I said.

"Good," Edie said. "Just checking." She continued reading.

"The next thing she knew, a small girl was standing over her.

"'Who are you?' the girl demanded. 'And why are you here? You do not belong here. Do you not know that this is the field of the fierce Queen Goren, who can take a shape as small as a beetle or as big as a cloud? Who has eyes that can see for miles and miles? Who can send out her messenger flies to see what is happening wherever she wants? Queen Goren, who is evil and powerful? And dangerous?'

"Francesca looked up at the girl. She was thin and pale, with white skin and black hair and eerie black eyes. As she spoke, she hovered over Francesca, moving closer and closer toward her.

"'I meant no harm,' Francesca said sleepily to the girl. 'I just wanted to see where the tallest tree was, but I fell asleep. I really should be going. My father will be waiting for me.'

"As soon as she said it, Francesca realized she had revealed something she shouldn't have. Her heart sank.

"The girl glared suspiciously at Francesca. 'Why do you need to know where the tallest tree is?' she hissed.

"Francesca remembered the old woman's words. Tell anyone about the butterfly's secret and she would lose her voice. Forever. 'I'm sorry,' Francesca replied. 'It is a secret.'

"'Secrets are for fools and old women,' said the girl. 'And because you are not an old woman, you must be a fool.'

"'I am not a fool!' insisted Francesca.

"'Then tell me your secret!' spat the girl. As soon as the words came out of her mouth the girl screeched in agony and her arms and legs stretched out long and black like a spider's. A halo of flies began to swarm around her head, and her teeth and eyes turned yellow.

"'Wh-who are you?' stammered Francesca.

"'I am Queen Goren,' the creature screeched, her spindly arms flailing. 'How dare you defy me! You will tell me your precious little secret!'

"Francesca recoiled with horror as Queen Goren's long arms reached toward her and the flies crawled over Queen Goren's black withered body. She seized Francesca violently.

"'Please, let me go!' Francesca pleaded. 'I cannot tell you anything! I beg you! My poor father will be wondering where I am!'

"'Curse your stupid father!' Queen Goren cried. 'From this moment on, you are my prisoner and you will go in search of the tallest tree! And whatever you find there, you must give to me! To see that you return, one of my flies will watch over you! And if you try to escape, my pretty little fly will kill you with one deadly bite!'

"At Queen Goren's command, a fly leapt out of the thick band that swarmed around her head and flew straight toward Francesca. Francesca tried to brush it away, vainly waving her hands in the air.

"Queen Goren laughed: a deep, dark, horrible laugh that cackled like fire from her throat.

"'Now be gone!' she commanded to Francesca. 'But remember this! If you disobey me, not only shall you die, but so shall your father!' Queen Goren angrily shook Francesca. 'Is that clear?' she ordered.

"'Yes!' Francesca answered, looking away in fright. 'Yes! Please don't hurt my father! Please! He has done nothing. I'll do whatever you say!'

"Queen Goren dropped Francesca carelessly to the ground. 'Now go.'

"Terrified, Francesca gathered herself together and ran from the field. Now not only did she have to give whatever she found under the tallest tree to the horrible Queen Goren, but if she didn't, she would die—and so would her father."

Edie stopped reading and closed the black book with a solemn gesture. There was a fluidity to her movements, a sense of ceremony.

"That's it?" Megan said as she watched Edie put the book away.

"For now," Edie replied. "But come back again next week and I'll tell you more."

Megan groaned. "That's what you said last week—"

"And that's probably what I'll say next week, too," Edie said. "I'm very sorry, but right now I have a date with the most handsome man in the universe."

Edie picked up the remote and turned on the television. On the screen, Bob Barker was welcoming another contestant to come on down, his slim microphone poised elegantly between his fingers.

"Oh, darlings," Edie sighed. "Isn't he just a dream?"

As we walked home from the hospital, Megan and I took turns eating our "Steal of the Week" from St. Teresa's: a large box of Junior Mints. Swapping it back and forth, we each ate handfuls, our mouths gobbed with dark minty goodness.

Each week Megan and I scored at least one kind of candy. Afterward, we always expressed our deep concern to Sister Maria that something on the cart must have been miscounted. Clueless, Sister Maria always took the blame herself, making excuses for her senility and poor memory, not once suspecting that maybe Megan and I might have done it.

"How do you solve a problem like Maria?" Megan sang at the top of her lungs.

"How do you catch a cloud and pin it down?" I sang back.

Under the bare black branches of the trees, we danced down Megan's street, doing goofy exaggerated pirouettes.

Suddenly Megan stopped dancing. The expression on her face was one I had never seen before. As if she was nervous. But terrified, too.

"What is it?" I asked.

Megan stared down the street.

"My mother," she said. "My mother. She's home."

I looked toward Megan's house, observing the black Mercedes sedan parked in the driveway, wondering why I had never seen it before. Finally, I thought, I would get to meet Mrs. Chalmers.

"I have to go," Megan said.

"What?"

"I can't explain. But I have to go. Right now."

"Megan —" I said.

"Look, just go, OK?"

"I don't understand —"

"There's nothing for you to understand," Megan said.

"But I wanted to —"

"Please. Please," Megan insisted, her voice shaking. "Just *go.*"

"OK," I said. "OK."

I watched as she ran down the street to her house and stopped at the bottom of her driveway. Then she walked slowly toward the front door and disappeared inside the house.

The following day, Megan was absent from school. I wondered if it had something to do with her mother being home. But I couldn't understand what all the secrecy was about.

Megan's absence did not go unnoticed by MAL, and at lunch they cornered me outside.

"Without your master today?" Laura teased.

"Whatever will you do? You're like a dog without a leash," said Angela.

"And about as ugly as one, too," Meredith said.

I turned away from them and started walking toward the front doors, but Laura jumped in front of me and stood in my way.

"Where do you think you're going?" she said.

"Inside," I answered quietly.

"What was that you said?" Laura asked me. "I didn't hear you."

"Inside," I said again.

I tried to walk around her, but Meredith and Angela boxed me in.

Laura laughed. "Oh, I don't think so," she said.

"Please," I said.

"Please," Laura mimicked. Meredith and Angela laughed. Then Laura pushed me. Hard.

"Oops," she said as I fell to the muddy ground. "I'm, like, *so* sorry about that. Here, let me help you up."

Laura extended her hand and pushed me down again. Harder.

"Omigod!" she exclaimed. "Like, really, I am *so, so, so* sorry . . ."

MAL laughed. Then I stood up and pushed Laura back.

Before I knew what was happening, I was rolling around on the ground, kicking and hitting and punching Laura Mitchell.

Finally, I heard Mr. King's voice. He came between Laura and me and pushed us apart, telling me to break it up. *Now.*

Expertly, Laura began to cry.

I watched in silence as Meredith and Angela told Mr. King that it had all been my fault. That Laura hadn't done anything. That I was the one who had started it. Mr. King looked at me disdainfully and sent me to the principal's office.

Mr. Carter told me he was shocked by my behavior—absolutely shocked—and how in his day no girl my age would ever be caught fighting. He was truly disappointed by what he clearly saw as my dangerous, delinquent behavior and assured me that my father would be contacted.

When Mr. Carter asked me if there was anything I wanted to say, I suppose I could have told him what he wanted to hear: about how sorry I was supposed to be and how bad I was supposed to feel. But the fact was, he had already made up his mind about who I was and what he thought I was fighting about.

I imagined him expressing his shock in the teachers' staff room after school, shaking his head with weary disillusion. Because we were *girls*, after all, he would say. And girls aren't supposed to fight. Girls don't war.

It wasn't worth telling him the truth.

When I got home from school that day, my father was waiting for me in the living room, sitting on the couch with a pained expression on his face.

"I got a call from Mr. Carter today," he told me. "He said you were in a fight with another girl." He stood up and paced back and forth in the living room. "Is that true?"

"She pushed me first," I said, standing still. "She started it."

My father sighed deeply. "I don't care who started it. Just answer the question, please. Were you or were you not in a fight with another girl at school today?"

I nodded silently.

My father put his hands on my shoulders and looked at me.

"Is there something going on at school that you want to talk about?" he asked. "I know I haven't been around much, but I'm here for you when you need me."

I couldn't believe he was saying this to me now. It seemed a little late, considering what had happened. And I wasn't about to tell my father about MAL, anyway. His reaction would be the same as Mr. Carter's. He could never understand.

"Whatever," I replied.

My father removed his hands.

"What did you say?" he asked.

"Nothing," I answered.

I took a step back.

"What is wrong with you?" my father asked sharply.

"There's nothing wrong with me, Dad," I replied. "What's wrong with you?"

His face contorted with anger. "If your mother were here, you'd never speak to me like that!"

"You know what, Dad?" I cried. "You're right! If Mom were here, I'd never speak to you at all!"

I grabbed my coat and ran out the door. I didn't even know or care where I was going. I just had to get away from him. Be anywhere other than where he was.

The first place I went was Megan's house, but there was no answer when I knocked at the door. No lights were on and no one was home, not even Rose.

When I realized I didn't have anywhere else to go, I went to the fort in the woods. I ran my finger along the candy wrapper wallpaper that Megan and I had taped to its inner walls. The names of different candy bars fused together in a complex design of colors and words: *AlmondJoyWhatchamacallitKitKatBabyRuthPayDay*. Without Megan around, there seemed to be nothing to do. I slumped down on the floor and stared into space, trying not to think about anything.

When it started getting dark, I began to walk home. I

dreaded facing my father, but I had no choice. Hopefully I could sneak past him and go straight into my room. Hopefully he would be asleep.

As I walked out of the forest and onto the street, I saw a figure in the distance coming toward me. It was Blake Starfield.

"Hi," he said, stopping.

"Hi," I said shyly.

"I didn't know you lived around here."

"I didn't know you did, either," I said.

There was an awkward pause.

"What are you doing?"

"Nothing. You?"

"Nothing."

For a second my eyes met his one good eye, while his other lazy eye peered off into the distance.

"I saw what you did today," he said.

I put my hands in my pockets and looked down at my feet. "What do you mean?"

"Fighting Laura." He smiled. "It was cool."

I shrugged. "Whatever," I said quietly. "It was nothing."

I took a deep breath. My pulse was racing.

Blake looked up at the darkening sky. "You like stars?" he asked.

"What?" I asked, quickly looking around. Even though I knew no one was watching us, I was still afraid that MAL or someone else from TWS would see us together. Me and *Quasi*. I could almost hear the cruel ridicule.

"Stars. You know. Do you like them?"

I looked into his face again. It seemed enormous, as big and bright as the moon. And then he smiled at me. I soon forgot everything.

"Yeah," I said, looking up.

"Know what my favorite constellation is?" he asked.

I shrugged my shoulders.

"Orion. The Hunter." He pointed. "Right there. See it?"

I craned my neck back, searching the sky above.

"It's the one with three stars in a row," he said. "Right up there."

"Where?"

He moved closer and stood right beside me. Our shoulders touched. Then he took my hand, raised it up in the air, and directed it above our heads.

"There," he said, moving my hand with his, drawing out the constellation. "There's the bow. And the arrow. And the belt. See it?"

"Yes," I said. "I see it."

Blake showed me more constellations: Cassiopeia, Perseus, Pegasus. Then, when I realized how late it was getting, I said goodbye. I didn't say we'd talk to each other the next day at school. I knew we wouldn't.

When I arrived home, my father was asleep on the couch, just as I had hoped.

My usual duty was to tell him to go to bed. But instead I knelt down beside him. I stared at his closed eyes, watching them flutter in REM sleep. He looked so vulnerable. As if his face were a mask, engraved with sadness. Suddenly, his whole body jolted. I backed away, fearful that I might have woken him. But within a moment, his body was released from its nocturnal grip and he resumed his state of slumber. I wondered what he had dreamed of.

I went upstairs to my room and closed the door. As I undressed in the dark, I looked outside my bedroom window.

I stepped toward the glass and exhaled on it; my breath frosted the pane. Beyond the window, far into the universe, was Orion, just where Blake had shown me. Drawing with my fingertip, I traced it on my windowpane, connecting the dots from one part of the universe to another.

METAMORPHOSIS

MEGAN DID NOT COME TO SCHOOL AGAIN the next day or the following day. I tried calling her. Both days. But there was never any answer. When she didn't come to school the rest of the week, I began to worry. Then Mr. King approached me and asked if I knew where Megan was.

My first thought was to tell him the truth. But I realized I didn't really know what that was.

"Her grandfather died," I told Mr. King. "In California."

"Oh," he said. A look of confusion passed over his face. "Do you know where?"

"In San Francisco, I think."

"Oh," he said again.

"Is anything wrong, Mr. King?" I asked.

"No. I'm just concerned that Megan will fall behind. Do you know how long she'll be gone?"

I thought of my mother's funeral. It had all happened so quickly.

"No," I answered.

"When she comes back, will you help her catch up?" Mr. King asked me.

"Sure," I said, relieved that he had believed me about Megan. "Of course."

Later that day, I wrote out the lessons and exercises we had done in math and science. I took detailed notes and photocopied all of them at school, preparing everything in a file folder for Megan. It was extra work, but it made the day pass more quickly. And it helped to take my mind off MAL and my father.

Megan was gone for days, so for days I followed the same routine: I wrote out the day's lessons, wedged my notes in a folder, and dropped them off at her house.

My life without Megan was just survival. I got up, I ate, I went to school. I avoided MAL. My father was never around. His work consumed him. Every night he would pace up and down the hallway, walking in his sleep. And every night I would get up and guide him back to bed. It was during those nights I missed my mother the most. It was only after my mother went to the hospital that my dad started sleepwalking. It was almost as if he were out looking for her, wandering around the house at night. When she finally moved back, into the spare bedroom, his sleepwalking worsened. She would tease him about it, joking that she had to get cancer in order to get him out of bed. Her sense of humor always helped to lighten things. I never realized how much she anchored our lives. I yearned for her sturdy reasoning, her warmth and assurance. To hear her laughter again.

One afternoon after school, I sat alone in front of the television and watched the news and cartoons, flipping back and forth between both. I was hungry. Bored. Tired. I needed something. Then I remembered the bag of candy that Megan had given me. Just in case of an emergency. I went up to my room and dug it out of my underwear drawer.

Somehow it seemed dishonorable to eat the remaining candy without Megan. But I could not resist. I ripped the bag open and pulled out a marshmallow banana. It was sweet, and chewy, and stuck between my teeth. Then I ate another. And another. And another. Until the whole bag was gone.

When I was finished, I realized I was still hungry for more. And that was when I knew I was no longer afraid of eating candy.

From then on, every day, before, during, and after school, I ate candy. I consumed chocolate before the morning bell. Chewed gum during class. Filled my lunch bag to the brim with an assortment of sours, just in case I needed a quick fix. When I went to bed one night with a peppermint wedged in my mouth, I realized I had successfully made the transformation.

Once I had been trapped within the boundaries of my identity—of who I was and who I didn't want to become. But through Megan and her candy stories, I was permitted to transcend those boundaries. To transform myself. Like a butterfly that had crawled out of its chrysalis, I spread my candy-colored wings, proud of my spectacular metamorphosis.

That week I went to visit Edie alone. As I pushed the cart into her room, I found her sitting up in her bed, clutching the remote control. Above her, Bob Barker was asking a contestant about his recent trip to Las Vegas. Edie made her usual number of candy selections and placed them on the bedside table.

"Where's Megan?" she asked.

I thought about lying to Edie the way I had lied to Mr. King, but it didn't seem right.

"I don't know," I replied.

"Hmm," Edie said thoughtfully, opening a box of chocolates. "Well, don't worry, she'll be back soon." She extended the box with her hand. "Go on, darling, take one."

I took a chocolate and savored it in my mouth while I watched "The Grocery Game."

"Now, Beverly," Bob Barker said, "how many cans of Maxwell House do you need?"

Beverly fretted anxiously. "Four, Bob."

The *Price Is Right* model rang up four cans of Maxwell House coffee on an old-fashioned cash register.

Edie watched me carefully. "I see you've seen the light," she observed.

"I beg your pardon?" I replied.

"The candy, darling, the candy!" she exclaimed. "I always knew you could be saved. Congratulations! I'm so proud of you!"

"Thanks," I replied.

"Sixteen dollars and eighty-eight cents. Now, Beverly, what other product—"

Edie turned off the television with the remote.

"It's a repeat," she explained. "I've seen it at least a dozen times. Beverly chooses the Rice A Roni, which is her fatal mistake, and she doesn't win the dining room suite. Now come, darling. Sit down."

I approached the bed and sat down on the edge of the mattress. Edie held out the box of chocolates again.

"Go on, darling. Help yourself. No need to be shy. One is never enough!"

As I took the box from her hands and began eating a chocolate caramel creme, Edie once again removed her small black book from her bedside table drawer.

"Now, where were we last time?"

"Francesca fell asleep in a field," I answered, finishing the caramel creme and picking a chocolate-covered cherry, "and was threatened by Queen Goren—"

"Yes," Edie said.

"And one of Queen Goren's flies was sent to follow her," I went on, my mouth full.

"Very good," said Edie, opening to the place in the story. "Exactly right."

She took the box of chocolates out of my hands and picked one for herself. As she put the whole chocolate in her mouth at once, she rolled her eyes dreamily.

"*Mmmmm,*" moaned Edie, devouring it. "Lemon cream. My favorite. Tart but sweet. Tangy and delicious!" She winked and put the lid back on the box of chocolates and picked up her black book.

"Now, are we ready?" she asked.

"Ready," I said.

Edie cleared her throat and began.

"Francesca longed to see the face of her father once again. She had been wrong to go walking in the forest that day, wrong to follow the butterflies, wrong to wish she had known one of their secrets, wrong to put her life in danger. She should never have listened to the old woman in the cave, who

Francesca now was sure must have been a witch. Neither should Francesca have been so greedy as to want treasure she knew she would never have. She looked around her. The forest was immense. Where would she begin?

"Francesca heard the fly circling her head. It had been with her since she left Queen Goren's field, haunting her with its droning buzz that constantly reminded her of what Queen Goren had said: the fly would kill her if she didn't obey the queen's commands. How Francesca longed to run away from it! But she knew it would mean the end of so many things — her father's life being the most dear. She stared into the fly's tiny black eyes. Oh, how she detested it! How she longed to destroy it! But she knew she could not.

"Hungry and exhausted, Francesca noticed some mushrooms and berries nearby. As she dared to eat them, a few small pieces fell from her hands. The fly flew to them and began to eat ravenously. As the little fly fed, Francesca was transfixed by the silver-gray sheen of its wings and the deep blue-green hue of its body.

"When she had finished scavenging for food, Francesca continued her search for the tallest tree. Her journey took many days, and the fly buzzed next to her at all times. It ate her food when she ate and drank her drink when she drank and slept near her ear when she slept.

"Then one day, when she was desperately lonely and could not bear it any longer, Francesca buried her head in her hands and sobbed. Perhaps she and her father had been poor, but at least they had each other. Francesca missed him so much. Finally, when she could cry no longer, Francesca lay perfectly still, listening to the silence. But there was no silence. Instead she heard a soft, low buzzing sound. A singing, almost. A strange kind of singing. At first she was afraid, but the sound became so surprisingly sweet and soothing that she raised her head. She looked in the direction of where the sound was coming from.

"It was the fly! And as it continued to sing, Francesca felt lighter and lighter until she realized she was floating. It was as if she were riding a magic carpet! The fly's song lifted her up into the sky until she could see over the whole forest. What a beautiful sight it was: the sun spreading its light over the trees like wings. Then she saw it again. Right there, almost directly in front of her. Just as it had been the first time, on the edge of the woods. The tallest tree.

"'I see it!' Francesca exclaimed to the fly. 'I see it!'

"As she drifted back down to the ground, Francesca was overcome with joy. She cupped her hands together and the fly flew down and rested in her palms, rubbing its legs together and cleaning its wings.

"'Oh, dear little fly,' Francesca said. 'How good you must be to have sung such a sweet song! And to show me the tallest tree! It must have been right there in front of me the whole time, and I've been walking in circles around it!'

"The fly looked up at her, tilting its tiny head. Francesca was ashamed to think of how she had doubted this little creature before, of how ugly she thought it was and how she had hated it, how she had even wanted to kill it.

"'Never shall I doubt you again, my little friend!' Francesca exclaimed as she looked down on the fly with tenderness. 'I shall give you a name. But it shall not be any ordinary name. It will be a noble name. A name of a prince I once heard of in a story, long ago. I shall call you Ferdinand.'"

As Edie's voice lingered with the last word, I looked down at the storybook where it rested between her hands.

"Is there more?" I asked.

Edie smiled. "Yes," she assured me. "But I don't want to tell you *too* much without Megan."

"Oh," I said, disappointed.

"Besides," she said with a wink, "I don't want to give the whole story away!"

Edie lay back against her pillows and closed her eyes. "Now, darling," she said, "please go. I need my beauty sleep."

On my way home from St. Teresa's, I made a quick stop at the T'n'T Variety. The last time I had been there was with Megan.

I feared that the same woman who had threatened me would be working, but when I stepped up to the front to pay for some Gobstoppers, a skinny woman with sharp, high cheekbones and dark feathered hair was standing behind the counter. Her eyelids were heavily rimmed with black eyeliner, her lips glossy red.

"You like those, eh?" she said. Her voice was hoarse, and her fingers were yellowed with nicotine stains.

I nodded, digging in my pockets for change.

"Yeah, I used to, too, you know, but I can't eat 'em no more 'cuz of my stupid teeth." She raised her hand and lifted her upper lip. There on the left side of her mouth was a dull silver crown.

"See that?" she garbled with her open mouth not giving me

time to answer. She leaned forward so I could see. "Root canal, twice over. My tooth was so rotted from eating so much candy, it almost fell right out my jaw." She stood upright again. "Dentist said I was real lucky."

She took my money and gave me my change.

"It hurt so much," she barked, "I thought I was seeing an angel when the dentist bored that drill into my tooth. It was like he was mining for diamonds. So I said that's it for me: no more candy."

I read the woman's nametag. It said: T'N'T VARIETY! MORE BANG FOR YOUR BUCK! Underneath: HI MY NAME IS YVONNE.

"I sure do miss it, though," she said, dropping my purchase into a small brown paper bag. "Gobstoppers were my favorite."

As she handed the candy over the counter, Yvonne looked at me with a wistful expression, as if she were going to cry. If I ever had to stop eating candy, I decided right there and then that I would never spook kids out with creepy teeth stories. I grabbed my bag of Gobstoppers and walked out.

That night, I had a terrible dream.

Megan's house was made out of candy, covered with gumdrops and peppermints and jellybeans. Red licorice tiles covered the roof, and in the garden were steppingstones made of sugar cubes.

When I knocked and asked if Megan was home, a woman who must have been Mrs. Chalmers answered the door dressed in a black business suit and said to me in a soft soothing voice, *Why certainly, my dear. But why don't you come inside for a while? Surely you must be tired and hungry from such a long day at school. Would you like something to eat?* I said yes.

Inside the house there were marshmallow chairs and

chocolate sofas, licorice rugs and toffee floors. When I asked Mrs. Chalmers where Megan was, she told me that Megan would be there very soon. *Why don't you eat some candy while you wait?*

I said OK, and Megan's mother brought me a big bowl of licorice allsorts. I had never tasted anything so delicious, and I ate and ate until the whole bowl was empty. When Megan's mother came back into the room she said, *My, what a big appetite you have. Would you like some more?*

I said that would be fine, and she brought me another bowl of licorice allsorts, and no matter how much I ate, I never got full. All the while I kept asking her when I could see Megan and she kept replying, *Very soon, very soon.*

When I had finally finished eating the last bowl of licorice, Mrs. Chalmers said, *I'm baking a cake for dinner — would you like to see?* and so I went into the kitchen and stuck my head inside the oven just to have a look. Next thing I knew, she had tied my arms and legs together with a string and shoved an apple in my mouth and thrown me inside the oven. With shock, I realized that Megan's mother was going to eat me.

Suddenly, appearing out of nowhere, came Megan, sneaking up behind her mother with a big shiny kitchen knife. Except that Megan wasn't Megan — Megan was me — and when I looked into the oven, Megan was the one who was trapped inside.

Megan's mother cackled with delight. And then I knew. Mrs. Chalmers wasn't really Mrs. Chalmers, but an evil witch. I lunged at her with the silvery blade of the kitchen knife, but she vanished. I ran to the stove and helped Megan out.

Quick, quick, Megan said as she grabbed my hand. *We have to get out of here before she comes back!*

But I killed her, I said to Megan as we ran out the door.

No, Megan said, *you can't kill her! She'll only come back and take on another shape, another disguise!*

I turned around and looked back at the house. It was no longer coated in candy, but was made of rotting wood, covered with skulls and eyeballs and gaping mouths and severed arms and legs. And just as Megan had predicted, the witch reappeared, chasing after us. But she was not Megan's mother. Now she was my mother. Blue and emaciated, she had two hollow pits for eyes, and her skin was hanging off her bones.

As she got close, I felt Megan tugging at my arm, shouting, *C'mon! C'mon! It's a trap, a trap!* But it was too late. My mother's skeletal arms squeezed tightly around me.

I shot out of bed, waking in the cold darkness of my room, my heart pounding. I peered into the shadows, listening. My father was still asleep. Quietly I got up and looked out into the night.

It was snowing. Over the streets and the forest and the frozen ground, over all the world outside my window. On my mother's grave. I thought of her there under the earth, all alone. Buried in all that cold, dark silence.

I hoped Megan was OK. And that she would be back soon.

THE CANDY DARLINGS

THE NEXT MORNING AT SCHOOL, damaged bodies of snowmen dotted the schoolyard. Territories were designated, divided by borders of mounded snow. What snow remained was used for fights. A steady crossfire of snowballs, cool as comets, sailed through the frosty air.

Across the schoolyard I saw MAL huddled together in a tight circle, insulating one another from the cold. Since the incident, they had kept their distance. But I knew that wouldn't last for long. They were probably already scheming their next attack.

Then I saw a head of blue hair bobbing between the cars in the parking lot.

Megan.

I thought she must have been sick, because she looked blue, and not just sad but actually blue; the color of her skin was as pale as a winter sky. Then again, maybe it was just the new blue dreadlocks.

"Megan!" I shouted, running to meet her. "Where have you been?" I asked. "You've been gone for more than a week! I called, I came by your house, every day! I was getting worried—"

"About what?" Megan said coolly. "My mom had to go away on business. She just wanted me to go with her." Megan opened her jacket to reveal a T-shirt emblazoned with I ♥ NY.

"You went to New York City?"

"Yeppur."

"Wow."

I looked into her face, expecting to hear some details of her trip. An animated story about a cab ride in SoHo. Lunch in Central Park. An elevator ride up the Empire State Building.

"Yeah, it was great. I love New York. It's like my second home. We have some family there." It sounded as if she went all the time.

"Mr. King didn't know where you were. He asked me and I didn't know. So I had to lie and tell him you went away for your grandfather's funeral—"

Megan was intrigued. "Really?"

I nodded. "Didn't you get my messages?"

She looked at me with vague suspicion. "No," she replied.

"But I left you one every day."

"Oh," she said casually, "that must have been when our answering machine was broken."

"Your answering machine was broken? When?"

"When we came home—"

"When did you come home?"

"A few days ago."

I was confused. "But I came by your house every day and no one was there—"

"I know."

"But how did you know if you were away?"

Megan looked at me. "The homework you left me, stupid."

"Oh. Yeah. Right."

"What's with the cross-examination?" she asked.

It wasn't just the blue dreadlocks. Something else was different about her. But I couldn't tell what. Some things didn't make sense. The answering machine, for instance. And the homework. Something wasn't right.

Megan's eyes darted across the parking lot, then flickered over my face.

"You got any candy?"

I searched my pockets. Finally, triumphant, I found a piece of Bazooka. I put it in my mouth and chewed. Then I pulled half out of my mouth and gave it to her. Unflinching, she took the masticated goo and put it in her mouth.

"Did you really tell Mr. King that I went to my grandfather's funeral?" Megan asked.

"Uh-huh."

She laughed. "That's really good. I'll have to remember that one."

We chewed our gum in silence, honoring the exchange of each other's saliva.

"It sure is good to see you," she said.

"Yeah," I replied, relieved she was back but suspicious of the reasons she had left. "It's good to see you, too."

That afternoon Megan and I forged a path through the snow toward the fort. As we walked, I told her about the fight I had with MAL. And about my father. And the part of the Francesca story she had missed. I didn't tell her about Blake. Or the dream I had about her and her mother. It was just too weird.

When we got there, Megan lifted a small Mason jar half full

of red liquid out of her backpack. I watched as she took out a can of Hawaiian Punch and dumped it into the jar and swirled it around. When she finished, she carefully poured half of the mixture back into the can. Then she took out two cherry Twizzlers and bit the ends off—one for each of us—to use as straws.

"Here," she said, passing me the can. "'It's called 'The Surely Tempting.' Sorry I don't have any little umbrellas or maraschino cherries."

I took the can of Hawaiian Punch and held the licorice stick between my fingers as I took a sip. It was sweet, but with a sharp kick at the end.

"What's this?" I asked, shuddering.

"Cherry brandy, gin, Southern Comfort, and grenadine."

I took a couple of long slurps and nibbled on the end of my Twizzler. "It feels like my belly's on fire."

"Uh-huh," Megan said as she took a sip. "That means it's working. Or at least that's what my cousin Gabe said. He's the one who gave this shit to me. And this . . ." She pulled a thin hand-rolled cigarette out of her pocket.

"What's that?" I asked.

"A joint," she replied.

"What?" I answered, shocked. "You mean marijuana?"

Megan laughed.

"Yessiree—pot, tea, grass, ganja, weed, reefer—whatever you want to call it, that's what it is."

I had never smoked pot before. I couldn't tell if Megan had either. But she seemed to know what she was doing. I watched as she stuck the joint between her lips and lit it with a match.

Pinching it between her thumb and index finger, she inhaled deeply. Then she smiled and passed it to me. Nervously, I took it and did as she did and passed it back.

I coughed uncontrollably. My throat was burning. I grabbed my can of Hawaiian Punch and drank quickly, forgetting that it was spiked. I coughed again.

"How did your cousin Gabe get it?"

"Let's just say he has connections." Megan coughed also.

"Really?" I asked.

Megan raised her eyebrow. "Oh, yeah. He was the one who showed me how to smoke it. This was his goodbye gift to me."

The air was thick with smoke. The back of my throat felt as if it were coated with shellac. But I smoked some more, then coughed some more, then drank some more, too. I watched Megan take a few more tokes, and then, when she was sure it was done, she threw the joint outside the entrance to the fort. In a delirious haze, I watched it smolder in the snow.

I looked back at Megan. With her new dreadlocks, she was a vision, bathed in an aura of blue light. As I looked at her longer still, she seemed to levitate off the ground, suspended in midair.

"You look like you're floating," I said.

She looked at me and laughed.

"So do you."

There was a pause.

"Here," she said. "This is for you. Special delivery from the Big Apple." She reached into her backpack and pulled out a snow globe, putting it in my hands. I held it up.

Inside was a miniature Statue of Liberty, bright green against the gray and black New York cityscape. In the background was bright blue sky; in the foreground, bright blue sea. At the base of the dome was the phrase *I Left My Heart in New York City*. Inside, a tiny red heart floated amid a blizzard of little white bits. I shook the globe and watched the flurry around the Statue of Liberty, her little torch a bright yellow beacon.

"It's beautiful," I murmured.

"I knew you'd like it!" Megan beamed. "I thought it looked like candy inside, you know?"

I examined it again, this time through Megan's eyes. Inside was a candied New York City in miniature: the glazed buildings, the heart, the blue sea, the white flakes spinning through the sky. It was a world sweet enough to eat.

"I'm hungry," I said.

Megan laughed again.

"You've got the munchies!" she sang, teasing.

"Fuck off," I said, giggling.

Megan flashed me a fake affronted look, pouting.

"Fuck on and you get better results," she said as she took a big slurp from her jar and burped loudly, nibbling on her licorice stick.

Then I suddenly remembered that I had some Mike and Ikes. From my pocket, I pulled out the box and opened them.

"Mmmmm," I said, filling my hand. "These are *sooo gooood.*"

"Hey, gimme some of those," Megan said.

"Never!" I teased.

She lunged at me and wrestled me to the ground, tickling me.

"No, no, no," I protested, laughing. "No tickling! Please, stop!"

Breaking free from her grip, I rolled away, catching my

breath. In a haze, I realized I had had nothing to eat all day but candy. Delirious, I reached for some more Mike and Ikes.

"Would you like to hear a story, little girl?" Megan asked.

I looked at her and nodded. "Please," I said.

She smiled.

"Nose pressed against the glass," she began, "Melody watches Lucifer, the prize black angel, swim in the aquarium before her. Fringed with sharp black spikes, his spiny fins fan slowly through the warm blue water, disappearing and then reappearing among the long, thin strands of seaweed.

"In the apartment outside the four walls of Lucifer's underwater kingdom is a bedroom, the door to which is closed. From her seat on the couch Melody can hear the sounds within the bedroom. The heated words. The heavy breathing. The dark, urgent moans.

"In her hands, Melody carefully squeezes one piece of candy out from the long package of Lotsa Fizz, then drops it into the tank. It hits the water fizzling, like a hot stone being thrown into a cold sea.

"Smiling, Melody watches it sink downward. Tiny pearls of air escape from its sides like seeds, spitting upward toward the surface. Like a fissured jewel, the candy cracks; swirls of syrup dissolve.

"Working quickly, Melody adds the remaining Lotsa Fizzes to the water. Lucifer parades before her, gliding serenely, oblivious to his forthcoming demise.

"When she is finished, Melody goes and waits by the window, staring at the gleaming skyscrapers, listening to the steady gurgle of the aquarium. Above the city skyline, the sun hangs like a hot pearl in the sky.

"The sounds from the bedroom do not stop."

Megan drank the last drop of red liquid from her jar. Then she looked off into the distance. I realized then that maybe Megan hadn't told me everything. Why did she have to go to New York City, anyway? And who was her cousin Gabe? She'd never mentioned him before, but then again I'd never asked. I was confused. Maybe she hadn't told me everything, but at least she was back. And the proof that she had gone to New York was in my hands. I shook the snow globe above my head, looking at a candied world, and watched the little heart whirl wildly in the falling snow.

The following day, Mr. King gave us an assignment for an independent painting project based on an image from our dreams. As Tracey Reid walked dutifully up and down the rows of seats with an armful of white paper, spreading one sheet on each desk, Mr. King directed his attention to Megan.

"Nice to see you back again, Miss Chalmers," he said.

"Nice to be back, Mr. King," Megan replied.

"I'm sorry to hear about your grandfather," he said. "But I trust you've been catching up with your homework?"

Megan's eyes welled with tears as she looked at Mr. King. Her face was a perfect mask of grief.

"Please don't hesitate to come and see me if you have any problems," said Mr. King. "Or if you just want to talk."

Megan's performance was almost worthy of an Oscar. And Mr. King had even called her "Miss Chalmers." It was unbelievable.

For my assignment, I decided to paint the candied gingerbread house I had seen in my dream. My painting would include a lemon yellow sun with rich chocolate ground below and peppermint trees on all sides. On the reverse side of the paper would be the same house but with eyeballs and skulls and severed hands. I already knew what I was going to call it: *Sweet Dreams*.

From behind me, Blake raised his hand and asked what he could use to make his painting. Mr. King raised an eyebrow and said, "Do you mean what medium, Blake? You can use whatever you want."

Gathered at our desks, we lined up paints and paintbrushes and began to sketch out our drawings. Mr. King was busy helping us, attending to our questions, giving individual suggestions. And then we heard the abrupt rattling knock on the window.

We all looked. It was Blake.

He was in the parking lot, standing on the hood of Mr. King's car, his face pressed against the classroom window.

Mr. King liked things organized and efficient. When we put our papers on his desk, he preferred them in a neat pile, all the corners matching. He diligently checked attendance every morning right after the national anthem. He did not like carelessness. And he especially did not like it when someone deliberately disobeyed him.

"Miss Reid," Mr. King said to Tracey, "would you mind watching the classroom for a moment, please? I'll be right back." He glared at all of us. "And don't think for a minute that Mr. Carter won't hear you from down the hall." Mr. King turned his attention to David Pierce. "If Blake comes back inside, keep him here. Got it?"

"Yeah, right," David Pierce said as Mr. King left the room, "if we can keep him here. We need a cage for that psycho retard." He laughed loudly at his own little joke and high-fived Jason Cutler.

Blake pulled back from the window and jumped off the car. All of us rushed to the window to watch.

"What's he doing?" Adam Diamond asked.

Blake ran to the center of the parking lot and turned around and faced us. Then he undid his zipper and pulled his pants down to his knees.

"Oh, my—" Tracey Reid gasped.

"Shamalamadingdong!" Megan whistled. "Check it out!"

Then, fully exposed, Blake began to pee in the snow.

It seemed to last forever. And as he kept urinating, it looked as though he thought it was summer and he was watering the lawn with a garden hose, the stream of steaming pee whizzing into the air. I watched in awe, stunned at the sight of his thin white thighs exposed against the cold starkness of the snow. Blake's face was manic with glee.

"Quasi must have drunk a gallon to piss that much," Jason Cutler said. "What a freak!"

Meredith McKinnon was horrified. "That is *so* disgusting."

Tracey Reid was speechless. Megan moved closer to the window to get a better look. The rest of the class cheered him on.

But I noticed there was a pattern to Blake's movements. He was not just peeing randomly, but stopping and starting, creating a specific design. In the snow, I could see the outline of a frame and some intersecting lines accented by a series of circles and spirals. It was, I suddenly realized, his painting.

When he had finished, Blake turned to the window and looked at our class and waved, an ecstatic smile on his face.

"Qua-si! Qua-si! Qua-si!" Jason Cutler chanted.

Just then, both Mr. King and Mr. Carter appeared outside without their coats on, skidding across the parking lot, their thin ties flapping in the wind. Their faces grim with moral conviction, they stopped and seized Blake and made him pull his pants back up. Following that, they hauled him away and out of sight, as stern as executioners. The class stopped cheering.

It was not the first time Blake had had such an episode. But this time it was different. This time it was serious. Punishment was inevitable.

And so was medication.

That week, as usual, Megan and I found Edie sitting upright in bed, watching *The Price Is Right*. When we came into her room, she turned and stared at Megan.

"What in God's name have you done with your hair?" she asked in disbelief.

"Dyed it," Megan said.

"Darling, I can see that—but *blue?* Why blue?"

"I wanted a change," replied Megan as she wheeled the cart beside Edie's bed, letting her buy her weekly supply of candy.

"And what do your parents think?" she asked.

"My mother doesn't care what I do with my hair," Megan asserted coolly. "She doesn't care what I do, at all."

Edie thought about this for a brief moment. "I see." She turned to me: "And what would *your* mother think?"

"She wouldn't," I replied quietly. "It's just me and my dad. My mom died last year."

Edie was silent. She looked at both of us. "Well, then, darlings," she said brightly, "who cares about hair, anyway? Let's continue with our story."

On the TV, the *Price Is Right* models glided across the showroom floor to unveil a matching washer and dryer. A contestant with the nametag BERNICE jumped up and down with hysterical wonder, giddily clapping her hands.

"See?" Edie said, emphatically pointing to the TV. "See how happy she is?" It was true: pure ecstasy was all over Bernice's face. Edie smiled and shut off the television.

"It's what I find so wonderful about *The Price Is Right*," she said. "Not a day goes by without someone winning. It gives me hope about humanity."

She reached over to her bedside table and took out her little black book.

"Did you tell Megan about what happened in the story?" Edie asked me.

"You mean about Francesca finding the tallest tree?" interrupted Megan. "She did."

Edie nodded. "Good. Now, where were we?"

"Francesca had just named the fly Ferdinand," I reminded her.

"Ah, yes," said Edie as she flipped through the pages. "Noble Ferdinand." Megan and I sat down beside her, taking our usual seats. "Yes . . . here we are. Now, ready, darlings?"

"Ready," Megan said.

And so Edie began:

"Now that the tallest tree was right in front of her, Francesca raced through the forest toward it, Ferdinand flying close behind. How happy she was to have finally found it! As she made her way through the woods, she thought again of the butterfly's secret: *In the forest under the tallest tree, here you will find the most precious treasure of me.* What could it mean? What was so precious? Francesca's heart fluttered with excitement.

"When at last she reached the tallest tree, Francesca stood in awe before it. It was enormous, and the ground below its branches was sheltered by its sweeping shadow. Francesca searched under its lower branches, but she found nothing.

"She looked at the tree, studying its great system of roots. Perhaps 'under' really meant *under* the ground. Francesca began to dig at the base of the tree, scooping up small handfuls of soil. As she was digging, she discovered a small hole against a root, and as soon as she pushed the earth aside it collapsed. Francesca crashed downward, swallowed up into the hole.

"Down, down, down she fell, past layers of earth and rock and sediment, past roots and clay and stone. Down, down, down. Francesca began to wonder if she was getting near the center of the earth, for the hole seemed to go on forever, when — *thump! thump!* — she landed on a bed of knotted roots. The fall was over. Francesca strained her eyes. She was enveloped in complete darkness.

"'Ferdinand,' she cried out in panic, 'are you there? Ferdinand! Where are you?'

"Francesca had once dreaded his presence, but now she listened closely for him. Soon she heard the soft hum of tiny wings beside her ear.

"'Oh, Ferdinand,' Francesca cried. 'This is a horrible place. How will we ever get out?'

"Buzzing excitedly, Ferdinand flew away from Francesca,

then flew back to her. Then he did it again, even more energized than before. Suddenly she realized that he was asking her to follow him.

"Step by step, through the darkness, Francesca followed Ferdinand until very faintly in the distance, beyond her outstretched hands, she saw a golden light, like the glow of a lantern, beckoning her.

"Francesca stumbled toward it. When at last she came closer, she realized it was no lantern at all but a nest of snakes, their skins gleaming bright. They were very tiny—no longer than Francesca's finger—but there must have been a thousand of them, sleeping coiled side by side, twisted around one another.

"Afraid she might wake them, Francesca stood very still. At first she was fearful of them, but as she looked closer she saw how beautiful they were, with red speckled heads and bodies ringed with gold. As she looked more closely, she saw that the rings were more than just markings; they were real gold. And the red speckles on the snakes were rubies.

"So this was the butterfly's secret, Francesca thought. This was the precious treasure. Francesca stared in awe at the snakes' beauty and riches. But soon she remembered she had to give Queen Goren whatever she found under the tallest tree or both she and her father would die.

"'Ferdinand,' Francesca cried. 'Whatever shall I do? Somehow I must take all of these snakes to Queen Goren. But how? There are so many of them. And what if they are poisonous?'

"And then, as he had done before, Ferdinand began to sing. It was the same sweet voice Francesca had heard before, and as he sang the snakes began to awaken. One by one they slithered to life and rose up into the air in a rope of golden light, hypnotized by the little fly's voice.

"In the same instant Francesca also began to rise, just as she had before. As she floated higher and higher, she emerged through the same hole she had fallen into, up into the sky.

"When she was above the tallest tree, Francesca's heart filled with wonder, for she saw a magical sight. There, awaiting her in the clouds, were the beautiful golden snakes in the formation of a magnificent golden carriage, their heads and tails magically forged together. As the door swung open, Francesca drifted inside the carriage and sat on its golden seat. With Ferdinand singing beside her, they rode over the tops of the trees, through the waves of sunshine.

"From her field down below, Queen Goren could see something glinting brightly in the sun. Because she was used to looking upon only dark ugly things, she shielded her eyes from the dazzling brilliance. Knowing it could only be Francesca, the queen was filled with rage, for secretly she had hoped the girl and the fly would die. But against all odds their quest had been successful.

"Still hypnotized by his singing, Francesca and the carriage of golden snakes were guided by Ferdinand to Queen Goren's field, where they landed at her feet."

Edie became silent. Megan and I stared at her, waiting.

"So what happens next?" I asked.

"Yeah," Megan said. "Can't you read a little bit more?"

Edie smiled and closed the book.

"Next week, darlings," she said. "I promise."

That afternoon as we walked home from St. Teresa's, I asked Megan if she thought Edie had some magic power.

"Excuse me?" Megan said, stunned.

"You know. Magic power. Like a fairy godmother or something."

"I'll say she's got magic power," Megan said. "It's called those little pills she pops every day. *Darling*."

Megan smiled and removed our "Steal of the Week" from her backpack. It was our all-time favorite treat from St. Teresa's: the large box of Junior Mints.

"Mint? Junior?" Megan asked, offering the box.

I took it and poured some into my hand.

"Thank you, *darling*," I replied as I passed them back to her.

"No, *darling*, thank you," Megan said.

We looked at each other and laughed. Then we toasted Edie. We were both her darlings.

The Candy Darlings.

Later that night I woke to the sound of my father's footsteps outside my bedroom.

I got out of bed and opened the door and watched him shuffle up and down the narrow hallway, sleepwalking again. He passed in front of my door and walked to the end of the hall before turning around again.

Slowly, I moved toward him and put one hand gently on his elbow and the other on his back. He was mumbling something, but his words were unrecognizable.

Somehow sensing my presence, my father let me guide him back to his bedroom. As I nudged him toward his bed, he took his cue and lay down. I pulled the blankets up and over his shivering body.

Soon, I knew, he would stop mumbling. And then, as he always did, he would surrender back into sleep, his body shuddering as if he were about to fall from a great height, dropping into nothing.

I sat beside him on the edge of the bed, holding his hand, waiting for the fall.

SNOWBALL

THE FOLLOWING WEEK, Mr. King announced the annual assembly and dance at Woodland to celebrate the upcoming holiday season. They would be held in the afternoon on the last day of school before the Christmas holiday. It was expected that we would all attend.

I recalled other dances at other schools: the dim lights, the streamers, the balloons, the music. The whole awkward ceremony of it all.

"So," Mr. King asked, "who would like to volunteer to decorate the gym this year?"

Tracey Reid shot up her hand. Like that was any big surprise.

Mr. King smiled. "Miss Reid," he said. "Excellent."

"That is the most fucking retarded thing I have ever heard," Megan said at lunch, offering me a candy cane. "A Christmas assembly *and* dance? Golly gee! Is the glee club gonna show up, too? Pa-rum-pa-pum-pum!" Megan crunched up her candy cane in her teeth. "This school is *so* archaic."

She offered me another from the bouquet in her hand.

"Where'd you get so many candy canes?" I asked.

Megan smiled. "Santy Claus. I went to the mall and sat on

his knee, and when he asked me if I'd been naughty or nice, I told him that I'd been naughty. That I was a *very* naughty little girl . . ."

"You did not."

"Oh, yes I did! And when he told me to reach inside his pocket, right there, beside his big ole woody, was a big ole stash of candy canes. So as I smiled for the camera I stroked ole St. Nick—"

"You did not!"

"Did too! And when I was finished, Santa said that I could take as many candy canes as I liked."

"Yeah, right," I disputed, smiling at her. "Very funny."

"Just be glad I wiped off all the Santa spunk," Megan said, smirking. "But then again, maybe I didn't."

"You are so gross," I said, swatting her. "You actually expect me to believe that?"

Megan smiled and sucked on her candy cane, sliding it in and all the way out of her mouth. "What? That I jerked off Santa Claus just to get candy canes?" She looked at me with total earnestness. "Of course I do. I want you to believe every story I tell. Every character. Every detail. *Everything.*"

"But you've already said I shouldn't believe everything you say."

Megan laughed. "Just because something isn't true doesn't mean you can't believe it!"

I stopped smiling. "What's that supposed to mean?" I asked.

"Nothing. C'mon! I'm just joking around! I'd never lie to you. With the candy cane in her hand, she quickly criss-crossed her hand over her heart. "Cross my heart and hope to die."

∽⟨§⟩∽

On the day of the Christmas assembly, Megan and I had to hand it to Tracey Reid. Even though we had wanted to say she did a lousy job, the gym looked beautiful.

It was decorated in the theme of "White Christmas." Icicle lights were strung everywhere: up and down in loopy swags across the stage and on the walls, within doorways and from basketball hoops. On the stage, white felt was stuck to the floor to make it look like snow, and Tracey had created a family of fake snowmen from Styrofoam. A disco ball, struck by a single beam of light, slowly rotated above the stage, its small shiny dots flickering around the darkened gym. From the ceiling dangled hundreds of paper snowflakes.

Before the dance started, Tracey came bounding over to Megan and me. "Merry Christmas!" she said. "What do you think?" A little silver bell jingled on the top of her white faux fur hat.

"I'm blown away, Tracey," Megan said. "It's so ho-ho-ho and fa-la-la-la-la-la-la-la-LA. Oh, if only dear old Bing could be here!"

Tracey's face screwed up into a tight little smile. It was hard to tell whether her feelings were hurt or if she was just confused.

"You did this all by yourself?" I asked.

"Oh, no!" Tracey said. "Amanda Fletcher and Caroline Schaefer were a big help. And so was my mom!"

I imagined Tracey and her mother working side by side, laughing together. I remembered how my mother used to help me with my homework and class projects, before she got sick.

"Candy cane?" Megan offered Tracey.

"Thanks, Megan," Tracey said, honestly touched. "Thank you."

"No, thank *you,* Tracey," Megan said. "You've worked hard. You deserve one. Courtesy of the Woodland Hills Mall Santa Claus. Let's just say he granted me a few extra special ones."

"Oh, really?" Tracey said. "Why'd he do that?"

"Just watch out for the jizz," Megan warned. "It can get pretty sticky."

"The *what?*" Tracey said with disgust.

Before Megan could tell Tracey anything more about Santa spunk, MAL made their entrance into the gym, moving across the floor toward us, toward Tracey.

"Satan's helpers at six-six-six o'clock," Megan observed aloud.

Ignoring Megan and me, Meredith said, "Tracey, Laura and Angela and I just wanted to tell you how pretty the decorations look. You did a wonderful job. It looks so *festive.*"

Tracey Reid was awestruck. "Gee, thanks, Meredith," she gushed.

Megan and I looked at each other with raised eyebrows. Any minute Tracey would fall to her knees and kiss Meredith's feet.

"What are you doing hanging out with these losers?" Angela said, stepping aside and taking Tracey's arm. "You deserve better."

"Yeah," Laura sneered. "Come with us."

In the flickering lights of the disco ball, Megan and I sucked on our candy canes as we watched MAL whisk Tracey away.

"Well, isn't that just swell," Megan commented. "Just like a

mutant alien creature being hatched—*ta-dah!* It's the birth of
MALT."

Riding a candy cane–induced high, Megan and I watched
the rest of the Christmas dance unfold from the back of the
darkened gym. Cheery, goofy songs like "Jingle Bell Rock"
and "Rockin' Around the Christmas Tree" blared out of the
speakers.

It was only when Mr. King, dressed as Santa Claus, ho-ho-
hoed his way through the gym that things finally got interesting.

"Well, deck the halls! Check out who's playing the fat man
in the red suit," Megan wryly observed. "Further proof that
this school is trapped in a time warp."

But as Mr. King threw handfuls of candy canes and chocolate kisses, we clamored around him, pushing and shoving to
get as much candy as we could. When at last it looked as if the
big red felt bag was empty, we retreated to the back of the gym.

While we were eating our stash of free goodies, Tracey
Reid—joined silently by MAL—stepped onto the stage and
announced to everyone that there was going to be a special
"Snowball" dance. It was a tradition from the 1950s, Tracey
said, that her mother had suggested. She explained that a
"Snowball" was when the names of a boy and girl were randomly picked to dance together. Tracey removed the white
faux fur hat from her head and MAL filled it with tiny slips of
paper. Then Tracey mixed them up and held the hat in front of
Meredith's hand.

"And the first name is . . . Blake . . . Blake Starfield!" Meredith crooned.

I had seen Blake before the dance started on the opposite side of the gym, leaning against the wall. Since the episode in the teachers' parking lot, he had changed somehow. He was still quiet. Aloof. But he seemed sedated. With a sad, easy confidence, he pushed himself off the wall and moved into the spotlight. As he shuffled out into the middle of the gym, Adam Diamond, Jason Cutler, and David Pierce chanted their usual *"Qua-si! Qua-si! Qua-si!"*

I was so busy watching Blake that I didn't hear Meredith announce the next name.

It was only when I felt the hot white light shining in my eyes and bathing me from head to foot that I knew it was too late to run. I, too, had been chosen for the "Snowball." I stood there, frozen. Then Meredith said the name again—my name—and insisted I move to the middle of the gym.

Panicked, I looked at Megan. She shrugged her shoulders.

"Don't be afraid, darling." She smiled. "Get out there! Poor Quasi's waiting."

I turned around. It was true. There, in the middle of the gym, was Blake, his head bowed, all alone in the spotlight. He raised his face and looked in my direction. I couldn't leave him out there.

Hesitantly I walked to the middle of the gym and stood in the spotlight with him. He gave me a shy, nervous smile. We danced together, slowly, painstakingly moving back and forth. We dared not speak. When the music finally ended, we broke away from each other and pretended that nothing had happened. I headed straight to the back of the gym and took my place beside Megan. My humiliation was complete.

"Well, that was brave," she said, "for some stupid dance ritual out of the fucking dark ages."

I could see MAL on stage, standing behind Tracey, laughing.

"Too bad Quasi didn't whip it out like last time," Megan concluded. "Then we could have really seen something."

Christmas was a special time at St. Teresa's. From the painted nativity scenes in the windows to the colored lights strung down the hallways, the sisters did everything within their power to celebrate the birth of their savior.

When we went to visit Edie she was sitting up in bed, staring out the window. As we entered her room, she turned and looked at us, her eyes twinkling.

"Oh, darlings!" she exclaimed. "I do love it when it snows! It's so magical! The whole world sparkles!"

Megan looked at me and rolled her eyes as she pushed the cart beside Edie's bed. "Oh, it's magical, all right," she replied.

Edie looked at us with a strange smile as she made her weekly candy selection.

"I know it seems hard to believe," Edie said, "but magic happens. Is happening. All the time. All around us." She waved her hand through the air and reached over to her bedside table, pulling out her customary fifty-dollar bill. As Megan handed her her change, Edie got out the little black book.

"Now. How about some more of our story?" Edie said. "Can you girls remember where we finished off last week?"

"Francesca fell down a hole—" I recalled.

"And found these *freaky* golden snakes," Megan interrupted.

"And then," I added, "she flew in a magic carriage to Queen Goren's field."

"Very good!" Edie offered us a bag of Christmas Hershey's Kisses. Megan and I each took a handful and sat on either side of her mattress. The thick fuzz of chocolate melted on my tongue in waves of delight.

Then Edie began.

"As Francesca landed on Queen Goren's field, the snakes slithered apart and resumed their original nest formation.

"'What kind of trickery do you dare bring before me?' demanded the queen.

"'No trickery,' Francesca insisted, trembling. 'Only this treasure of golden snakes.' Francesca fell at Queen Goren's feet. 'Now, please, I beg you, let me go!'

"'Not quite yet,' Queen Goren said cruelly. 'There is still one more thing you must do.'

"Francesca shuddered as she looked up into Queen Goren's cold yellow eyes.

"'And what is that?' Francesca asked, cowering.

"'You must remove the rings of gold from the snakes.'

"'But how?' cried Francesca. 'What you ask is impossible! What if they are poisonous? Surely they will kill me!'

"Queen Goren laughed and then turned on Francesca with fury. 'Do as I say!' she snarled. 'Or do I need to remind you of how I shall dispose of your father?'

"'Please, please! Don't punish my father! He is all I have!' Francesca pleaded. 'He had no part in this! It is not his fault!'

"'Then do as I say! Remove them!' Queen Goren demanded as she reared above Francesca, her flies swarming around her. 'Now!'

"Francesca looked down at the nest of sleeping golden snakes. She was terrified of harming them. They were so beautiful. Finally she reached out and picked one. It began to lash its tail, and then it drew back its head and reared its fangs, biting the back of Francesca's hand. She screamed and threw the tiny snake down, staring at the two pinpricks of blood where she had been bitten. Instantly the snake withered up and disappeared in a cloud of gold dust.

"Queen Goren seized Francesca by the shoulders and shook her.

"'You stupid girl!' she roared. 'Look how careless you are! You're useless! You deserve to die!'

"As the poison spread throughout her body, Francesca fell to her knees. She pleaded for mercy, but Queen Goren did nothing. As she looked up at the swarm of flies surrounding the queen's head, Francesca wondered where her dear little friend Ferdinand had gone.

"Then a remarkable thing began to happen. Francesca began to feel stronger. Somehow she felt larger, as if her arms and legs were becoming longer. She sat up and looked down at her body. Francesca had not died from the snake venom after all, she realized, but had grown from it. Her hands and feet and body were at least twice their normal size.

"Francesca looked again upon the golden snakes, this time with wonder. How big might she grow from another bite? From two or three bites? From one hundred? From all of the them?

"Gathering her courage, Francesca bravely leapt into the pile of snakes, surrendering herself to them. And as they coiled about her, slipping through her arms and twisting themselves around her fingers and toes, she felt as if she were being stung by a thousand bees, pierced by a thousand arrows. It was an exhilarating feeling.

"And then, just as the first snake had died, so too did all the others that had bitten her, withering and disappearing in an enormous cloud of gold dust. When it finally settled, Francesca looked down on herself. She was a giant, taller than the tallest tree!

Queen Goren shrieked with terror. With one giant swoop of her hand, Francesca scooped her up and brought her close to her face. She watched with delight as the little queen clung to Francesca's thumb, her voice a tiny frantic squeak.

"With the biggest breath she could take, Francesca filled her massive lungs with air. And then she blew Queen Goren away. Francesca watched as the queen's minuscule body spun away like a black dot over the horizon, disappearing forever.

"Francesca looked around her. The sky was a deep, radiant blue, the woods and fields a deep, misty green. She looked down at her feet and hands and studied their grooves and wrinkles, the great fault lines of her flesh. How big she was! How huge and giant! The world was hers to roam!"

Edie stopped reading and closed her book.

Then I remembered her words from earlier that afternoon: *Magic happens. Is happening. All the time. All around us.*

Magic, indeed.

That afternoon after we finished our rounds, Sister Maria eyeballed Megan and me as we restocked the cart. While we tallied each candy bar, I noticed as she noticed the absence of any

Good & Plenty. I wondered if she was starting to suspect that something funny was going on.

"Busy today?" she asked.

"Sort of," Megan replied. "Steady. But we had a real blowout on Good & Plenty, as you can see."

"Yes," said Sister Maria, who hovered over us, hawklike, as we counted each package of candy.

"Remember, girls," she warned. "This is a holy house. He is watching you."

In December, it snowed and snowed for days, turning the whole world white.

The first day it stopped snowing, Megan and I went to the fort after school, our backpacks stuffed with blankets and provisions. Once we got there, we bundled up and stayed out for hours, even after dark. Of course the flashlights helped. The candy, too: the constant flow of sugar like rocket fuel in our bloodstreams.

"All we'll really need for food," Megan said one day, "is Astro Pops. Once we absorb the powers of the Astro Pop, our bodies will transform into spaceships that can travel through time at the speed of light."

She looked at me and grinned, handing me my Astro Pop. I stared at its sharp cone shape, its rainbow stripe of colors.

"Then we'll be able to fly and communicate telepathically," Megan said. "Which will be very important," she added, "if one of us gets sucked into a black hole. Not everyone gets to do this," she said. "Not everyone gets chosen."

I put it in my mouth, initializing the countdown, preparing for the transformation.

We pretended we were part of a secret religious order, forbidden from disclosing to anyone any of our activities, our ceremonies, our rituals. There was only the two of us. But the world we created was ours. And as we told each other stories, myths and legends were born.

Just before Christmas, my father made a big fuss over getting a tree. We drove to a local gas station and I had to stand outside and watch as he haggled with the guy who was selling them. Eventually—after my father failed to negotiate the price he wanted to pay—we loaded the overpriced tree into the trunk and drove it back to the house.

In the living room, he cursed as he struggled to put it in a stand. I was sent upstairs to find the decorations.

It was amazing how well my mother had packed everything away. Each decoration had been individually wrapped in tissue paper, arranged by color. I had forgotten this about my mother, how organized she had been. I stared at the labeled boxes, reading her handwriting, running my fingers over the letters.

When I went downstairs, my father asked me what had taken so long.

"Nothing." I shrugged, handing him a box.

"Is that all you got?"

"I didn't think we'd need more."

He shook his head, his disappointment in me obvious.

I watched as he opened the box and unwrapped a silver star and hung it on the tree. He stood back and stared at the solitary ornament, holding the crumpled tissue in his hand.

I recognized the star instantly. It has always been my mother's favorite Christmas decoration.

"Maybe we should string the lights first," I suggested.

My father didn't turn around. "OK," he said.

After we finished decorating the tree, we sat side by side on the couch in the living room, awash in the pale glow of the lights. We had said hardly a word to each other.

"The tree sure is pretty," my father said finally.

"Yeah," I answered.

Just before I thought I had given him the allowable limit of what I had come to understand as our father-daughter quality time, he said, "I wish your mother could be here. She should be here to see this."

I looked over at my father. His head hung; his hands were clasped.

I felt my chest cave with sorrow. It was true. She should have been with us. All I wanted was to have her back. For things to be the way they were.

I would not cry, I said to myself. At least not in front of him. I ran upstairs to my room.

"Wait—" my father called after me. But I had already closed the door. Tears streamed down my face.

I would be glad when Christmas was over.

A LIKELY STORY

ONE DAY AFTER THE SCHOOL HOLIDAYS, when it was too cold to go outside, Megan suggested that we go snooping in Rose's apartment again. She was still at work, Megan said. She wouldn't be back for hours. There was nothing to worry about.

"C'mon," she said, leading me downstairs. *"Trust me."*

Like thieves, we entered the apartment and went from room to room. With the lights turned off, we skulked in the kitchen, the bathroom, and the living room. Then we went into Rose's bedroom.

I watched as Megan opened Rose's closet and inspected her wardrobe.

"Check this out," she said, holding up a full-length blue velvet gown with fake ermine–cuffed hems and sleeves. "How Snow White can you get?"

The dress was too big, but Megan tried it on anyway. I watched as she strutted around the apartment in Rose's high heels, two pink hand towels stuffed down the front of the dress to make enormous breasts.

"Oh, dah-ling," Megan said in a high, lusty voice, thrusting her chest in front of my face. "Would you mind fixin' me a drink? I'm absolutely parched."

I donned a suit jacket and hat and stuffed a couple of pairs of Rose's socks down the front of my jeans.

"Of course, darlin'," I replied. "G'n'T?"

Megan lowered her eyes at me and batted her lashes, tossing her hair over her shoulder. "No, dah-ling," she purred. "A Manhattan."

Megan stretched out on the bed in Rose's bedroom, starlet-style. I pretended to give her a glass.

Megan lifted the pretend glass to her lips, drinking it in one shot. I slurped my own, watching as she placed her pretend glass on the bedside table and opened her arms.

"Come to me, dah-ling," Megan said, lying back. I leaned over her and peered down into the fuzzy garden of her cleavage.

"You sure do smell beautiful, darlin'," I told her.

"Do I?" Megan replied breathily, pulling me down on top of her. "It's called *Eau de Rose.*"

I buried my nose in her chest and inhaled deeply. *"You smell so . . . red . . . so rosy."*

"Oh, *dah-ling,*" Megan moaned, reaching out and grabbing the socks in my jeans. *"I want you."*

We fell into each other, shrieking with laughter, and rolled off the bed onto the floor. I pulled a hand towel from Megan's dress, freeing it into the air. As I waved the soft pink towel in my hand, Megan screamed and giggled and chased me down the hall.

After we put the clothes back in Rose's closet, we lay on the shag rug under the forest mural and made up some stories of what we thought had happened to Rose.

Mine was mainly the stuff of soap operas: Rose had once

been betrothed to a rich, handsome man, but on her way home from work one day she had caught him with another woman. In a blind rage, Rose got into a terrible car accident, which explained her limp and slightly hunched appearance. In a coma for years, she finally awoke and found her betrothed had long since married. Poor and deformed, she was doomed to live alone in dingy basement apartments for the rest of her life.

Megan's version was much more sensational. In her story, Rose had been born the oldest of two children to immigrant parents. Talented and resourceful, but not beautiful, she was a loner at school. Tragically, when she was a teenager, her parents died in a car crash. To keep her remaining family together, Rose quit school and got a job, caring for her younger brother, who had never quite recovered from the shock of their parents' death. Desperate for guidance, her brother soon became involved with a local gang. Rose did everything she could to stop him, but it had become his replacement family. Years passed. The brother married, started a family, and tried to live a normal life. But he knew too many secrets. Suddenly, tragically, her little brother was murdered — and Rose vowed revenge. She planned to kill those who had killed her brother, so she infiltrated a rival gang. But just before Rose had struck alliances with some key players in the organization, her infiltration scheme was discovered and she had to begin a life on the run. Broke but not broken, and with nowhere else to go, Rose moved into a cheap basement apartment below a professional woman and her young daughter to try to survive and escape her past.

"And the Snow White dress?" I asked.

"Nothing more than a prom date that never happened."

I thought about the white cylindrical object we had found in Rose's drawer. "And the *thing?*"

"The dildo?" Megan shrugged. "Nothing more than the evidence of a lonely and horny old maid."

"But what about the vow of revenge against her brother's murderer? Did she kill them?"

Megan's lips curved into a cryptic, knowing smile.

"Now that," Megan said, "that is another story."

"What do you mean?"

"I'll tell you another day." Megan sat up. "C'mon—we should split. Rose will be coming home soon."

As we made our way upstairs, I noticed the only room in the basement that Megan and I had never gone into.

"You don't want to look in there," Megan told me firmly. "There's nothing in there. C'mon, let's go back upstairs to my room."

"Just a peek," I said, opening the door and turning on the light. The room was being used for storage, its corners stacked with boxes of varying shapes and sizes.

Behind me, Megan emitted a dramatic, exasperated sigh. "See?" she whispered. "Nothing. Now let's go."

I was not so easily convinced. Perhaps there would be some real clue to Rose's life hidden somewhere among the boxes. I stepped inside the room and approached the closest one.

"Get back here!" Megan demanded.

I opened the top and looked inside.

"What the fuck are you doing?" Megan said angrily.

But I didn't listen to her. Inside the box were photographs. Men and women sitting in a restaurant, glasses raised, the words CONGRATULATIONS, JOE AND CATHY on a banner against the back wall. A wedding: the men dressed in baby blue tuxedos with big collars, the women plump and curvy with permed hair.

"Look at this," I said to Megan as I took a photograph of a little girl out of the box. She was standing in a sprinkler on a green lawn, holding her arms up, squealing with laughter.

"Put that back," Megan urged as she pulled my arm. "I mean it."

There were others: a row of girls in white dresses at a communion; a man with dark, unsmiling eyes leaning against an old stone wall. Then there was one, more recent, of a group of older men all dressed in suits. I recognized one of the men — the one from the previous picture, with the dark, unsmiling eyes — standing in the middle. There was an air of importance about him. And danger.

"What are you," Megan said, "fucking deaf or something? Let's go. *Now.*"

"What's the big deal?" I said, joking. "Don't you want to find out about Rose?"

Finally I pulled out another picture of a small girl standing in a courtyard, staring defiantly into the camera. There was something about the look in the girl's eyes that seemed familiar, one that I recognized but had not seen in any of the other photographs.

"Megan," I asked, "is that *you?*"

"Give me that," Megan demanded, snatching the photograph out of my hand. "Now, can we go, please?"

"No," I said, taking it back. "I want to see — "

I turned the picture over. On the back was written: *Mea. 3 years old. Brooklyn.*

"Who's Mea?" I said, confused.

"That's not yours," Megan replied, not answering my question. Seeming panicked, she snatched the picture back again. I wondered what Megan's picture was doing in an old box of photographs in Rose's apartment. And why she was called Mea.

Then, from behind us: a door opening. Then the sound of footsteps on the stairs. It was too late to run.

"What are you girls doing?"

We turned around. Rose was standing behind Megan.

"We, uh—" Megan began.

"—We were just looking at old photographs," I interjected.

"I'm not talking to you," Rose said to me, looking at Megan. "What have you done? What have you told her? What does she know?"

"Nothing!" Megan said in a flustered voice. I had never seen her act so nervous. "I tried to tell her not to come in here," Megan explained, "but—"

"But what?" Rose demanded.

Megan was silent. It was almost as if she was *afraid* of Rose.

"It's true," I said. "She told me not to come in. I was the one who wanted to see what was in here. It's not Megan's fault. Blame me."

"A likely story," Rose huffed. She turned to Megan again. "I'm going to have to tell your mother about this one!"

Megan's eyes glazed with panic. "No. I can explain—"

"I'll bet you can," Rose replied. "You always can."

I wondered what Rose meant by that. It was a strange thing to say to someone she wasn't supposed to know. As I stared at Rose, I saw for the first time how large and rounded her nose was. How dark her eyes were. The waxy grain of her face.

"Well, you can explain everything to your mother," Rose continued. "She's coming home tonight." Dejected, Megan hung her head. Rose looked at me. "You'd better leave now."

"What's going on here?" I said, looking at Megan.

"You have to leave," Megan said, not looking up.

"But why?" I asked.

Megan raised her face and looked at me with tears in her eyes.

"What? Megan—"

Before I could say anything more, Rose gripped me by the elbow and led me up to the top of the stairs. I was confused, and scared for Megan.

"Please tell me what's happening!" I cried.

Rose looked at me. "She didn't tell you anything?"

"Who?" I asked.

"Megan," Rose said.

I shook my head.

"I can't explain. You have to leave." Rose pulled me forward and opened the door.

"But wait," I implored. "I don't understand! *Please!* Tell me! What is going on?"

"Look," Rose said, "I'm sorry." Her eyes softened. "I know it's not your fault—"

"But what's going to happen to Megan?" I demanded.

Rose looked at me again. "Just go home," she said. "And forget what you think you saw."

Before I could protest, Rose pushed me outside and shut the door.

❧

That night, I was worried about Megan. Who *was* Rose? If she was just supposed to be renting the downstairs apartment, why did she know so much about Megan and her mother? I tried calling Megan, but there was no answer. Frantic, I replayed the scene over and over in my mind. What, exactly, had Rose meant about me forgetting what I thought I saw? What did I see? And who was Mea?

Before school the next morning, I went to Megan's house, but there were no cars in the driveway and no one came to the door. I stared at her window, hoping to see something or someone, but the curtains were drawn, straight and unmoving.

That day at school I kept expecting Megan to show up, but she didn't. As soon as classes were over, I ran to her house and banged on her front door again, but there was still no answer. I didn't understand what could be happening. How could Megan just disappear like that, again? I knocked on Rose's apartment door, but there was nothing. No one was home. The house was impenetrable.

I started home. I still couldn't understand why Megan would be so secretive over some old photographs. Or why Rose would care. As I walked down the street in a daze, I heard someone say my name. I stopped and raised my head, surprised. Blake Starfield. Again.

I almost couldn't believe it. We were standing in almost the same spot as when we had looked at the stars together.

"Hi."

"Hi."

Although he sat behind me every day, we rarely spoke to each other. I recalled our "Snowball" dance before Christmas.

Not knowing what to say, I looked down awkwardly at the ground.

"What are you doing?" he said.

"Nothing," I replied. "What about you?"

"Nothing."

We looked at each other.

"It sure is cold," I said.

"Yeah," he replied. "Sure is."

Our eyes met. He smiled at me, then looked down. I was overcome with a sudden desire to kiss Blake Starfield.

"Hey," I said, feeling peculiarly brazen. "I know a place in the woods. Wanna go?"

As I led Blake through the forest, our footsteps were soundless in the snow. When we came to the fort, Blake stared with wonder at the walls. Our candy wrapper wallpaper had been growing.

"This is where you and Megan come?"

"Uh-huh."

I watched as he ran his fingers over the walls. "Where do you get it all?" he asked.

"Get what?" I replied.

"The candy."

I watched his breath curl in the cold silence.

"Oh. You know," I said. "Here and there. Do you want some?"

"Want what?" he asked.

"Candy."

I took a step closer to him and reached into my pocket, pulling out a blue Tear Jerker. I put it in my palm and offered it to him. "Here," I said. "For you."

"I shouldn't," he said.

"You don't like candy?"

"No. I do. It's just that, you know, I'm on this medication." He paused, looking down at his feet. "I'm not supposed to eat sugar. It makes me too hyper. I don't know. The doctor says the medication will stop me from doing all that crazy shit, you know?"

I thought of one of the first things Megan had spelled out to me: C-O-N-S-P-I-R-A-C-Y.

"Oh. Too bad."

"So, what do you do here?" Blake asked.

"Tell stories," I replied.

"Really?" He smiled. "What kind of stories?"

I pointed at the candy wrapper wallpaper arched above our heads.

"Candy stories."

Blake looked up. "What? That's all you do?"

"Yeah," I said. "And eat it, too."

I held up the Tear Jerker to offer it to him again.

"You know, Megan has this theory," I said. "About kids and candy. And how all adults just want to control us." I paused. "One won't kill you, you know," I said. "Trust me."

He looked at me and smiled shyly.

"OK," he agreed, blushing. "But just this once."

I smiled back. Then I held the Tear Jerker up in front of his mouth. "Close your eyes."

He did as I said, and when his lids were closed, I gently pressed my index finger down on his bottom lip, slowly prying open his mouth. I took the blue gumball and brushed it on the inside of his lips. He laughed and said, *Hey, what are you doing* and I said, *Nothing* and put it inside his mouth, watching it stain his lips and teeth and tongue the color of the sky. Then I leaned forward and put my lips to his, and kissed him long and slow.

When we walked back hand in hand through the forest, there was no conversation between us. I knew once we were out of the woods, Blake and I would go our separate ways and pretend nothing had happened.

We let go of each other's hand as soon as we reached the sidewalk. As I watched him walk away, I could still taste him in my mouth; my lips still tingled from his kiss.

When I headed home, I saw someone far ahead of me, standing in the street, watching. A girl. My heart stopped. I didn't know how long she had been there or what she had seen. I started toward her in the hopes of recognizing her, but she ran down the darkened street.

It was clear she had seen everything.

Megan was not at school the next day. Or the next day after that. I wondered where she had gone this time, where her mother had taken her.

I went to her house every day, but there was never an answer at the door. And there were no cars in the driveway. To make matters worse, whenever I called, an automated voice told me the number I had dialed was no longer in service.

Ever suspicious of unexplained absences from his classroom, Mr. King asked me again if I knew where Megan was. I'd already played the death card. So I told him the truth. I didn't know, but I would still keep her homework for her. This answer

—which was obviously the correct one—seemed to please him. He said he would speak with Megan when she got back.

Days passed.

I fantasized about breaking into Megan's house, sneaking downstairs to Rose's apartment to look at the photographs in the storage room. I imagined how I would open each box, investigate every picture, analyze every word. Upstairs I would search through closets, cupboards, drawers, rooms. Looking for the one thing that would explain everything and unlock the mystery of Megan's past.

But I couldn't do that. Instead, I went to her house every day, trying to believe everything was all right. Hoping she was OK.

The truth was, without Megan around, I had no protection from MAL. Once again I had been left alone, and it was my fault that I wasn't watching when MAL came up behind me at lunch and knocked me face first into the snow. As I struggled to stand up, MAL laughed. Before I could even get up on my knees, Laura pushed me down with her boot.

Meredith kneeled beside me. "Guess what we heard?" she said. "That you have a boyfriend. A very *special* boyfriend."

My heart pounded with fear.

"I don't know what you're talking about," I said.

"Don't play dumb with us, dead girl," Laura told me. "You know *exactly* what we're talking about. And who. We know all about it. And we're going to tell *everyone*."

I barreled over on my side and displaced Laura's foot, throwing her off balance. As she fell to the ground, she toppled over Meredith. I pulled myself up, but Angela was waiting for me. As she grabbed me, Meredith and Laura got back on their feet and knocked me down again.

Then I saw Blake. From out of nowhere, he crashed into Meredith with a solid thud and pushed her away from me.

"Don't touch me, Quasi!" she shrieked. "Don't touch me, you freak!"

Instantly, Jason Cutler and Adam Diamond and David Pierce were on the scene. As soon as they came up behind Blake and pulled him off Meredith, Blake started swinging punches with his fists, fighting the three of them. A crowd gathered, watching. Then Mr. King came and tore the fighting boys apart, pulling Blake away. Blake flailed against Mr. King, kicking and screaming.

I watched as Mr. King forced Blake to his knees, pushing him to the ground.

"What happened here?" Mr. King demanded.

"He pushed me!" Meredith shouted. "He tried to hurt me!"

"He's dangerous!" Jason shouted, pointing at Blake. "And a freak, too!"

Blake exploded with fits of nervous laughter, his eyes rolling back in his head.

"That's enough from you," Mr. King said to Blake. His eyes hardened with scorn. "Don't you have anything to say for yourself?"

Blake continued laughing.

"Let's see how funny you think this is in front of Mr. Carter," Mr. King threatened. Just then, the bell rang and Mr. King cast his eyes over the crowd. "All right, let's break it up, people. Inside, *now*."

As we filed into the school, I watched Blake being led by Mr. King down the hallway to Mr. Carter's office.

Blake had stopped laughing.

Soon after that day Blake was moved to sit right in front of Mr. King's desk, in a special kind of relocation: to a place where he could be monitored more closely, contained and observed like an animal in a zoo.

No one could predict what he would do next. One afternoon Blake suddenly began screaming. Beating his head on his desk. For no apparent reason.

Some days he wouldn't talk at all. He no longer answered questions. He refused to do his assignments.

Then one day Blake just started throwing books across the classroom, pulling them off the shelves in great armfuls of rage and hurling them into the air, their pages flapping before they landed in a huge crash on the linoleum floor.

After each outburst, he was sent to Mr. Carter's office. There were no explanations. No excuses. And when he came back, his eyes were full of only a hollow, deadened fury. Medicated into total submission, Blake had become someone else.

I felt sick with helplessness.

TRUTH

When Megan returned to TWS, I first saw her waiting in Mr. Carter's office. She had changed her hair again. This time, it was a shaggy blunt cut, dyed black. Green eye shadow and thick black eyeliner completed her new look. She had been gone for almost ten days.

But she was not alone. Someone else was in Mr. Carter's office. A woman. I wondered if it really could be Megan's mother. I stayed out of sight. Watching. Waiting.

When the woman stepped out of Mr. Carter's office, I was stunned.

It was Rose.

When Megan saw me later that morning she pretended to be cheerful and happy, as if nothing had ever happened.

"Hello, dah-ling!" she exclaimed.

"Megan, what happened? Are you OK? Where have you been? I was worried—"

Megan laughed. "About what?"

I couldn't understand why she was acting this way. The last time I saw her she had tears in her eyes. There were so many questions I wanted to ask her. About the storage room. The photographs. About Rose. Her mother. Her.

"Where have you been? There was no answer at your door—"

"Yeah, so?"

"And your telephone was disconnected . . ."

"My mother forgot to pay the bill. It happens sometimes," Megan said casually. "Because she's away so much."

"On *business*."

"Yeah. On *business*."

I glared suspiciously at Megan.

"OK," Megan said. "You got me. You want to know the truth? Here's what happened. My mother got called away on business, again, except this time it was a different kind of business—you know, top secret, really hush-hush. So rather than leave me alone or take me with her, she sent me to my grandmother's house."

"Your grandmother's?"

"Yeah."

I said nothing.

"And when I got to her house and knocked on her door," Megan continued, widening her eyes, "I said, *Why, Grandmother, what big eyes you have,* and she said, *All the better to see you with, my dear . . .*"

She stopped, waiting for me to pick up her story, but I was not going to play that game this time.

"Megan, please tell me," I said. "What is going on?"

She looked into the distance. "My mom got called out of town again. That's all. LA."

"Los Angeles?"

"Yep. Ocean waves. Palm trees. Blue skies. It was beautiful."

I stared at her with disbelief. I wanted the names of hotels, streets. Her daily itinerary.

"But what about Rose?"

Megan flashed me an accusatory stare. "What about Rose?"

I couldn't hold back any longer. "I saw you. This morning. With Rose. Standing outside Mr. Carter's office."

Megan was uncharacteristically silent. I searched her face for the answer, but she wasn't giving anything away.

"Why did she have that picture of you?" I demanded.

"What picture of me?" Megan answered defensively.

"You know the one I'm talking about. The one that was downstairs, in the box, with all the other boxes, in the storage room, in *her* apartment."

"That picture wasn't of me," Megan said. "That was a picture of my mother."

"Why would Rose have a picture of your mother?" I asked.

"She doesn't have the picture of my mother, stupid," Megan answered. "We're just storing the boxes down there in the extra room."

"Is Rose your mother?" I blurted out.

Megan burst out laughing. "Oh, that is good!" she howled.

I crossed my arms. "Well, is she?" I demanded.

"No!" Megan said, still laughing. She pointed to her upper lip. "Tell me. Do you see any foreshadowing of the hereditary Rose'tache?"

"I'm *serious*," I said.

Megan stopped laughing and lowered her head and looked at the ground. "OK. Truth?"

I looked at her. Finally. "Yes. Truth."

"You know when I said Rose was a teacher? Well, she's not. She's my mom's cousin." Megan paused and took a deep breath. "She's got this whacko personality disorder where she thinks she's someone else."

"*What?*"

"I know. Rose thinks—get this—that she's on the run from some gang because she was witness to some murder, and now she's under some kind of protection from another rival gang. She's scared shitless that someone is going to find out who she really is and that the big bad gang will hunt her down and kill her. That's why she freaked out on you the other day."

I was speechless. Megan shook her head sadly.

"She's *crazy,*" Megan said. "Totally fucking looped. And when she doesn't take her medication on time, sometimes she gets a little weird. My mom just rents the place out to her because she feels sorry for her. That's all."

I thought about Rose's reaction to the photographs. Her words to Megan in the storage room. It all made sense.

"But why did she bring you to school?"

"Sometimes she just does stuff like that. When my mom can't."

I was stunned. "But—"

"But what?" Megan said.

"Why didn't you tell me?"

"Because," she said quietly, looking down. "I didn't want you to think we were weird. You know. Renting out to crazy cousins and everything."

"Oh."

Megan searched her pockets.

"Got any gum?" she asked. "I'm totally out."

I looked in my backpack. "Nothing."

"Oh well, that's OK," she replied sadly. "I didn't really want any, anyway."

"Liar," I said, the accusation hovering in the air between us.

After school that afternoon Megan and I went to the fort. We cocooned ourselves inside it, huddling under our blankets to stay warm.

Megan talked about LA, painting vivid pictures of her and her mother "going shopping." Her and her mother "taking long walks." Her and her mother "lounging poolside." It all seemed idyllic. Perfect. Almost too perfect.

It wasn't that I didn't believe Megan. I did. But there was something in the way she described the trip that made it seem as if what she was telling me had already been told before, like a memory that had been selected from a stockpile of memories, culled from movies and television, stolen from other people's lives. There was truth to what she was telling me. I just didn't know whose.

Just as it was getting dark, Megan looked at me and said, "Can I tell you a story?"

She had never asked for my permission before. It made me wonder what kind of story she was going to tell me.

"Sure," I said.

And then she began: "Once upon a time, in a land not too far away, there was a girl named Melanie who lived with her mother. Melanie's mother had a very special job that took her to many different hotels across the city, and on the days when Melanie's mother couldn't get a babysitter, Melanie would sometimes have to go to work with her mother.

"Melanie's favorite hotel was the Seven Dwarfs Inn. She loved each of the small brown cottages with their white-shuttered windows and little picket fences, their knotty pine furniture and lace curtains. She also loved the pool in the middle of the courtyard, surrounded by the rose-covered trellis."

Megan stopped and leaned against the wall of the fort, making herself more comfortable.

"OK?" I asked.

"OK," she replied. Then she continued.

"As soon as they checked in, Melanie changed into her swimsuit to go swim in the pool. Melanie's mother would soon be expecting her friends to visit, and Melanie was not to disturb them, no matter what. Before they arrived, Melanie's mother would walk around the dark cottage in her high heels, smoking cigarettes and carefully dressing, making sure not to spoil her nails or her hair.

"'*Mirror, mirror, on the wall,*' her mother would say, '*who's the fairest of them all?*'

"And Melanie would look at her mother and say, '*You are, Mother, you are.*'

"When her mother asked her to fetch some ice, Melanie skipped down the cobbled lane to the ice machine, white plastic bucket in hand. When she went back to the cottage, her mother would be sitting on the bed with a glass, holding the bottle of Southern Comfort she had brought. Melanie would drop one, two, three ice cubes into the glass and watch as her mother poured the bourbon over them. She always drank two glasses: one very fast and then another one very slowly. While her mother was drinking, Melanie would read her stories from her favorite fairy-tale book.

"After she finished drinking the two glasses, Melanie's mother would look at her watch and tell Melanie it was time for her to go to the pool because the first of Mommy's friends was going to be there any minute. *'Besides,'* Melanie's mother would say as she drew back the lacy white curtains and looked out into the sunny afternoon, *'it's a beautiful day.'*

"From the pool, Melanie watched the first of her mother's friends arrive. She had never met any of them, but she imagined them carrying armfuls of flowers for her mother. Through the lens of her scuba mask, Melanie watched them disappear behind the door of the cottage, reemerging a half-hour later into the bright afternoon.

"When the last of her mother's four friends had left, Melanie left the pool and went back to the cottage. The ashtray was full of cigarette butts, the bottle of Southern Comfort almost empty. Melanie would lean over the edge of the bed and stare down at her mother and wake her.

"Drowsily, her mother's eyes would open.

"*'Mirror, mirror, on the wall,'* she would say to Melanie, *'who's the fairest of them all?'*

"*'You are, Mother,'* Melanie would reply. *'You are.'*

"Then Melanie's mother would sit upright on the bed and hold out a glass. Melanie would drop one, two, three ice cubes into the glass and watch as her mother poured in some Southern Comfort. Just as before, she always drank two glasses: one very fast and then another one very slowly."

Megan stopped. It was dark outside. Snow, thick and wet, drifted silently to the ground.

"Where's the candy?" I asked.

"What?"

"You know, the candy. I thought every story was supposed to be about candy."

"You didn't like it?" she said.

"It wasn't that I didn't like it. It just sounded so . . . *real.*" I shivered with cold, rubbing my hands together. "Is it true?" I asked.

Megan drew her blanket tighter around her shoulders. "Does it matter?" she answered.

I thought about this for a moment. "No. Yes."

"Why?"

"Because if it was true, it would be a different kind of story."

There was a brief silence. I blew on my hands to warm them.

"So?" Megan said. "It's still a story, isn't it?"

I felt her eyes staring shrewdly at me, looking, waiting.

"I'm not so sure anymore," I said.

"Not so sure about what?"

"About what's true. Because there's no difference between what's real or unreal. All that matters is the truth."

"No," Megan said. "Everything exists, real or unreal. The truth is only a matter of perspective."

"Yes, but—"

"But what?"

"Is it true?"

I strained my eyes to see Megan sitting in the fort beside me, but the shape of her body had become indistinct in the darkness.

Megan paused, considering her answer.

"You decide," she said.

❧

The following day we went to see Edie. When we entered her room, the curtains were drawn and she was lying in bed sleeping; the TV was turned off. It was odd to enter her room without hearing the clapping and cheering of studio audiences. Megan and I stood behind the cart, watching her sleep, her breathing soundless and eerie. We didn't want to disturb her, so we carefully turned the cart around and tiptoed toward the door.

"Aren't you forgetting something, my darlings?"

Megan and I stopped and turned. I noticed Edie looked weak, tired. Megan wheeled the cart beside her bed.

"You weren't really going to leave me without candy for a week, now were you?" We watched as Edie picked out her usual favorites, selecting each candy slowly and carefully.

After she had paid, she took out her little black book from the bedside table. As she opened it, her fingertips lingered lovingly over the words. I stared at her hands. They were wrinkled and milky white, the fingernails as round as moons.

Then I saw the tattoo. On the inside of her left forearm, just above her wrist.

A rectangular set of numbers. Faded and dark blue. I quickly looked at Megan and our eyes met. She had seen it, too.

"Now," Edie said calmly, turning over a page, "we must continue with our story. Do you remember where we finished off last time?"

I tried hard not to stare at the tattoo, but I couldn't stop myself.

"Francesca had just been turned into a giant . . ." I answered.

"And then," Megan added, "she blew away Queen Goren."

"That's right," Edie said, turning the page. "Aha. Here we are. Right here—"

"Are you sure you want to read today?" I asked, interrupting her. "Because if you're feeling tired, we can do it another day."

Edie looked up at me and smiled. "Nonsense, darling! I feel perfectly fine!" She looked at the open book under her hands. "Now. Are we ready?"

Megan and I nodded and sat down on the edge of the mattress beside her. Story time was about to begin.

"Francesca, who was now taller than the tallest tree, raised her foot and took a step. The earth trembled and shook as if from an earthquake, the field buckling in waves beneath her. When she picked her foot up again, Francesca was alarmed to see that she had cleared an entire stretch of forest in her colossal footprint.

"Her head above the clouds, Francesca looked all the way down at her feet and shuddered to think of the deer and birds she had trampled on, what trees and flowers she had destroyed. With every movement of her body she wreaked chaos and destruction.

"Sadly, Francesca now realized she could never return home. For how could she see the small house in the woods without stepping on it and crushing it—and her poor father inside? Because of her size, all the world and everything Francesca loved in it was in peril.

"Tears like tiny oceans fell from her eyes. And as her teardrops touched the ground, trees and vines and ferns began to magically appear, sprouting full grown. Within moments

Francesca was standing in a wild garden, her giant arms and legs tangled with green. But Francesca, so afraid of harming anyone or anything, did not move. She remained standing, as still as a statue.

"Now, you may think it would be hard to stand that long. But after the first few hours it became second nature to Francesca. The weeks and months passed. And, gradually, Francesca's feet became submerged in the earth. As the ground gave way beneath her, her ankles became engulfed. Then her legs. And as she sank farther and farther down, her chest became buried, then her arms, until the earth had almost swallowed her up, its moss and ambling vines spreading over her. Only her head remained visible.

"The years went by. And there grew a garden so dark and dense around Francesca that the features of her face were barely noticeable; the slope of her nose and the gentle curve of her mouth were hidden behind a great wall of green.

"It would not be long before the earth would claim Francesca entirely. She would sink, inch by inch, into the ground, the roots of the forest penetrating her flesh, forking out through her heart and lungs.

"But Francesca was not afraid.

"Then one day she heard a peculiar sound. It was high and frantic, as if it was a little voice speaking to her. But Francesca ignored it, thinking it was only the sound of the wind in the trees.

"If Francesca could have turned her head she would have seen that it was a fly, so tiny against the cavern of her ear that it seemed like a speck of dust wavering in the air.

"It was Ferdinand. He was alive."

Edie stopped and closed the book and took a long, deep breath.

"And then what happens?" I asked.

She gave me a wry sideways glance.

"Have patience. The end will come. And when it does, remember, endings aren't always what you want them to be. Or what you expect." Edie reached for the remote. "That's how life is. That's how stories are." She looked at me and smiled sweetly. "Everything ends." I watched as Edie secured the book in her bedside drawer.

Once again I saw the tattoo of dark blue on her forearm. Noticing the direction of my stare, Edie reached for a tin of candy.

"Black currant drop?" she asked Megan and me as she turned on *The Price Is Right*.

I stared at Edie with wonder and fascination. What did the Francesca story really mean? To her? And who told it to her? So long ago? During a very dark time?

Above us, on the television screen, contestants ran and leapt with joy, their faces bursting with happiness.

As our eyes met, I reached forward and took a candy. The dark sour flavor was sharp on my tongue.

TRAP EERHT
EHT DNE

MAGIC LOVE POTION

ON VALENTINE'S DAY, Mr. King gave everyone a special assignment for art class. Using images from newspapers and magazines, we had to create a collage about an object or activity that we loved. David Pierce joked that if Blake was going to make a picture about what he loved, Quasi would have to go home to get some of his own "magazines." Mr. King ignored him.

As we gathered our materials, I looked across the room at Megan. I knew her collage could be about only one thing. Candy: her beloved one and only.

In the time that I had known her, I had never seen Megan eat anything else. She didn't eat food. Not real food, anyway. She was a machine fueled by sucrose, dextrose, glucose, and Red Dye No. 5.

It had been a few weeks since Megan's last disappearance, and in that time we hadn't been to her house—or Rose's apartment—once. We went to the fort instead. I assumed the reason for this was that Megan was embarrassed about another possible encounter with Rose, but there were still so many unanswered questions.

Whenever I tried to ask her anything—about her mother or

Rose or her life before she came to Woodland Hills—she evaded my questions. Eventually I just stopped asking her.

For our collages, Megan and I worked beside each other, flipping through the pages of glossy magazines, scissors poised in our hands. Every now and then we stopped to recharge ourselves with candied cinnamon hearts. Our hands were stained bright red, thick with the scent of cinnamon.

Megan turned and faced me, sticking out her tongue. I knew Tracey Reid was watching, and I should have cared about who saw us, but I didn't. I stuck mine out at her, too. The rapid snip-snip-snip of Tracey's scissors was right behind us—Tracey had engineered her own assembly line: images fell and scattered at her feet like fallen leaves.

"Hey, Tracey," Megan said. "Wanna suck face?"

Tracey looked up and gave us a smug, knowing smile.

After Mr. King's strategic relocation of Blake to the front of the classroom, he had decided it would be best to place Tracey Reid in Blake's former seat. With her behind me, I was suddenly under constant scrutiny. One afternoon while I was responding to a note from Megan, I caught her peering over my shoulder. Later that day, Megan and I witnessed her meeting MAL in the schoolyard, apparently passing on information to gain favor with them.

Tracey had always wanted to be friends with Meredith and Angela and Laura. Finally, she had something they wanted. And now she was their spy.

Later that afternoon, I found two valentines slipped into my desk. One was from Megan: a pink paper heart outlined with real cinnamon hearts. The message said GNILRAD EB

ENIM. The other, which was on a sheet of lined binder paper, had only a small cluster of black stars drawn in the shape of a heart.

As we walked home from school, Megan asked who had given me a valentine.

"Just you," I lied.

"Nothing from Quasi?"

"His name is not Quasi," I said.

"So you did get one." Megan smirked.

"So what if I did?"

"I knew it!" She laughed, clapping. "What did it say?"

"I'm not telling you!"

"C'mon—"

"No!"

"*Pleeeeeze?*" Megan batted her eyelashes up at me. "I prom- ise not to laugh."

I knew she couldn't be serious. She was only mocking me.

"You *will* laugh!" I protested.

"I won't!"

"Really?"

"Really."

"Promise?"

"Promise. Girl Scout's honor." She struck a solemn salute.

"You were never a Girl Scout!" I cried in disbelief.

"I was, too!" Megan protested. "At least, until I got kicked out."

"For what?"

"For saying I didn't want to be part of some fucking weird Hitler Youth kind of thing." She grinned. "Now tell me. What did Quasi say? Anything about his future plans to be a porn star?" Megan began to pant heavily. "Oh you're *soooooo* big and you're getting bigger and bigger and *ohhhhhhhhhhhhhhh*—"

Abruptly, she stopped panting. "Well, looky who's a-coming," she said.

I turned around. Tracey Reid was walking toward Megan and me, pretending to ignore us.

"Hey, Spy Girl," Megan said. "Where you going?"

"Wouldn't you like to know?" Tracey said.

"Yeah, I would," Megan replied, grabbing her arm.

"Let go of me!"

"Not until you tell me where you're going." Megan kept a firm grip on Tracey's arm. "Can I tell you a secret?" Megan said in a hoarse whisper.

Tracey's dark brown eyes widened with interest.

"The fact is, Tracey," Megan began, "you're just too nice to be friends with Meredith and Angela and Laura. It doesn't matter what you do or say—they will never, ever accept you as one of them. No matter what you tell them. Or who you try to be. Face it, Spy Girl. They're just using you."

"That's not true!" Tracey said defiantly. "As a matter of fact, I'm going over to Meredith's house right now. She's having a special Valentine's Day party. For her closest friends. Which includes me, not you." Then, as an afterthought, she added, "You fucking *loser.*" Tracey's words hung in the air with an astonishing ferocity. It was so unlike her.

In a quick gesture of surrender, Megan released Tracey's arm. Tracey walked brusquely away, turning around and giving us the finger.

Megan laughed.

"C'mon," she said, turning to me, her eyes sparkling. "Let's go back to my place. I have an idea."

When we got to her house, Megan went straight through the front door into the kitchen and pulled a chair away from the table and butted it up against the wall. Stepping onto the counter, she reached her hand into the highest cupboard.

"What are you doing?" I asked, looking around the kitchen for proof of Mrs. Chalmers's presence.

"Looking for"—she pulled out a white plastic medicine bottle—"these." She grinned.

I studied the sink, the countertop, the kitchen table, trying to find evidence. But there were no empty coffee cups. No dirty dishes. Nothing.

"What are those?" I asked.

Megan jumped off the chair and dangled the little plastic bottle in front of my nose.

"What are they?" I asked, still looking around for some remnants of Megan's mother.

Megan shrugged. "I dunno."

There were no pictures on the refrigerator. None on the wall. But I had never seen any photographs anywhere in their house. Except in Rose's apartment, downstairs.

"What do you mean, you don't know?" I pressed.

"I mean I don't know," Megan rebutted. She winked at me and smiled, forcing a southern drawl. "But it'll shore be real interestin' to find out, now, won't it, darlin'?" She paused as she noticed my surveying eyes. "Whatcha lookin' for?"

"Oh, nothing," I said, turning all my attention to her and

the plastic bottle. "But they could be anything," I warned Megan. "Maybe they're *drugs*."

Megan looked me straight in the eye. "No, really," she said. "What are you looking for?"

Then I remembered something she had once said. "Oh, you know, skeletons, dark secrets, body parts," I said nervously.

Megan gave me a funny smile and shoved the bottle of capsules in my pocket.

"Of course they're *drugs*, dum-dum," she said. "We just don't know what kind."

"I'm not taking those," I said.

Megan laughed as she pushed me out of the kitchen. "Oh, they're not for you, darling. Or me."

"What?" I said as I took a quick inventory of the living room. Still nothing.

"Just think of it as a magic love potion. It *is* Valentine's Day, after all." Megan struck a pose in the front hallway: Cupid with his bow and arrow.

"What are we going to do with them?" I asked as I followed her out the door.

Megan grinned and draped her arm around my shoulder. "You'll see."

When Megan rang the bell at Meredith's house, Mrs. McKinnon answered the door. She was dressed in a velvet pantsuit, gold chains dripping from her neck. She had dyed her hair a dark red, her lipstick and fingernails in a complementary shade. In her left hand she cradled a glass with only ice cubes at the bottom. Smoking one of her French cigarettes, she smiled wearily and helplessly gestured us inside.

"It's lovely to see you again, Margaret." Megan beamed. "Happy Valentine's Day!"

A bewildered look passed over Mrs. McKinnon's face. It was obvious she didn't remember who we were.

"It's nice to see you, too . . ." she fumbled, searching Megan's face for a name.

Megan stepped forward. "Marcia."

"Oh. Of course. And—"

"Jan," Megan said, smiling, pulling me beside her. "Our little sister Cindy couldn't make it."

Obviously drunk, Meredith's mom studied us intensely, lowering her eyebrows and pursing her lips together as she staggered slightly.

"We're here for Meredith's party," Megan assured her.

"Ah. Of course," she said. Meredith's mom stared blankly into the room.

"Margaret?"

"Oh, just over there," she slurred, rattling the ice cubes in her glass. "Downstairs."

As we watched Meredith's mom sway through the living room toward the sofa, Megan leaned over and whispered into my ear, "Cupid, aim your arrow. It's time for *love.*"

Needless to say, when Megan and I descended the staircase and made our way into Meredith's rec room, MAL was shocked.

"What the . . . ?" Angela gasped.

"I don't believe it!" cried Laura.

"What the fuck are you doing here?" Meredith demanded, getting up. "You weren't invited. Get out of here," she ordered. "Right now."

Megan and I looked around. Besides MAL, Tracey Reid was there. And Jason and Adam and David, too. All of them were sitting on the floor and on the couch, in the darkened glow of red light bulbs, listening to some dance music. In the corner was a refreshment table heaped with bowls of chips and candy. In the center of the table was a punch bowl filled with red juice. Stuck on the walls were cut out paper hearts. Blood red streamers were twisted into the corners of the room, cascading down the walls. It looked like a cutesy Satanic clubhouse.

"What? Not invited? But that's not what Tracey told us," Megan stated.

MAL shot Tracey Reid a condemning look. "I didn't say anything!" Tracey said, defending herself.

"But Tracey," Megan said, pouting, "you said we could come, too!"

"What do you want?" Meredith demanded.

Megan stood boldly before her. "I want to join you," she said.

Meredith laughed hysterically. "Who? You? Join us? I don't think so."

My heart pounded. This was the part of Megan's plan that I was worried about. Her making them believe that she wanted to join them: to defect and join the dark side. Sure, I had told Megan that we might be able to get into the party. But we might not be able to get out.

"Hey, princess," Jason said to me, "where's your knight in shining armor? Sir Quasi?" He paused. "He could really *bone* up on his partying."

While MAL and Tracey laughed, Megan dropped to her

knees and bowed before Meredith. She raised her arms up and down, her body swaying in the eerie red light.

"What the hell?" Laura said.

Mesmerized, the group stood watching. Meredith's icy blue eyes glowed as if she were possessed. It was almost as if by shocking them Megan had hypnotized them, too.

"Omigod," Tracey said. "This is so weird—"

Then, suddenly, Megan's eyes turned white, rolling back in her head. She crumpled to the floor and began convulsing, her whole body shaking violently on the carpet in a spastic fit.

This was my cue.

"Omigod!" Tracey screamed. "What's happening?"

Everyone, including the boys, crowded over Megan, watching.

"She's having a seizure," I cried. "She just needs her medicine!"

I grabbed the plastic medicine bottle from Megan's pocket and ran toward the refreshment table. As I poured Megan a glass of punch, I dumped the powdered contents from the mystery capsules into the bowl, then ran back to her side. From my pocket I produced an identical plastic medicine bottle filled with tic tacs. As I forced one into Megan's mouth with a gulp of punch, her body shuddered in my arms.

"Is she OK?" Tracey asked.

"Wait," I said. "Wait."

Finally, Megan's eyes opened. Silence pervaded the room.

"Are you OK?" I said. Megan and I had determined that would be the code phrase if my mission to the punch bowl was successful. If it was a failure, the alternate code was *"Do you need more medicine?"* Then we would have left. Immediately.

Megan smiled.

"Yeah, I'm OK," she said, slowly sitting up. "I just need to rest. It must have been the lights."

Meredith narrowed her eyes. Then she leaned over and whispered something to Laura and Angela and Tracey. Immediately they busied themselves with pouring cups of punch and distributing them to everyone except us. Megan and I remained sitting on the floor, held hostage by our own operation.

"I don't know what you're up to," Meredith said, "but let me make three things clear. One: you can *never* join us. Two: I don't fucking *care* if you drop dead. And three"—Laura handed her a cup of punch—"I still don't want you here. So as soon as you can get your sorry ass up, spaz, I want you out of here. And that goes for you, too, dead girl."

Meredith raised her cup ceremoniously in the air.

"I'd like to propose a toast," she called out. "To friends." She saluted, bowing to Laura and Angela and Tracey and Jason and Adam and David. "And *enemies*," she said, referring to Megan and me.

United against us, MAL clinked their cups of punch in the blood red air above our heads, and drank.

Soon after that, just as we had been ordered to, we left the party. But we didn't go far. Instead, after saying goodbye to Mrs. McKinnon, Megan and I sneaked around to the back of Meredith's house and secretly watched the rest of the party unfold through an outside basement window. They were, as Megan said they would be, the best seats in the house. We could see almost everything.

It all started with Tracey Reid, who looked as if she had decided she didn't need to wear her shoes. Or socks. All of a sudden she started dancing, swinging her arms in the air and twirling around in crazy pirouettes. Following her lead, Laura and Angela took off their shoes and socks, scrunching up their toes in the carpet, convincing Meredith to do the same. She was hypnotized by the red lights and the twist of red streamers in the center of the room, captivated by the walls of paper hearts.

It didn't take long for Jason and Adam and David to take off their shoes and shirts. Then they turned up the music. The girls oohed and aahed, admiring the way the boys danced, slow and goofy in the dim glow of the red light, their lean, hairless torsos undulating to the music, their heads thrown back in abandon. Meredith danced her way around them, urging Laura and Angela and Tracey to do the same.

Soon all of them were dancing in various states of undress, moving to the rhythm of the music, their eyes closed. They all danced together. Then alone. And as they danced, they drank more punch. And as they drank more punch, they danced.

David raised his arms from his sides as if he were flying. Adam jumped up and down with a handful of streamers. Jason gyrated in front of the red lights. Meredith spun around and around, making herself dizzy and falling to the floor, collapsing with laughter. Laura put her ear against Angela's chest as if she was trying to hear her heart beating inside her body. Tracey looked as if she thought the walls were throbbing.

Then all of them suddenly must have gotten hungry.

Megan and I watched as they all followed Meredith to the refreshment table and scooped up handfuls of candy, feeding one another. Adam placed a chocolate heart on David's tongue;

Laura and Angela ate cinnamon hearts out of each other's hands. In a weird threesome, Tracey and Meredith fed Jason Cutler jellybeans as he lay on the floor, laughing. Then Tracey and Meredith got down on the floor with him. Then Adam. And Laura. And Angela. And David.

Then Adam was kissing David and David was kissing Laura and Laura was kissing Angela and Angela was kissing Jason and Jason was kissing Meredith and Meredith was kissing Tracey, and they all started kissing and licking and touching one another.

A demon Cupid, Megan had created a human pyramid of spontaneous erotic combustion, fueled by candy and charged by lust. She smiled in the red light.

"Isn't it delicious?" she whispered, her dark eyes dancing with devilish delight.

I studied her profile, mesmerized. She was really enjoying watching MAL's humiliation. I looked through the window, then looked away again. I couldn't bear to watch. What had we done? And why had I gone along with her? I could have stopped her. But I didn't.

Entranced, I nodded, secretly afraid of what we had unleashed.

SWEET REVENGE

ON MONDAY MORNING, MAL did not come to school. Neither did Jason Cutler, David Pierce, or Adam Diamond. Or Tracey Reid.

Mr. King matter-of-factly informed the class that they were absent because they had all come down with the same illness, which was apparently from some kind of food poisoning. Megan and I exchanged glances across the classroom.

The truth was, Megan didn't know that the punch had already been spiked, thanks to Adam and David and Jason, who had been hoping for some heated rounds of spin-the-bottle. Unbeknownst to Megan and me, the powder we added from the blue capsules only enhanced their psychedelic love cocktail, making it a true magic potion.

We fantasized about the look on Margaret McKinnon's face as she staggered downstairs to find her daughter and her friends eating cinnamon hearts out of one another's mouths and licking chocolate off each other. We imagined with great delight the dull edge of them coming down: struggling to remember what they had done, trying to find their clothes. The embarrassing phone calls Meredith's mother had to make. Trying as soberly as possible to explain to Mrs. Pierce and Mrs.

Diamond and Mrs. Cutler what their sons had done. Or explaining to Tracey Reid's mother why her daughter didn't know where her underwear was. Or trying to remember who Marcia and Jan were.

When MAL did return to school, something in them had changed. There were no more stabbing stares at lunchtime; there was no more name-calling. No bullying. Nothing. Just a strange, eerie silence. Even Tracey Reid had been transformed, haunted by what had happened.

It didn't matter what Jason and Adam and David had done to MAL. Or what they had intended to do. As boys, their promiscuous actions were both expected and forgivable. But what Megan and I had done was unacceptable. We were truly the guilty ones. And what we had done was more than just humiliate MAL. We had shamed them. And we were going to pay.

At first I thought their silence was a sign of surrender, an acknowledgment of their defeat. But, like any warring tribe, they were only building up their reserves, planning their revenge. There was no way I could have predicted the force of their wrath.

One week later, after school on an unseasonably warm winter day, Megan and I walked through the forest toward the fort. Everywhere the snow was melting into soft icy slush. Megan packed some snow into a plastic cup, poured some grape soda pop over the top, and crunched the grapey crystals of ice between her teeth. The world was her giant Sno-Cone.

When we got inside the fort, I took out a Popeye Candy Stick and held it between my fingers, studying the reddish pink dye around its small stubby end. I nibbled at its tip while Megan pulled out a package of Thrills gum.

"Want some?" she asked.

"Sure," I replied.

Megan held out the package.

"They taste like soap, you know."

"What are you talking about?"

"Thrills. The soap candy. They taste like soap."

I took the package from Megan's hand and stared at the small purple squares of gum in my palm.

"He was too small a man," Megan announced. "Too small and too short with too clean a pair of hands. Mercer couldn't stop thinking about those hands, so soft and fine, the fingernails neat and trim and bloodless."

"What are you talking about?" I said.

Megan stood up and hunched her back. "'That's him?' Spider asked." Megan used a thin and whiny voice. Then normal again: "Mercer studied his apprentice, appraising his long thin arms and legs, his white womanly fingers."

"Are you telling a story?"

Megan's eyes flared. "Just shut up and listen!"

I was silent.

"'I don't get it,' Spider said." Megan used the whiny voice again. "'*Him*, a murderer? No way. I mean, look at him.'"

"Spider scuttled across the windowless room and stood before the man in the chair, whose head was hooded, his hands and feet bound. Laughing, Spider placed his hand between the man's legs and crunched his fist. The man cried out in a high, muffled shriek."

Megan paused for effect.

"'See?' Spider laughed, looking back at Mercer. *'No balls.'* Spider flashed Mercer a toothy, arrogant smile. The piercing black of his eyes like two piss holes in the snow. Wearily, Mercer reached into his pocket.

"'Whatcha got?' Spider asked.

"*'Thrills,'* Mercer replied.

"'Oh, yeah,' Spider said, lighting a cigarette, 'Thrills. The candy that tastes like soap.'

"'No, they don't,' Mercer said.

"'Yeah, they do,' Spider replied."

Megan fixed her gaze on me.

"Mercer looked Spider in the eye. Then he opened his mouth and put the small purple square of gum on his tongue. Spider's black eyes stared, watching Mercer's mouth move.

"'Well,' Spider said, 'taste like soap, don't they?'

"Mercer looked at the man in the chair. He was well dressed. Well groomed. *Clean.* The flavor of Mercer's gum was already fading.

"Spider dropped his cigarette on the floor and squashed it with his heel. 'They said he said he was innocent. That he didn't kill Joey. That he loved him like a brother. That he'd been set up, you know. Likely story. Oh, and that he had a wife and kid, too. You want me to waste him?' he asked.

"In the chair, the man rocked violently back and forth, rage suffocating in his throat. 'They always fight back in the end, eh, Mercer?' Spider said, catching a fly with a quick swoop of his hand.

"Mercer watched as Spider raised the insect to his lips and swallowed it in one bite.

"Spider was right, Mercer thought, sickened. They always fought back in the end. Especially the innocent ones. But he had a job to do.

"He got up and walked toward the man in the chair, then steadied his gun against his head. Then Mercer pulled the trigger, feeling it squeeze tight and then spring back sharply against his finger. The man's head slumped forward, the hooded cloth black with blood.

"Mercer leaned over and spat out the lump of gum at the dead man's feet.

"'You're right,' he said to Spider. 'They do taste soapy.'"

My gum turned gray and waxy in my mouth. "Ewww," I said. "That's so *gross*."

Megan looked away. "Yeah. Fucked up, isn't it?" she said quietly.

As she pushed back a lock of black hair from her face, I noticed she had flecks of green in her eyes. And in that instant, I realized I didn't really know who she was.

It was getting dark. Cold. I folded my arms around me. I looked at Megan again. I didn't know what the Thrills story meant. What she was trying to tell me. Since her last disappearance, I had listened more closely to the details of her stories. But I didn't know how to ask her what the real truth was. I searched her face again, hoping she would tell me.

"Why are you looking at me like that?" she asked. "It's *just* a story."

Suddenly she grabbed my hand and looked over my shoulder, her eyes wide with fear.

"What is it?" I said, turning around, my heart pounding.

There, standing in the doorway, were the three masked pigs, each of them wielding a shovel. With them was Tracey Reid, her hands bound and her mouth gagged, her face full of panic.

Whoever says they haven't met a terrorist doesn't know the heart of a teenage girl.

MAL were wearing the same masks they had worn at Halloween: the same hideous identical plastic pig masks. Their bodies were again covered in long black coats; black boots were on their feet and black gloves on their hands.

Megan and I may have been faster than they were, but before we could make a run for it it was too late. MAL stormed into the fort and kicked us to the ground. We were outnumbered, again. As I struggled to stand on my feet, one of them jumped on me from behind and twisted my arms behind my back. I swerved my head around, trying to identify who was who, but it was impossible to tell. I squirmed on my stomach while my hands and feet were bound with duct tape. The sound ripped inside my ears. I watched as the other two pinned Megan to the ground, sitting on her back, holding her arms and legs.

"You fucking bitches!" she shouted.

I craned my neck to look at Tracey Reid, kneeling in the corner of the fort, weeping. Her face was a swollen mess of tears.

Before I could say anything, one of the pigs pulled me up by the hair and pushed me outside the fort. Then the pigs shoved Megan and Tracey out of the fort behind me. As my body landed with a thud on the ground, my face was forced down in the snow. The cold crystals burned my forehead. Then I felt the sharp tip of a shovel pressed into the back of my neck. Megan was forced to the ground beside me. As the other two pigs held her down, she was still shouting, ordering them to let us go.

"Shut up!" the pig holding me yelled at Megan, cold and heartless. It was Laura. "Shut up," she said again.

"Once upon a time," another of the pigs began, "there were three girls." It was Meredith. "Three girls and three little pigs."

"Who went for a walk in the woods—" The third pig's voice. Angela.

Laura: "And they walked deeper and deeper into the woods, where no one would ever find them—"

Angela: "Because the three girls and the three little pigs were going to play a little game with each other—"

Meredith: "And the three girls would lose."

Angela: "And the three little pigs would walk away—"

Laura: "Leaving the three girls in the woods—"

Angela: "Alone—"

Meredith: "To *die*."

Megan laughed hysterically.

"Yeah, right! You don't scare me, you fucking pussies!" she yelled. "Go on! I dare you—just try to kill me, you bitches!"

I turned my head and watched Megan try to break free, but Meredith stopped and caught her, throwing her back down against the snow. Megan struggled like a bug on her back, try-ing to get upright again.

"Megan!" I cried out, but Laura pushed my face back into

the snow and nudged the tip of the shovel even harder into the back of my neck. She breathed into my ear. "Shut up, dead girl. Shut up." She pressed my head into the snow again, the cold slush scraping against my face.

"Now," I heard Meredith say presumably to Tracey, "start digging. Three holes. Here, here, and here." I heard the sound of duct tape being torn apart.

"What?" Tracey answered.

My heart thumped with panic. What was happening?

"You heard me," Meredith said calmly. *"Start digging."*

Tracey started sobbing uncontrollably. "But you said no one was going to get hurt," she begged. "Please, I can't—"

"Now," Meredith ordered.

I struggled to turn my head to see what was going on, but Laura pressed her foot on my neck. "Don't even try it," she said.

Laura scooped snow into her hand and rubbed it in my face. It was cold and sharp. I looked at Megan. She was lying face-up in the snow; Meredith's black boot was on her throat.

"Leave them alone!" Megan said. "If it's me you want! Let them go!"

"Silence!" Meredith shouted, pressing her boot down harder on Megan's throat. "I don't want to hear one more fucking word from your fucking stupid little mouth!"

Megan was gagging and coughing, her face turning red, eyes bulging.

"Stop it!" I screamed. "Stop it! Stop it!"

Meredith laughed and released her boot. Then Megan spat at Meredith. Instantly, Meredith kicked her over with her foot, forcing her face into the snow.

"Let me go!" Megan shouted. But Meredith had her pinned

to the ground. Like me, she couldn't move. I felt sick and help-less.

Laura threw a shovel at Tracey's feet. "*You* told them about the party. *You* do it," she ordered. "*Now.*"

Whimpering, Tracey slowly bent over and picked up the shovel. I tried to see what she would do with it, but again my face was forced back into the snow. The ice was burning cold.

"Don't worry, dead girl," Laura whispered ominously, "you'll get to see soon enough."

For a moment there was only the sound of Tracey sobbing. Then: the sound of the shovel. Over and over again, the dull, ceaseless chip of the steel blade cutting through the icy snow. And Tracey crying.

"Hurry up!" Meredith yelled at her. "You're taking too long!"

I heard the sound of footsteps crunching through the snow. Then another shovel digging. It must have been Angela. After a moment, the sound stopped, then resumed again.

"Now here," Meredith ordered. "And here."

The digging started again. Then stopped. Then started. What were they doing? After some time, the digging of both shovels stopped. I shivered with cold. My face was numb.

Forcefully, Laura pulled my head up by the hair so I could see. Then Megan.

There, side by side in the snow, were three shallow graves, crudely dug.

"Oh very nice," Megan said. "And just my size, too—"

"Shut up!" Meredith shouted.

The three of them dragged Megan, me, and Tracey to our separate holes. As we were pushed into the graves, MAL carelessly shoveled the snow back over us, burying us up to our necks so that only our faces were exposed. I shut my eyes as the snow landed on me. It was muddy and wet and cold.

Next to me, Tracey began to weep. Again. "No! Please, Meredith! No!" she implored. "You can't do this!"

"Me?" Meredith laughed. "Oh, no—it's not me, Tracey. It's *you.* Just like Laura said. *You* invited them to the party—"

"But I didn't," Tracey sobbed. "I didn't, I didn't!"

"You *lied* to us," Angela said.

"We thought you wanted to hang out with us. We thought you wanted to be a part of us," Laura taunted.

It was the same speech MAL had given me. I lay there speechless with terror, listening, the snow a cold concrete blanket, smothering me.

Meredith's blue eyes appeared above my face through the slits of her pig mask.

"So we hear you like candy," she said. "How about some Pixy Stix?" I watched as she rooted in the pocket of her black coat, lifting out a handful of colored paper tubes.

"You won't get away with this," I said, shivering.

She laughed.

"Oh, but we are getting away with this," she said. "Now. Open your mouth, nice and wide."

I turned my head away, keeping my mouth shut tight. Next thing I knew my jaw was being pried open by Laura while Meredith ripped off the tops of the Pixy Stix and rammed a handful of tubes into my mouth. The powdered crystals of sugar tasted bitter, as if there was something else in them. I tried spitting them up, but I couldn't. I gagged and coughed, choking, before I finally swallowed. The acrid powdered sugar burned in the back of my throat.

"Those aren't just Pixy Stix," I heard Megan shout beside me. "What did you put in them?"

MAL laughed.

"Very clever," Meredith said. "Let's just say you're getting a taste of your own medicine."

Megan laughed. "I'm not eating those," she said. "And you can't make me." Laura and Meredith moved toward her.

There was the sound of a struggle. Then I heard Megan gagging.

"Megan!" I shouted. "Megan!"

Finally Megan coughed. And spat. Then spoke. "Go on!" she dared Meredith and Laura. "Give me more, you pigs! Just try me!"

So they did. Again and again. And every time they did, Megan spat it back up.

"See? What did I tell you?" She laughed. "You can't make me! You can't make me!"

When they were finished with all the Pixy Stix, Megan still shouted at them for more. Beside me, I heard Tracey Reid puke, then her uncontrollable weeping resumed.

"Wait'll I tell your mom about this party, Meredith!" Megan yelled. "I'm sure Margaret would *love* to hear all about it!"

Hovering above me, Meredith glowered at Megan. "Shut up!" she hissed. "You're not going to tell my mother! Or anyone! Not a soul. Because you're not going back home. Not now. Not ever. Or don't you remember our little story? The one I just told you? About the three girls and the three little pigs?"

"Yeah, I remember it," Megan said, laughing deliriously. "It *sucked*."

Meredith lurched in anger and swung at Megan with her shovel. There was an awful crack. My stomach heaved.

"Megan!" I screamed. "Megan!"

Angela and Laura rushed to Meredith's side. The three of them hovered over Megan in a black swarm.

"Omigod!" Angela said.

"Is she OK?" Laura asked.

There was a horrible silence from Megan. I felt sick to my stomach. My head was throbbing. Tracey screamed.

"Shut up!" Meredith shouted at her. "Or you'll be next!"

In fear, Tracey quietly whimpered. Everyone else was silent. Then Angela said to Meredith, "Did you—"

"Did I what?" Meredith asked frantically. "Did I what?"

"Did you . . ." Angela said slowly.

"No!" Meredith insisted defensively.

Then Laura said, "But what if she's . . . you know—"

"She's not!" Meredith shouted.

"Meredith," Angela said, "look. She's *bleeding*."

"I didn't hit her *that* hard, stupid," Meredith said coldly. "She'll be fine."

I tried to free my arms and legs, but the snow was too heavy. I couldn't get out. I strained to lift my neck and look over. Megan's head was slumped backward, blood trickling down her face onto the snow.

"Meredith! Please!" I begged. "This isn't funny anymore! Megan! Megan! Megan!"

"She's right," I heard Angela say, her voice filled with panic. "Maybe we should get help—"

"What?" Meredith said in disbelief. I noticed the flutter of panic in her voice. "Don't be ridiculous! They'll be fine. We're sticking to our plan. Let's go. *Now.*"

"No! Meredith! No!" I screamed. "You can't leave us like this! We'll die!"

Meredith looked upside down over my head and smiled. "No, you won't. But if you do, you'll finally live up to your name, won't you? *Dead girl?*" She laughed. "You know, it's true what they say. Revenge is sweet. So, so sweet."

And then without another word, Meredith stepped out of view and disappeared.

"Laura! Angela!" I cried, hoping they would heed my pleas. "Do something! Please!"

But they were conspicuously silent.

I listened to Meredith's footsteps crunch like broken glass in the snow. Laura and Angela followed after. My mouth went slack. I felt dazed. My whole body was numb.

Alone in my cold grave, I tried to scream but couldn't.

Beside me, Tracey Reid erupted into sobs.

It got darker. And colder.

"Megan?" I said, my voice weak. I raised my head, straining to look. Megan's head was still slumped backward, the blood black on the snow. "Megan? Please, *please* wake up."

I looked over at Tracey. She had been silent for too long.

"Tracey?" I pleaded. "Please, wake up."

I listened, hoping to hear Tracey breathe—talk, cry, anything—but she was soundless.

I looked up through the cover of trees. The forest was very quiet. All I could hear was the stuttered, panicky sound of my breathing. My body was frozen. I struggled to free myself once again, but I couldn't move. I called Megan's name again and again. But she wouldn't wake up. Then I knew. We would get cold and fall asleep, and we would freeze to death.

A light snow started to fall, and I thought about what Edie had said about how the whole world sparkles when it snows. I watched the snowflakes as they floated down from the sky, each one unique and spectacular. Crystalline kisses, they fell from heaven, spinning and swirling like granules of sugar through the air, landing on my face.

And suddenly, the falling snow wasn't snow—it *was* sugar. The snow hanging heavy in the dark chocolate trees was gooey marshmallow topping. And the drifted mounds in the green gumdrop forest were white royal icing. The icicles, meringue. Then, all at once, as if by magic, it stopped snowing. Through the trees I saw the moon, one star after another shining in the sky, glittering hard and cold and bright. Before my eyes the moon became a great glowing white peppermint, suspended in an ocean of stars that sparkled like confetti.

I felt as if the sweetness of all the candy I had ever eaten was swimming through my veins—as if my entire insides were composed of nothing but sugar.

I wondered if this was how my mother had felt.

I'd been told she had gone to a better place, somewhere where she was herself again. But I knew the truth was that my mother was lying all alone in the cold dark ground, nothing but her best dress to cover her bare bones.

My body writhed with anger and sadness, locked in the snow, buried beneath the weight of all that sugar pressing on my chest, crushing me with its sweetness.

I started to cry.

Just then I heard a voice. "Don't worry, darling, everything's going to be all right." I looked up. In disbelief, I saw Edie: her tiny fairylike body, in a shiny silver dress, hovering over my head. Through my tears I stared at her blurred figure, entranced. She smiled gently.

I tried to speak, but my voice was gone.

"Ssshh," she said. "Save your strength. You're going to need it."

I looked up at Edie again, her tiny body flitting like a butterfly. Slowly she waved her hands together and produced her little black book.

"It's time," she said. "For you to hear the end of our story." In a daze, I watched as she opened the book and flipped through its pages. "Here we are," she exclaimed. "Just when Francesca has given up all hope and Ferdinand has returned."

I watched Edie hover in the air above me. And then, after a moment, I heard the sound of her voice, the thread of the story like a band of light weaving in and out of the darkness, through the cold and the snow, keeping me awake, keeping me alive.

"Francesca continued to ignore the sound in her ear, not realizing it was her long-lost friend and companion, Ferdinand. Unbeknownst to her, Ferdinand had traveled a great many miles to return to her. Since Queen Goren's death he had been cast adrift upon the air, blown over many mountains and oceans, his life threatened many times. Now, trying desperately to attract Francesca's attention, he buzzed frantically outside her giant ear. But still Francesca did not hear him. So Ferdinand began to sing.

"Slowly, Francesca opened her eyes. Her heart was bursting

with happiness. She wanted to tell Ferdinand how glad she was that he had returned, but she was afraid she had lost her voice, just as the old woman in the cave had foretold.

"A large tear welled up in the corner of her eye, and Francesca realized she did not want to die. She wanted to run, to jump, to sing and dance and be alive. But what could she do? It was hopeless. She had been buried in the earth for too long. It was only a matter of time.

"Yet what Francesca did not yet know was that Ferdinand had a secret he had carried with him over many years, a secret that would free them both.

"Francesca listened as Ferdinand began to sing. She had almost forgotten how sweet his voice was; and as she surrendered herself to his strange and beautiful serenade, Ferdinand entered the dark mossy hollow of her ear.

"Then a most curious and remarkable thing happened. As Ferdinand sang inside her inner ear, the vibration of his song tickled her and Francesca began to laugh. And then, miraculously, as she laughed, she began to get smaller. And smaller. And smaller. As she shook with laughter, the years of cold black earth fell away from her body. Her skin drank the sweetness of the air! The spell of silence had been broken. And when at last she had returned to her original size, Ferdinand came flying out of her mouth in one last final laugh. And there, right before her, he transformed into a handsome young man.

"Anxiously, Francesca looked down on her body, gazing at her arms and legs. She was exactly the same as she had been before she was transformed. As if she had never been buried at all.

"'Who are you?' Francesca asked.

"The young man bowed before her.

"'Dearest Francesca. You know me as Ferdinand.'

"'But I don't understand!' Francesca cried.

"He smiled. 'Please, let me explain. Many, many years ago, this field and these forests and all the ground we stand upon was my ancestral homeland. This was my father's kingdom.'

"'Kingdom?' Francesca said in disbelief.

"'Yes,' he replied. 'My real name is Prince Henrik. Legend had it that this forest was formed by the magic of a thousand and one golden snakes.' The prince stood up before Francesca. 'It remained only a legend, until one day, many years ago, I was traveling through the forest with my army when we discovered the nest of the golden snakes. As we set about to capture them, an evil witch appeared who wanted to keep the snakes for herself.'

"'You mean—'

"'Yes,' the prince confirmed, nodding. 'Queen Goren lived in these woods. And when I said that the snakes were part of my rightful kingdom, she declared that the forest was her kingdom and that she was the queen. The snakes were hers. But as soon as she tried to capture them, they slithered out of her grasp. For you see, the snakes could only be claimed by the true heir. Me.'

"The prince looked deep into Francesca's eyes.

"'Wild with rage and jealousy, Queen Goren cast a spell on the snakes, banishing them to a place where their light could never be seen again, ensuring that the whereabouts of the snakes would remain a secret. Forever.'

"'And you?' Francesca asked.

"The prince bowed his head in shame. 'I became a fly,

trained to sing for Queen Goren's cruel amusement. She was jealous of my power, and she persecuted me for who I was and what kingdom was mine to claim.'

"Then Francesca asked, 'But what about me?'

"'Before she turned my army into a legion of butterflies,' the prince replied, 'in her haste Queen Goren neglected to cast a spell upon one last soldier who knew the secret of the golden snakes. Time passed, and at long last that butterfly was found, and chosen, and the snakes' secret location was revealed.' The prince looked at Francesca with gratitude and admiration. 'To you.'

"'But your precious golden snakes were destroyed!' Francesca said. 'Why? Could you not have claimed them?'

"'Sadly, no. For as long as I was a fly, neither I nor my ancestors could possess their power. And because Queen Goren wanted to use them for an evil purpose, the snakes relinquished their power to you. Their strength, their power, their riches, are in you. Now that Queen Goren is dead, you have saved my life. And for that, I am eternally grateful.'

"'Oh, dear, kind prince!' Francesca exclaimed. 'It is *you* who has saved my life! For you have rescued me! For all that you have done, I am forever in your debt.'

"Prince Henrik stepped forward and took Francesca's hand.

"'Many years ago, my ancestors held a proverb: *In the forest under the tallest tree, here you will find the most precious treasure of me.* And that is where I found you. You are my destiny, Francesca. Be my bride. Help me to reclaim my kingdom and be my beloved queen.'

"And so she did. And while Henrik became king, the army who had turned to butterflies became men again, and throughout King Henrik's kingdom, all was as it had been. His kingdom was justly returned to him, and Francesca became queen.

"Like the tallest tree, Francesca had towered over her troubles and prevailed against the forces of evil. As queen, she was heralded for being both strong and brave and honored for her courageous defeat of Queen Goren. Francesca eventually came to understand that the precious treasure was within her, that it had been inside her all along, and that that power would always be with her.

"After many years, Francesca was reunited with her father. Magically, as though not a day had passed, he looked no older than the last time she had seen him, and he was welcomed with much love and joy into the royal palace, where he lived out the rest of his days in peace and perfect harmony.

"And they all lived happily ever after.

"The End."

The air was filled with the quiet finality of the story's ending. Edie looked down at me and smiled. I thought of my father, alone, at home. He would be wondering where I was. Would he be worried about me? I wondered.

"It's almost done," Edie told me. "I don't have much more time."

I wanted to ask her what she meant, but I still couldn't speak. Above me, she extended her arm. "Give me your hand, darling," she said. "Before I go, I want to show you one last thing."

For a moment I wondered how I was supposed to do that, but astonishingly, Edie reached through the snow as if it were invisible and took my hand. Then something remarkable happened.

I felt myself leaving my body, slipping out of my skin, flying into the air.

"Come with me," Edie said.

I held her hand. As we sailed into the night sky, leaving the forest behind, I looked down at the fields and roads surrounding our subdivision, seeing all the little rooftops, like game pieces against a bigger grid of green. There was TWS and Megan's house and my house and St. Teresa's and all the hills sloping to the horizon in the distance. A cloud brushed past my ear. I turned toward the stars and felt as if I could see straight up into heaven.

It was then that I felt my mother looking down at me, watching over me. Protecting me. I felt an overwhelming sense of peace. I understood in that moment that it was only my mother's body that was gone. That she had always been there. And that she always would be. With me, in me.

"Do you see?" Edie asked.

I looked at her and nodded. It was just as Edie had said. Everything was going to be all right.

I looked down again at the forest, through the trees. There in the snow, with our eyes closed, were Tracey, Megan, and me. Despite what had happened, we looked strangely peaceful, like little dolls sleeping side by side in a row.

Then Edie said, "It's time. I have to go."

I wanted to tell her no, but she just looked at me and smiled. "Your story isn't over yet, darling. You still have yours to tell."

I watched as Edie let go of my hand. And I felt myself fall, falling back into my body, landing inside my skin with a solid thud. When I opened my eyes, Edie was gone. Then I heard Megan saying my name. My heart skipped.

"Megan?" I shouted, finally finding my voice. "Megan! Is that you?"

"Alive and kicking," she groaned.

I started crying and laughing at the same time. "Are you OK?"

"Yeah, I think so," she moaned.

"I was so afraid you were dead!" I said.

"What happened?" she asked groggily.

Then I remembered: the pig masks, the shovels. MAL had become a monster. I shivered with cold. "Meredith knocked you out," I said finally.

"Oh, yeah. Right. *Bitch.*"

I pushed against the snow that covered me, but I still couldn't move. I was encased within a coffin of crushed ice. I tried to stay calm.

"How's your head?" I asked.

"*Ouch.*"

"Can you get out?" I asked.

Another pause. "Who, me? The human Slushie?"

I wanted to laugh, but I couldn't. My throat and mouth were sore. "Please, I'm serious."

"No," she said. "I can't get out. Can you?"

I pushed again. This time harder. I couldn't feel my hands. My toes. My fingers. "No," I replied quietly.

"How's Tracey?" Megan asked hesitantly.

I looked over.

"Tracey," I said. "Can you hear me?"

"Yo! Spy Girl!" Megan shouted above me. "Wakey-wakey!"

Nothing. "Do you think she's . . .?"

"What? *Dead?*" Megan replied with a gruff laugh. "No way. But she is to blame."

"For what?"

"For getting us into this mess."

I remembered Tracey standing in the doorway of the fort, weeping, the look of terror on her face. "It's not her fault," I said.

"Oh, yeah? And whose fault is it?" Megan demanded.

I thought about it for a moment, then realized I didn't know how to answer that question. I called her name again, but Tracey still wasn't responding.

I looked at the moon, its familiar silvery face still hidden behind the trees.

"How are we going to get out of here?" I asked.

"I don't know," Megan quietly replied.

"Do you think we're going to get out of here?"

Megan didn't answer.

Then I said, "You know, I had the strangest dream. If it was a dream. I don't know. About Edie. And me. She was small, like a butterfly, and told me the rest of the Francesca story. Then we flew up into the sky."

"Oh, yeah? Tell me. Did Francesca live happily ever after?"

I stared at the trees surrounding us.

"Yes," I said. "Yes, she did."

Megan laughed.

"Sounds like you had a good trip."

"What are you talking about?"

"Duh! The dope that was in the Pixy Stix, dum-dum. I spit most of mine out. You were high as a freakin' kite!"

"Oh," I said, disappointed. "But it seemed so real . . ."

Suddenly I heard the sound of footsteps in the snow. My heart raced.

"Did you hear that?" I said to Megan.

"What?"

"Shh! That noise. Those footsteps —"

"I hear them," Megan said. "Who's there?" she shouted out into the darkness. "Who is it?"

I lay perfectly still and listened. The sound of the footsteps came closer. At first they were slow, then hurried. And then, like a vision, Blake Starfield's face appeared above me.

NOBODIES

BLAKE'S RESCUE FELL somewhere between divine intervention and blind luck.

Earlier that day, he had been walking home from school when he saw Meredith and Angela and Laura confronting Tracey. Knowing they were up to something, he followed MAL and Tracey from a distance and watched them enter the forest. Then, he waited.

When only Meredith and Angela and Laura came out of the woods, he became suspicious. So he followed their footprints back through the forest, knowing something was wrong. But it soon turned dark and Blake lost his way.

He searched through the woods for many hours, with just the faint light of the moon to guide him. It was only when he heard the sound of our voices that he finally found us.

We had been saved.

After he helped dig us out, Blake stood beside Megan and me in front of Tracey Reid's grave. We stared down at her. Her eyes were wide open, paralyzed with shock. Her lips looked purple.

"She doesn't look very good," Blake observed, as he stood beside me.

"No, she doesn't," Megan said ominously.

"Tracey!" I pleaded. "Please! Wake up!"

I looked at Tracey again and shuddered. I was cold and tired. I just wanted to go home.

Blake leaned over her and listened.

"She's breathing," he said.

"Tracey, can you hear me?" Megan asked, and she waved her hand over Tracey's eyes.

We waited. Nothing.

"Blink if you can."

Then, slowly, Tracey's eyelids blinked.

"Shit," Megan said, smiling. "She's alive."

The three of us quickly dug Tracey out, scooping up handfuls of cold icy slush with our hands. As we cleared the frozen snow away from her body and lifted her up from the ground, her eyes fluttered with panic. She was silent, traumatized.

We all hobbled back through the darkness of the woods, shivering, stumbling through the snow. Blake led us quietly through the trees while Megan and I helped support Tracey. As we made our way along the path, Megan stared moodily ahead.

"Can't you walk any faster?" she asked, dragging Tracey along.

"I-I—" Tracey stuttered. "I-I—"

"What?" I said.

"I didn't mean to hurt anybody," she whimpered. Deep, painful sobs rose in her chest.

"It's OK," I said.

But Tracey only cried more. "They said they just wanted to scare you," she said inconsolably. "To get back at you for what happened at the party."

"Did MAL put something in the Pixy Stix?" Megan asked Tracey.

Tracey nodded.

"I knew it!" Megan exclaimed. "What was it?"

"I don't know! I didn't see them do it! I just heard them talking about it!"

"You must have seen them! What was it?" Megan shook her.

"I told you! I don't know!" Tracey buried her face in her hands. "They only used me for information. Forcing me to find out about your secret club and where your fort was. It wasn't supposed to happen this way. No one was supposed to get hurt—"

"But how did you know?" Megan demanded.

"Know what?" Tracey replied.

"Where our fort was?"

Tracey stopped and looked at me, and then at Blake, and then back at Megan again.

"Because I saw them," Tracey said.

Blake turned around. I stopped walking. Our eyes met.

I knew then that it had been her. She was the one who had been standing in the street.

"Who?" Megan demanded.

"Her," she said, nodding at me, "and Blake. Walking out of the forest. One day. Together."

There was a moment of silence. Then Megan burst out laughing.

"Aha!" Megan exclaimed. "I knew it! You and Quasi! I knew it all along!" She continued laughing. Uproariously.

Embarrassed, Blake looked at the ground.

"Shut up!" I said to Megan. "It isn't funny!" I turned on Tracey. "So what if you did see Blake and me together!" I shouted. "What business was it of yours to tell MAL?"

"I'm so sorry," Tracey said. She bowed her head. Her shoulders began to shake.

I looked at Megan.

"What are we going to do now?" I said.

"Nothing. There's nothing we can do. Girls like Meredith and Angela and Laura never get into trouble. No one will believe us. There's no use trying."

"But we have a witness—"

"Who?" She looked at Blake. "Him?" she suggested. "Sorry. Nice try. But get real. No one's going to believe him, either."

"Why not me?" Blake asked. "I've got nothing to lose."

Megan smiled at Blake. "True. But it still won't work."

"What about me?" Tracey sniffled. "Mr. King might believe me."

"Maybe," Megan observed. "But why should he? When it's easier to believe nice white girls like Meredith and Laura and Angela instead? It's them against you, and I'm sorry, Spy Girl, but it doesn't matter how much you add it up: you're still outnumbered."

I recalled one of the first things Megan had said about MAL. Their unquestionable authority. Their gross pink talons of supremacy.

"But we have to do something," I said. "They can't get away with this!"

Megan's dark eyes glazed over in anger. "You don't get it yet, do you?" she said sharply. "People like us aren't special. We're not good in sports or good in school or popular or pretty.

We're just there. A part of the class, a part of the picture that gets taken every year—nobodies." She shook her head. "You know that stupid saying? 'Sugar and spice and everything nice'? That's what all the teachers and all the parents think Meredith and Angela and Laura are made of. And they know it, too. MAL can get away with anything they want." She stopped and looked up at us. "We're the forgettable ones, the expendable ones. And they know that, too."

She looked blankly ahead into the forest.

"No one cares what happens to us. Not even our own parents."

When I came through the door that night, my father was sitting up waiting for me. I stood before him, shivering cold. It was just after midnight.

"Where the hell have you been?" he demanded. "Do you have any idea what time it is? You better have a damn good reason for coming home at this hour, young lady! Have you been in trouble again?" he wanted to know.

I had hoped he would hug me. That he would have asked why I was so late and why I was so cold and wet. Then I would tell him about how scared I was, about all the horrible things that had happened, and how I missed my mother. Then he would say everything I wanted him to say: about how sorry he was about everything, and that everything was going to be OK.

But he didn't notice anything. He just looked at me and frowned. "I don't know where you've been or what you've been up to, but I can guarantee it's no good, isn't it?"

I hung my head and started crying. I was so tired. Of him, of everything he stood for.

"Well, answer me!" he said.

"Why do you care?" I blurted out. "You don't care what happens to me! You don't care if I'm alive or dead!"

His eyes filled with hurt. "Don't you dare speak to me like that! Do you understand me?"

My eyes burned with tears. How could he be so cruel? Didn't he know how much he was hurting me by just doing nothing?

"What about when you said you would be here for me when I needed you?" I cried.

I strained to make him see how much I needed him. But he wasn't looking at me. He was looking past me, at somebody else he wanted me to be. Some other girl who I might have been.

"Do you understand me?" he said again, louder. He hadn't even listened.

"No!" I shouted back, my voice breaking through my tears. "Do you understand *me?*"

I waited for his reply but he said nothing. Instead, he just turned around and walked away. I broke down sobbing.

For the next three days I stayed in my room. I did not see anyone. I did not talk to anyone. Not even my father. I lay in bed and slept, hiding from the world.

When I finally went back to school, MAL pretended that nothing had ever happened. I thought about telling Mr. King. But I didn't know where to start or what to say.

Megan had performed another one of her disappearing acts. No doubt her absence would be later explained by some exotic business trip somewhere with her mother. I wished she would tell me the truth—whatever that meant. But I don't think even she knew what that was anymore. In the days that followed, I tried all the usual strategies, including endless phone calls and knocks at her front door, even though I knew there would be no answer.

But amid everything else that happened, Blake had disappeared, due to a bizarre accident at school.

Incredibly, Blake Starfield was presumed dead.

From what Tracey Reid told me, David Pierce had dared Blake to eat ten packs of Pop Rocks with a Coke. Accepting this challenge, Blake stood in the middle of the schoolyard while Jason and Adam and David circled around him, chanting the usual *"Qua-si! Qua-si! Qua-si!"*

But then something happened. No one was really sure what. All Tracey heard was that Blake dropped to his knees and put his hands around his head as if he was in pain. They said that was when his lazy eyeball shot out of his head and fell into the snow. Some said it was because Blake had been sucker-punched in the eye by David or Adam or Jason. Kids started screaming, running in all directions, lifting up their feet and legs and sidestepping what they couldn't see in the snow: the lone eyeball of Blake Starfield, soft as a deviled egg.

No one actually saw it or even looked closely at Blake. But it was Mr. King who went over to him and said *Let's have a look at your face* and yelled at Tracey to call 911. *Now.*

As they all watched Blake Starfield leave TWS, strapped to the gurney, his head wrapped in a padded block—that was when the real speculations began. Maybe he had lost an eyeball. Maybe he had a concussion. Or perhaps he was in a coma. It was even further rumored that on his way to the hospital Blake had died from an aneurysm, his pulse mutating into a robotic blip and then flat-lining. But no one knew for sure.

I had no choice but to accept what I'd heard from Tracey to make sense of what had happened. In the end, I decided there had been no rampant eyeball rolling loose in the snow. No concussion. No coma. No aneurysm. Like someone playing a part in a magic trick, Blake had simply disappeared.

I chose to remember only the good things about him. The coolness of his hand as it held mine in the darkness of the gym. His smell, the taste of his tongue in my mouth, the strange stare of his eyes, his shy smile. How he had shown me the stars. And saved my life.

He had, I concluded, not really died. Instead, like a constellation, he had only been borrowed by the angels for a time and would soon return to earth.

I could not believe anything otherwise, no matter how hard I tried. For me he had already transgressed the real, evolving into myth and legend.

PROMISE

THAT NEXT TUESDAY when I went alone to visit Edie, I knew something had happened.

From the outset, I noticed the light in the hallway coming from her room was different somehow, brighter than usual. When I walked in with the cart, the bed was empty, stripped of its sheets. The plants were gone.

I must have been there for some time before Sister Catherine walked up beside me. I didn't have to ask where Edie was; I knew what had happened. But Sister Catherine said: "She went peacefully to the Great Maker. In her sleep. Last week."

I thought back to the night in the forest, trapped under the snow. Then I remembered seeing Edie—a vision in silver, flitting like a fairy.

"Do you know when she died?" I asked.

Sister Catherine turned to face me. "Let's see—it was eight days ago. Sometime during the evening."

A chill ran up my spine.

Observing my reaction, Sister Catherine said, "Don't be afraid, my child. She is at peace at last," and left the room.

I couldn't stop thinking about how Edie had appeared to me that same night.

I was shaking. I had to see Megan.

Without finishing my rounds, I went downstairs to see Sister Maria.

"Finishing early today, are you?" she said, inspecting the cart. She raised her eyebrow. "I see you're missing a box of chocolates."

Anxiously, I looked down.

"Am I? I must have miscounted them." It was true. I had miscounted them. Perhaps for the first time ever, I had not stolen anything. Remarkably, I was innocent.

Sister Maria, however, was not convinced. "Perhaps we should pay a visit to Sister Catherine," she said, smiling curtly. "There's no use trying to pull the wool over my eyes."

"But I didn't take anything!" I protested.

"Maybe not this time," Sister Maria asserted, "but I've suspected—no, I've known for some time now—that both you and Megan have been stealing since the beginning." Sister Maria was appalled and outraged by our irresponsible behavior. In her day, girls would never do such things. Girls understood their roles. Their duties. Their obligations. Blah, blah, blah.

I stood in front of her, listening, watching her wrinkly eyelids quiver, the pale pink hole of her mouth opening and closing like a fish's.

"You know what, Sister Maria?" I said. "Go ahead. Call Sister Catherine. Call Jesus. Call God. I don't care. I don't care about you or this stupid fucking cart or your stupid fucking rules! And you can take your stupid fucking ugly uniforms, too. Go to hell, you old bitch."

It felt good to swear. To say foul words that she found shocking. To disturb her. Then I opened my mouth and laughed. I laughed at her and her stupid panic-stricken face. I watched as her frail body cowered in helpless indignation.

The only thing Sister Maria wanted to enforce in me was the same set of rules everybody else wanted me to abide by. But I wasn't playing by her rules. I wasn't playing by anybody's rules anymore.

I grabbed a box of chocolates from the cart and tucked it under my arm. As I ran out of the room, I tore off my smock and threw it on the floor. But before I left, I turned around and gave her the finger.

As I walked out of St. Teresa's, tears streamed down my face. I couldn't believe Edie was gone.

I walked to Megan's house and banged on the front door. I banged again and again. And again.

"Megan!" I shouted. "Megan!"

After a moment, Rose opened the door. I wondered what she was doing upstairs, why she was answering Megan's door.

"Where is she?" I demanded. "I know you know where she is. I need to see her. Right now."

Rose was silent. Then she said, "I'm afraid that's impossible. She's away with her mother. Something important came up."

"When is she coming back?" I insisted. "I have to know."

Rose paused. "Not until tonight," she answered.

"What time?"

"I don't know," Rose replied. "Late. She probably won't be attending school tomorrow."

"Then give her this message," I told her. "Tell her to meet me tomorrow after school. She'll know the place."

I looked into Rose's eyes, searching for some sign of the manic instability Megan had told me about. But Rose just crossed her arms and looked at me, her eyes flat and unwavering.

"Listen," I said carefully, "I know about you."

Rose's eyebrow peaked. "Oh?" she said. "What do you know?"

"About your condition," I replied. "And that you're Megan's mother's cousin."

A tiny smile played on the corner of Rose's mouth. "Oh, is that what she told you?"

"Yes," I said.

Rose wearily shook her head.

"I haven't been the crazy cousin for a while," she muttered, almost as if she were talking to herself.

I was confused. This still wasn't making any sense.

"Excuse me?" I said.

"Whatever she told you," Rose said, "believe everything. And nothing." She studied my face with a knowing look.

Megan was right. Rose was crazy.

"Could you please just pass on the message?" I said.

"I'll see what I can do," she said.

The next afternoon I went to the fort to wait for Megan. It was strange being back there, in the woods again, after what had happened. As I walked along the path, the forest was eerily quiet. I kept looking up into the trees, checking behind me. My heart skidded when I thought I heard someone, but it was just a crow flying through the trees. I shuddered to think of our cold graves, their black, muddy hollows. I was glad when the fort was within sight, and I went inside and waited.

I wondered what future archaeologists might think of our fort. Despite the candy wrappers everywhere on the walls, the only other evidence of human activity was our blankets and a few stray pop cans. We had not crafted vessels. We had not fashioned tools. We had only, simply, told stories.

I reached into my knapsack and pulled out the box of chocolates I had stolen from St. Teresa's and broke the seal with my fingernail. Raising the box to my nose, I smelled the chocolate, closing my eyes. When I opened them, Megan was standing in the doorway.

I hardly recognized her. Her face was thin and drawn; her hair was dyed a natural shade of brown. She was dressed in a pair of plain blue jeans with a white T-shirt under a faded jean jacket. She wore no jewelry. No makeup. It was uncanny, looking at her. I felt as if I were looking in a mirror. She was dressed almost exactly like me.

"What do you think of the new look?" she asked.

"You look so different," I said, stunned. "So . . . plain."

"Rose gave me your message," Megan said.

"I didn't think you'd make it," I said. "You were away again?"

She nodded. "Yeah. We just got back. Yesterday. Late. That's why I wasn't at school today."

"Where were you?"

"D.C." Almost as an afterthought, she added, "Just for a few days, you know."

"Rose told me. Something important."

Megan came over and sat down beside me. I could still see the bruise where MAL had knocked her out, the braised red edge of the scab.

"Does it still hurt?"

"You mean this?" Megan touched her forehead. "Nah."

"What did you tell your mom?"

"That I hit my head on a tree branch."

"Did she believe you?"

Megan shrugged. "Probably not." She looked off into the distance. "It doesn't matter. It's the only thing she's going to get out of me, anyway."

I wondered what Megan meant. I waited for her to say something more, but she didn't.

"Blake's gone," I said.

"What? Quasi? MIA?" Megan remarked. "Too bad."

"I thought you didn't like him."

Megan smiled. "Are you kidding? The boy with the rocket in his pocket? C'mon!"

"But why didn't you say something?"

"Because I knew you liked him," Megan said, nudging me. "Did you guys ever, you know, make it?"

Before I could deny this, Megan looked down at the box of chocolates in my hands. "Where'd you get those?"

"I stole them," I confessed. "From St. Teresa's."

"Nice work," she said. "I see you've learned well. Now pass 'em over." She grabbed the box and ripped off the thin film of cellophane wrapping, taking a deep breath and inhaling the thick aroma of chocolate.

"They're for Edie," I said quietly. "In memory of her."

Megan raised her eyes and looked at me. "What happened?" she asked.

I bowed my head in silence. Megan was quiet for a moment.

"Oh," she said sadly. "Well, then. Which one do you want first? This one? A caramel? Or what about this one? I think it's an orange cream. I'm having the dark chocolate–covered cherry."

When we had both made our selection, Megan raised her chocolate. "To Edie," she toasted, "a great storyteller."

We touched our chocolates together and then popped them into our mouths. We chewed and swallowed in silence. Then we had one after another until both layers of the box were gone.

The inside of my mouth was bittersweet with chocolate. I felt both sick and delirious. For a while I just sat there, thinking about Edie. Megan looked at the empty box with dismay.

"We're going away again," she said.

"You and your mother?" I replied. "On some of her important *business?*" I did not try to hide the sarcasm in my voice. I knew that she was telling me a lie.

"Yeah," Megan answered quietly. "That's right. On business." She did not look at me.

"When are you going?" I asked, picking up the cellophane wrapper from the box of chocolates.

"Tomorrow," Megan answered.

I crumpled up the wrapper in my hands. "Oh."

Megan was silent.

"You remember that dream I had?" I said. "About Edie telling the end of the Francesca story? Edie died that same night."

"I told you, that wasn't a dream," Megan scoffed. "You were *hallucinating.*"

"Maybe," I said.

Megan leaned forward. "You don't think that it was real, do you?"

"No," I said defensively. "But I just can't help but think it's kind of creepy, you know, Edie dying the same night and everything."

"Well, that is true," replied Megan, her voice trailing off quietly. "It is kind of coincidental."

I kept thinking that there was something we should have been talking about—the night we spent out in the woods, why she was going away again, MAL—but I couldn't find anything to say.

"Promise me, if anything happens, you'll remember my stories," Megan suddenly said.

"What do you mean, 'if anything happens'?"

"Listen to me," she said as she reached out and grabbed my hand. "My stories. Our stories. You have to remember them. Promise me. You'll do this, no matter what."

"Why?"

"Just say yes." Her eyes were rimmed with tears.

"OK. Yes."

"Promise?"

"Promise."

As we walked out of the forest, thin bands of fog hung in the air. The snow was melting. Megan turned around and looked back at the forest through the mist.

"Where are you going this time?" I asked her.

Megan looked me in the eye. "It hasn't been decided yet.

We haven't been told. It's very hush-hush. You know, top secret and all that."

"Yeah, right," I said.

When at last we reached the usual place in the road where we went our separate ways, Megan hugged me and said, "I'll call you. When I get back, I mean."

"Sure," I replied.

Our eyes met.

"Megan—"

"What?" she said.

I wanted to grab her and shake her and make her finally tell me everything: about where she was going and why. Who Rose was. Where her mother was. Who *she* was. But as I looked at her—dressed in yet another style, another disguise—I felt somehow that I would never know.

Her eyes softened, and then she smiled at me. "Remember your promise."

"My what?"

"Your promise, darling," Megan said. "Don't forget!"

She started to walk away. I stood there and waved. As I watched her slowly disappear into the distance, I had the feeling I would never see her again.

SUCKER

When I woke up the next morning, I couldn't stop thinking about the promise I had made to Megan. What had she meant? Something was wrong.

Before school, I went to her house and knocked on the door. There was no answer, so I looked through the side window. When I couldn't see anything, I tried opening the front door, but it was locked. I went around to Rose's apartment door, but it was also closed. I went back to the front and banged my fist on the door.

"Megan!" I yelled. "Answer the door!"

I kicked the front door. When there was still no answer, I threw a snowball at Megan's window, waiting for her face to emerge from behind the curtains.

"Megan!" I shouted. "I know you're in there! Megan!"

I threw another snowball. Nothing. A feeling of dread overcame me. Why wasn't she answering the door? When she still didn't appear, I started throwing snowballs at the house, pelting every window.

"Hey! You! What the hell do you think you're doing?"

I stopped and turned around. A man with dark hair wearing a black suit and holding a magazine was zipping up his fly on the front porch. In his mouth was a lollipop; his eyebrows were furrowed with anger.

"Where's Megan?" I demanded.

The man pulled the lollipop out of his mouth and looked at me.

"Who?"

"Megan Chalmers. She lives here."

The man shrugged his shoulders, adjusting his belt buckle. His accent was rough and thick.

"I don't know who you're talking about. No one lives here by that name."

My mouth went dry.

"I want to talk to Megan," I insisted again. *"Megan Chalmers."*

"Look," the man said. "There's no Megan here, all right? No one lives here. It's *empty.*"

"What?" I said.

"Come have a look for yourself if you want." He gestured toward the front door.

I pushed past him and ran into the house, calling Megan's name.

I walked down the hall in a state of shock, staring at empty walls, empty rooms, empty closets. Everything was gone.

"Go ahead," I heard the man say, "take a good look around if you want."

I went through the kitchen and living room, then down the back stairs to Rose's apartment. As I stared into each empty space, my chest fluttered with panic. I rushed back upstairs into Megan's room. There was no furniture. No books. No clothes. No posters on the wall. Nothing. I looked in the closet, searching for some evidence of her, something she might have left behind. A pen, a hairbrush, a thumbtack—anything. But it was as if she had never even lived there.

When I emerged from Megan's bedroom, the man was sitting on a lawn chair in the front hallway. Beside him was a small tray table with a glass jar full of lollipops. When he saw me, he removed the lollipop from his mouth and twirled it between his thumb and index finger.

"Sucker?" he said, tempting me.

The man waved the lollipops under my nose. "Go on," he said. "Have one."

I felt numb. Slowly, I reached into the jar and took one.

"I apologize if I didn't hear you earlier," he said. "But I was detained in the facilities, if you know what I mean."

The man eyed me carefully. On his cheek I noticed a long white scar.

"So tell me," he said slowly. "About this Megan. Because so far as I know, there was no Megan that lived here. Unless of course you mean that woman with the kid—but her name wasn't Megan. But it did start with an M, I think."

"Wh-what did she look like?" I stammered.

"Skinny. Dark hair. Blue eyes." He looked me up and down. "Like you."

I was stunned. "That's her," I said. "That's *Megan.*"

The man repositioned himself in the chair.

"Did she tell you when she was leaving?" he asked nonchalantly.

I stared at the man's large, coarse hands. I didn't answer.

"Because they've been moving their stuff out of here for the past week," he informed me. "They split town last night." I watched as he helped himself to another lollipop. "That's the trouble with these damn things," he said to me as he ripped off the clear plastic wrapper and put it in his mouth. "I always end up eating them all." He paused, looking at me again. "Ain't you gonna have yours?"

I looked at the lollipop, thinking of all the stories Megan had told me. Then I remembered one, of the woman and her daughter at the Seven Dwarfs Inn. What had she been trying to tell me? Then I remembered some of her other stories. The girl in the backroom of the variety store. The girl who got hives at Halloween. The old lady who had choked to death. The man who had been murdered.

"What about Rose?" I asked.

The man looked at me in confusion. "Who?"

"Rose. You know—with the short hair. The limp?"

"Oh, *Rose*. Right. Yeah, sure. I just didn't recognize the name right away," he reflected. He twirled the lollipop between his fingers. "Did you see the other woman?" he asked.

"What other woman?" I said.

"Black hair. Fair skin. Red lips." He inserted the lollipop back into his mouth. "Just like something out of a fairy tale."

I guessed that he must have been talking about Megan's mother. It was the closest I would ever get to knowing who she was or what she looked like.

"No," I said. "I never did see her."

The man stood up from the chair and walked to the front door.

"Do you know where they went?" I asked him.

"No," the man said, looking out the window. "Though we did hear something about Canada. But we don't know for sure."

I imagined Mrs. Chalmers standing over Megan with garbage bags, ordering her to fill them. And I realized the scene would not be chaotic, with Megan frantically and tearfully stuffing the bags. Instead, she would know just what to do. Where to put everything in its right place, knowing what books fit into what boxes, what clothes fit into what suitcases, how to transport her belongings in the most efficient way possible. She had learned the quickest way to pack, to leave without a trace, to make herself disappear completely.

I knew then, too, that wherever they were going wasn't where they were really going. Like the rest of Megan's world, the cities were made up, too. Places where she could be free to invent herself as she pleased. Somewhere between fact and fiction, Megan's life was a story that changed as she changed, every time she moved.

Then I looked at the man and realized I still didn't know who he was or why he was there. My heart beat faster.

"What are you doing here?" I asked.

The man twisted around and looked at me, his face in shadow.

"I'm in real estate," he answered. The man gave me a crooked smile. "The name's Mercer."

I left Megan's house in a daze and ran to the forest. I didn't know what to do. What to believe. I felt panicky and out of breath when I reached the fort. Suddenly, it was all too much. I slumped in the corner of the fort and buried my head in the blankets and cried.

I cried for Megan and for Edie, for Blake and for me. I wept for my mother. And my father. And when I couldn't cry any longer, I just sat there on the floor and put my arms around myself, rocking back and forth. That's when I saw the message. Right in front of me, on the wall: *111515121621*. Backwards numeric code for *Look up*.

I shot my head up. I stared and stared. Then I saw it. Camouflaged among the candy wallpaper. Thin and rectangular, but bigger than the size of my hand, covered with candy wrappers. Fastened to the ceiling with duct tape.

A book.

I reached up and removed it, pulling away the tape. It was a journal. On the front were two words in ornate black script: *Eht Koob*. The Book. I opened it carefully, as if I were holding an ancient manuscript. Inside was a flurry of words and pictures, doodles and drawings. And stories—so many stories.

All of them Megan's. All of them about candy.

As I looked more closely, a distinct smell arose from the book. Inside were more candy bar wrappers, pressed flat against the dark flurry of words. I turned over the pages, mesmerized, taking in each word, each sentence, each stroke of black ink. Reading the flamboyant curves of Megan's handwriting was like reading an ancient alphabet. Some of the pieces of paper seemed untouched, while others looked as if they had been burned by fire or imprinted with chocolate.

They were all there. All the stories that I had been told— Fun Dip, Astro Pop, Ring Pop, Satin Chocolate-Covered Chicken Bones—all of them. There were also ones I hadn't heard: Nerds, Gold Rush, Lemonheads. So many others. I flipped through the pages, devouring them with my eyes. Every story, each word a clue, a piece in the puzzle of her life.

At the back of the book, on the last page, marked by a flattened Life Savers wrapper, was one final story. Written in the margin, in black ink, were the words *Dear Candy Darling—a story just for you* . . . I read with trembling hands. It was called "Life Savers."

In the darkness of early morning, the girl woke up and reached for the roll of Life Savers on the floor beside her. She had been saving them for moving day. And today was that day. Again.

The girl tore open the package of candy and put a red Life Saver in her mouth. It was tangy and sweet. In the warmth of her sleeping bag, she stared up at the ceiling, at the bare walls of her empty room. She had hoped to sleep more.

She sucked the Life Saver until it became a thin, flat round wafer, as delicate as glass. Then she looped it around her tongue and crunched it up in her mouth. Her life saved, the girl sat up and reached out into the darkness for her clothes, dressing slowly and quietly.

At her aunt's instruction, she had laid them out the night before, stacking each item, from the socks up, in a neat little pile beside her bed. This was just in case, her aunt said, they had to leave earlier than expected.

The girl unraveled another Life Saver from the roll and put them in her pocket. This time it was lime green, her favorite flavor. Her life would be saved once more.

She checked for the telltale sound of movement from outside her bedroom door. Both her mother and aunt were awake, too, making their preparations to leave. The girl rolled up her sleeping bag and packed the rest of her suitcase. It was full of all the

*things she'd need until they reached their next destination —
wherever that would be. It was for their own protection, her
mother told her. It was important that they never know.*

*The girl stood on her suitcase and looked out the window onto
the quiet, darkened street. Everybody else in the neighborhood
was still asleep. The girl took out another Life Saver. This time
it was orange. She turned around and sat down on her suitcase
and peered into the dark. She had liked this room. This town.
This school. Sadly, it was one of the only places where she felt she
had made a true friend.*

*In her pocket, the girl touched the roll of candy, its surface
round and smooth under her fingers. Every time they had to
move, the girl always took her Life Savers. They were the only
thing that could help her get through the day. The only candy
that could save her life.*

There was a knock on her bedroom door.

*The girl looked up and squinted as she stared into the light.
Standing in the doorway were her mother and her aunt.*

"Mea," her mother said. "Are you ready?"

"It's time to go," said her aunt.

*Mea touched the Life Savers in her pocket again and stood
up to leave. As she walked toward the door with her sleeping bag
and suitcase in hand, she turned back and looked behind her,
scanning the empty room. When she was sure that she had left
nothing behind, she took a deep breath and stepped forward into
the light.*

When I had finished reading the last word, I closed my eyes
and sank my face into the pages of the book, smelling its terrible sweetness, its unresolved secrets.

A LONG BLACK LINE

IN THE DAYS THAT FOLLOWED, I kept expecting Megan to just show up at school, her hair dyed a different color, a Tootsie Pop in her hand, telling me she had just returned from a long trip across the country. She would tell amazing stories: of her and her mother standing at the foot of Mount Rushmore, going horseback riding in the Grand Canyon, standing at the steps of the Lincoln Memorial, or driving up and down the narrow streets of San Francisco. But I knew that wouldn't be happening this time around.

I kept imagining where she might be and what she might be doing. What name she had taken. What new style she had adopted. What I did know was that whoever she had become, she had taken some part of me with her. I remembered the last time I had seen her, and I realized she had chosen me for her next persona; my personality had been added to her private cast of characters. And though I had read the book over and over again, Megan would always remain a mystery.

I was haunted by strange dreams. In one I was being buried alive under shovelful after shovelful of fine white sugar. In another, I was walking up and down the hallways of TWS, looking for Blake. One night I even dreamt that I saw Megan, but when I went up to her it was someone else, a stranger I never knew.

The only person I really talked to was Tracey Reid. After the night in the snow, she was a different person. The girl who had dressed up as Little Bo-Peep was gone. We had been hanging out together, for solace as much as for mutual protection. Both of us knew MAL wasn't going away anytime soon. As long as we were around, they would continue to bully us. For the first time, I was grateful that she sat behind me. She watched my back and I watched hers.

When I finally accepted that Megan wasn't coming back, I did everything I could to avoid MAL, but I knew it was only a matter of time. I was more vulnerable than before, and every day they watched me, waiting for the right moment to strike. As usual, Mr. King remained oblivious.

It seemed absurd to me that at one time I had wanted to be like MAL. To walk and talk and act like them. To be normal. Whatever that meant. Of any of us, Megan was the normal one.

I missed her more than anything. And I missed Edie, too. After Sister Catherine called to inform my father of my recent behavior at the hospital—and my subsequent dismissal as a volunteer—my father announced that he had given up on me. He wasn't even mad; he was just *disappointed*. He didn't know what to do. He had tried everything, he said.

Still, almost every night, I heard him pace up and down the hallway outside my bedroom door. He started out quietly, almost as if on tiptoe, and then he stepped louder and louder, as if he were marching. Sometimes when he got to the end of the hallway he just spun around and around in the same spot, trapped in his own twisted little circle. When that happened, I got up and helped him back to sleep. But sometimes, I just lay there in the darkness with my head on my pillow, silently listening to him struggle.

I knew all he had was me. But that didn't make it any easier. And although I knew I should have been doing something more to help him, I could only pity him. I didn't know what else to do.

I wished for a happy ending. I really did. But it would take him, too.

When MAL finally caught me, I was in the washroom during lunch, alone. I was at the sink, washing my hands, just as I had been the first time they confronted me.

"Well, look who's here," said Meredith, standing behind me. "And all by yourself. Not playing it very smart now, are you?"

"Yeah," mocked Laura. "Ever since your little girlfriend left you, you've had no one to play with."

"Except yourself," Meredith said.

"Well, you'd know all about that, now wouldn't you, Meredith?" I shot back nervously. "Party girl."

Meredith laughed.

"Oh, very clever," she said. "I see your little girlfriend taught you a thing or two. But guess what? She's gone now."

I turned around and tried to walk away, but MAL had encircled me.

"Not so fast," Laura ordered. "We're not finished with you yet. Not even close."

"Yeah," Angela echoed. "We've got *so* much to talk about."

They moved in closer. Panic thumped in my chest.

"And besides," Laura said, "we have to finish your story."

"Wh-what story?" I stammered.

"You know the one," Meredith said. "The same one. The one you've always heard. The story about the dead girl."

MAL erupted in ugly mocking laughter.

I wished Megan would walk in. Tracey Reid. Someone. Anyone. But I knew that wasn't going to happen. Not this time. No one was going to save me from them except myself.

"Oh, that," I said. My heart was beating wildly. I tried to think of something Megan might say. "I thought you meant the other story—about the three girls named Meredith and Angela and Laura who turned into a three-headed monster."

They stopped laughing.

"And?" Meredith challenged.

I could barely breathe.

"In your story, the girl gets murdered," I continued slowly. "But in mine, she never did. She was always alive. Even though they hurt her and terrorized her and tried to bury her alive in the woods. She never died. She's still alive. Today, right now. Here."

Meredith looked me in the eye. Angela and Laura were silent.

"Don't you see?" I said, gathering my courage. "I'm still alive. To tell the tale. For *everyone* to hear."

"How is that a story?" Meredith asked.

I took a deep breath. "It's not," I replied quietly. "It's the truth."

"Ha!" Meredith exclaimed, stepping toward me. "What truth? It's us against you! Do you expect anybody to believe your stupid little story? Your so-called *truth?*" Meredith burst out laughing. "They 'hurt her and terrorized her and tried to bury her alive in the woods'?" she said, mocking me. "Just who do you think you are? Do you think anyone is going to believe anything bad you could say about us?" She laughed out loud again. "Get real. Look at you! You're a fucking nobody."

Suddenly I couldn't move. My courage had been vanquished. Shame choked in the back of my throat.

"Hurt you?" Laura said deviously. "We would *never* hurt you!"

"And terrorize you?" Angela said. "Never!"

Meredith tossed her hair over her shoulder and flashed me a sly grin. "And what is all this silly nonsense about a three-headed monster and being buried alive in the woods?" She shook her head. "Sounds like *drugs* to me. Maybe we should tell Mr. King about all that *'candy'* you've been having lately."

Meredith stepped forward and put her arm around my shoulder. I shrank from her embrace, but her grip was leaden.

"Don't worry," Meredith said in a cruel whisper. "Even though no one else will believe you, we'll *always* be your friends."

With all my strength, I broke away from Meredith and ran out of the washroom into the hallway, where I ran straight into Mr. King.

"Well now, what's the matter here?" he asked, looking down at me.

"I-I-I," I began.

"Yes?" said Mr. King.

I wanted to tell him everything. But when I looked up into his face, I didn't know where to begin. How could I explain what had happened? And why? Megan and I were not innocent of anything.

"I think what she means to say is that she misses Megan. Things just haven't been the same without her." I turned around. It was Meredith. Standing beside her, as always, were Angela and Laura.

"Miss McKinnon, Miss Moyer, Miss Mitchell," Mr. King said, beaming. "Could you provide some assistance here, please? I think someone could really use a friend." Through his dark-rimmed glasses he looked down at me with a strange sort of pity. He had never called me Miss.

MAL looked at Mr. King and smiled. Their three-headed, hydralike oneness was rising up against me.

"Of course, Mr. King," Laura said sweetly.

"Anything," Angela answered.

"Don't worry," Meredith told him. "We'll take good care of her."

Mr. King sighed with relief. "Thank you," he replied with a smile. "I knew I could count on you. *As always.*"

MAL locked their elbows together and stood side by side. It was clear that I was expected to join them, fitting myself in like a link in a chain.

"Go on," urged Mr. King.

MAL tittered girlishly. And I knew then that Megan had been right—that she had always been right, from the very beginning.

MAL could get away with anything. Their authority was unquestionable.

And those were The Rules.

But I didn't have to play their game. Megan didn't. The choice was mine. I looked at Mr. King and MAL and laughed. Then I turned around and walked away.

Later, on my way home from school, I tried hard to resign myself to the hard truths that had become all too clear that day.

In the end, I knew, there would always be conflict between girls like MAL and Megan and me. But what I couldn't accept was knowing that MAL would always triumph and that no one would believe me. It wasn't right, no matter what anyone said. I couldn't give up that easily. Not after everything that had happened.

Megan knew about hard truths, some of them as enduring as stone. I thought about all of her stories and understood that they were more than just an interpretation of events; they acted in her defense, as a living record of her life and her memory. Together they formed a long black line into her past that weaved back and forth over the truth.

As I walked down the street, I wished there was some way that I could expose MAL for who they really were and all the harm that they had done. Tell Megan's stories. Blake's. Edie's. And then suddenly I remembered her last words to me: *"Your story isn't over yet, darling. You still have yours to tell."*

I realized then that I could tell others the truth. My truth. The way things really happened. Beyond the real, between the powers of yes and no, I could create my own transformation: I could write my own story.

I would not be powerless anymore.

∽⊚⌀

That night, I heard my father walking down the hallway. I got up and opened my bedroom door. As usual, he walked past me muttering nonsense. He was marching like a soldier again, his legs kicking out in front of him, his arms straight at his sides, a stern expression engraved in the lines of his forehead.

I stepped beside him and carefully slipped my hand into his, leading him back into his bedroom. After I helped him to his bed, I turned around and began to walk away. As I stepped gently out of the room, I heard him say something in a whisper.

"What?" I asked softly, not sure if he was still talking in his sleep.

"I'm sorry," I heard him say. His voice was small and delicate, trembling. "I'm so, so sorry."

I looked back. I could see my father sitting upright on the edge of his bed, holding his head in his hands.

"That's OK," I murmured. "I'm sorry, too."

I stepped toward him.

In the faint half-light of his room, my father raised his face and stood up and walked toward me, opening his arms.

EUGOLIPE

BLOOMSDAY

THE NEXT MORNING I noticed some of the bulbs my father and I had planted the previous fall were starting to come up. I thought of how they had spent the winter buried in the cold ground and how I had never wanted to see them again.

I put my hands in the pocket of my coat and felt something hard and small, like a stone. I lifted it out of my pocket. It was a small green and white striped mint. The one my Great-Aunt Elaine had given to me. I studied it for a moment and remembered how it had felt in my hand the day of my mother's funeral.

I stood in the sun and took a deep breath. The spring air was cool and fresh. For the first time, I noticed trees bursting everywhere. I looked at the flowers again. Sticking straight up out of the black earth, they were awkward, ungainly things: their tops flopping over this way and that, buds tightly sealed from view.

It was hard to believe that they had survived the winter, being buried there for so long under the snow and cold. But that dark frozen earth had cradled them, protected them. And now here they were.

I untwisted the clear cellophane wrapper and put the mint in my mouth. It was sweet and green. As I stood there, my father came outside and stood beside me. Humbly, he put his arm around my shoulder. I leaned into him, putting my arm around his waist.

As I savored the flavor of the candy in my mouth, I thought of an opening for my story: *Once upon a time, I saw the world the way I thought I was supposed to: as a place where the normal reigned and the weak perished under the strong. But I was wrong.*

I stared at the flowers. It wouldn't be long before they would bloom.

I could hardly wait to see what colors they would be.

ACKNOWLEDGMENTS

THERE ARE MANY PEOPLE I would like to thank for their help in creating this book.

First, to my husband, Paul Walde, my friend, my love, and my inspiration, who has made everything possible. Everything.

Sam Hiyate, as my first editor, my current agent, and my former publisher, was the first to believe in me and this project, and I am thankful to him for his faith and commitment to it, as well as for his friendship. I am grateful to him and The Rights Factory for all their hard work and enterprise.

I am also particularly grateful to Eden Edwards, who has been my greatest supporter. Her keen intellect, passion, and editorial insight have been an unfailing light that has guided me throughout the writing and revision process of this book, and I am forever indebted to her. I truly could not have written this book without her. Her bold vision for the Graphia imprint and Houghton Mifflin's support for this project have been both brave and unwavering.

I would also like to thank Helen Reeves of Penguin Canada, whose belief in me has been extraordinarily kind and encouraging, as well as the Lavin Agency of Toronto. I am also grateful to the former editor of Gutter Press, Ed Sluga, for his early support and guidance.

I am especially grateful to my families, who have made everything else possible: my parents, Rob and Sandra Mathieson, and David and Sandie Walde, as well as my extended family. Their love and belief in me during this project have meant so much. An especially big thank-you to all the members of the babysitters club: including Paul; my mothers, Sandra and Sandie; my sisters and brothers; and Bob, for taking Mr. Miles out. A special thanks to Sylvia Curtis-Norcross for looking after Zoe, too. And a big thanks to all the friends who listened or helped along the way. You know who you are, darlings.

I would like to thank some early readers of this work, including Julian Zadorozny and Erica Zappy, whose comments were kind and astute. I would also like to extend my gratitude to *The New Quarterly* for the first publication of three of the original candy stories. And I would also like to offer my sincere thanks and appreciation to the Ontario Arts Council for its early financial support and assistance.

There were a number of books that were both influential and instrumental in the creation of this work, and I wish to acknowledge them. For their wise reflections on storytelling and the power of narrative: Robert Fulford's *The Triumph of Narrative: Storytelling in the Age of Mass Culture* and A. S. Byatt's *On Histories and Stories*. For their insightful studies on girlhood: Rachel Simmons's *Odd Girl Out: The Hidden Nature of Aggression in Girls* and Naomi Wolf's *Promiscuities: The Secret Struggle for Womanhood*. Herbert S. Zim's delightful *Codes and Secret Writing* was also very helpful.

Finally, the following stories were originally published in slightly different forms in the following publications: "Lotsa Fizz" in *Descant*; and "Fun Dip," "Astro Pop," and "Tear Jerker Guts" in *The New Quarterly*. The chapter "Girls, Girls, Girls" was also previously published in a different form as "An excerpt from *The Howdy Club*" in *b+a*.